ISBN 9798420463291

Had to Be You

Cover design: Kim Bailey, Bailey Cover Boutique

Editing: Carolyn De Melo

Publicity: LitUncorked

HAD TO BE *you*

LILY MILLER

About the book

Let's get one thing straight: I don't believe in relationships, romance or any of that BS. My younger brother may have lost his mind over a woman, but that won't happen to me. I'm a shark in and out of the courtroom, and that's exactly the way I like it.

I worked my ass off to become Reed Point's #1 attorney and I'm not going to let any woman get in the way of my career.

It turns out, though, that Ellie Reeves is not just any woman. She's wild and infuriating and completely unpredictable. In other words, she's everything I don't need. Did I mention she's also sexy as hell?

I lost myself to Ellie once and I vowed never to let that happen again. But every time I think she's finally out of my head, I'll remember the feel of her skin, the taste of her lips. She's impossible to forget. And with both of us in the wedding party when my brother gets married in a few weeks, we're going to be seeing a lot of each other.

I know what I need to do. I need to stay far away

from Ellie if I have any chance of resisting temptation. And it works - that is, until I find myself alone with her and end up having the hottest night of my life. Now she's under my skin. Everything about her turns me on. Suddenly I'm breaking all my rules.

The trouble is, she's keeping a secret. All the passion in the world may not be enough to save me from getting burned.

But how do I walk away when Ellie may be everything I never knew I wanted?

HAD TO BE YOU

A small town enemies to lovers romance novel

LILY MILLER

For our readers
The ones who love to get lost in fiction and who love the romance genre endlessly.

Chapter One

Ellie

"I never want to see another penis again as long as I live."

"Having second thoughts, Liv? It's not too late to back out now."

Olivia, my best friend and the bride-to-be, scowls at me, taking another sip of her cranberry vodka drink. She scowls for a second time when her lips pop off the penis straw that I, like the best friend I am, made sure to add to her drink.

"Really, Ells? I'm starting to regret telling you that you could throw me a bachelorette party. This feels more like a giant penis orgy. There are penises *everywhere.* Penis necklaces, penis straws, penis-shaped shot glasses. And I think we all could have done without penis tattoos," she says, flipping her arm over to show me the one plastered to the inside of her wrist.

"I disagree. You specifically told me that you wanted to have fun and penises are the most fun."

Okay, maybe I took things a little too far with the party.

Out of the two of us, Olivia is definitely the reserved one whereas I am the definition of an extrovert to a T. That might be the reason we get along so well. She's the yin to my yang, the Ethel to my Lucy, the salt to my pepper. That's not to say that she's not a ton of fun - maybe just don't take her to a nightclub, cover her in penis paraphernalia and hire a stripper to grind his junk all over her leg. *Shit! I think I might have messed up this night.*

Olivia blows out a breath and turns to wade through the crowd towards our VIP table that her hot, uber rich, practically perfect fiancé Parker Bennett is footing the bill for. He wouldn't have had it any other way. When he's not sending her ridiculously expensive gifts or whisking her away on romantic weekend getaways, he's running the most successful hotel chain on the east coast with his father. He is the guy that every girl dreams of.

I follow Olivia, making a quick stop at the bar to order a round of shots to the table before squishing in next to Olivia's sister Kate, Parker's sister Jules and six more of the bride-to-be's closest friends. The plush velvet booth has a perfect view of the dance floor as well as a bouncer, per Parker's request, who is there to keep creepy guys from getting too close. A server arrives with the round of shots I ordered, plus a second round on the house.

"Cheers to Olivia!"

We raise our shots in the air toasting Olivia, and I watch as she laughs and tips her glass back. Maybe she's forgotten for a minute that she hates all of the penis bits and bobs. *Phew.* She flashes me a smile and in return I blow her a kiss. I'm determined that she has the best night ever. After all, if anyone knows how to have a good time, it's me!

"Round two!" We all toss the second round of tequila shots back and I wince as the burn of the clear liquid slides down my throat.

"Ladies, follow me. It's time we burn up the dance floor," Kate hollers over the bass that's thumping through the club.

"Kate, are you suddenly eighty years old, for Pete's sake? Nobody 'burns up the dance floor' anymore," I tease, sliding my body from the velvet bench. "I clearly need to get you out of the house more -especially since our three-pack is turning into a two-pack at the end of the month when Olivia gets hitched."

Kate rolls her eyes and follows our group past the bouncer to the dance floor. We spend the next hour dancing to top forty songs and occasionally fending off guys who seem to think we love it when they hump our legs with their bodies. *Why would anyone think that's a turn-on?*

My hands are in the air and my hips are swaying to the music when I hear our code word, "Pineapple," being called out from across the dance floor. Olivia, Kate and I had decided years ago that we needed a safe word to rescue each other from train wreck dates. And believe me, there have been plenty of those. I search the crowd, immediately laughing when I spot Kate smashed between two guys in a creepy testosterone sandwich. They are both hip thrusting their lower bodies into her, while she grimaces in annoyance. I've got this. Pushing my way through the crowded dance floor, I reach her and slip my hand in hers.

"Excuse me, boys," I say, looking in turn to the short guy behind Kate and the really tall one who's latched on to the front of her. "It's my turn to dance with my girlfriend. Right, future wife?"

The short guy backs away, his hands going up like a pair of stop signs. The tall one looks at me like I'm riding a motorcycle while doing a handstand and then turns and pads away. And that's how it's done, folks.

"Thanks, Ells. I didn't see that one coming," Kate shouts over the music.

"No one ever does, that's how they getcha!" We dance for a while until Olivia announces she needs a bathroom break. I follow her to the restroom, where we each slip into a stall.

"You've got to be kidding me, Ells," I hear Olivia shout in her annoyed voice from the stall next to mine. "Your name and phone number are *still* Sharpied on the back of the door."

"Oh my gosh, Olivia. Remember when I did that? Sarah Porter, who is now married with at least thirty three kids, dared me to do it. I was so drunk that night and remember- "

"Ells, I remember. I don't need my memory refreshed. You really need to get rid of this."

"Oh right, cuz I carry a permanent marker in my pocket with me everywhere I go. I'll get right on that." I shake my head like she can see me through the wall and make my way to the sink where she meets me seconds later.

At the sink, I meet her deep brown eyes in the reflection of the mirror. "Are you having fun, Olivia?"

"I am, Ells. Thank you for planning tonight. You are the bestest of the best. I've missed you."

"I've missed you more than you know," I tell her, because it's true. Olivia and I are more than best friends, we are also business partners. We opened the first location of our flower shop, Bloom, here in Reed Point shortly after college and our second just last year in Cape May, a small town roughly two and a half hours away. I run the Reed Point location and Olivia runs the Cape May one since she moved there to be closer to Parker. Unfortunately, that means we don't get to see each other nearly enough these days.

I apply another coat of gloss on my lips then turn to Olivia, pulling her in for a hug. "Are you ready for phase two of your bachelorette party to begin?"

"There are phases? I'm scared to ask," she says, pausing the brush of her lip gloss at the center of her lip.

"Oh, there are phases all right! Your night is about to get a whole lot hotter!" I smirk and give her arm a squeeze. She finishes applying the pale pink gloss and then turns to me with a murderous stare.

"Ells, I will stab you with the heel of my stiletto if it's what I'm thinking it is."

"You know you don't really mean that." I take her hand in mine and lead her out of the washroom. "Come on. You are going to love it."

OLIVIA IS SEATED in the center of Contact Club's private VIP room with the same murderous look in her eyes. The lethal gaze is directed squarely at me.

The rest of us girls are seated around her, taking in the dream of a guy who just walked into the room and introduced himself as Jay. He has thick brown hair and a chiseled jaw and is wearing a dark gray suit that is stretched across his muscular body. Kate appears to be drooling and our friend Amber looks like she is about to whip off her clothes and mount him.

"You must be the bride-to-be. Hello, Olivia." He slowly moves closer to her, flashing a sexy smile. "Are you ready to have a good time?"

Olivia swallows hard, but before she has a chance to say anything, the music starts, and Jay straddles her legs.

Good move on Jay's part, getting the show on the road before she has time to bolt. Leaning in closer, he whispers something in her ear and Olivia instantly turns a bright shade of red. He takes his time removing his jacket then unbuttons his dress shirt, one button at a time. He drops the fabric to the floor and that's all it takes for the girls and I to get out of our seats and get this striptease going.

Dollar bills begin to fly through the air as Jay swings his hips from right to left, never taking his gaze from Olivia's brown eyes.

He slowly steps back and starts to unzip his pants. The temperature in the room spikes to a bazillion degrees and we all lose our ever-loving minds. He shakes his toned, hard ass in a pair of black briefs as he slides his pants down his muscular legs. *Oh, fuck yes!*

I shove a handful of dollar bills down the back of his underwear, silently wishing I was the one sitting in that chair. *Olivia is one lucky girl. I seriously know how to throw a party.*

Jay turns to face us and pushes his ass into Olivia's lap. He smirks at us ladies, who would all give our kidneys to be in Olivia's seat right now, and that earns him a chorus of hollers and whoops. While the rest of us lose it, Olivia covers her eyes with her palms and squeals. It's safe to say that she would rather have a bath with a toaster right now than have Jay grinding his body on her. She is going to kill me for this. *Lord help me.*

Jay continues to work his magic for another thirty minutes, grinding and dancing and putting on a show. When he's done we snap a group photo with him - some sort of weird souvenir - and are then escorted back to our table by a hostess. There's a round of drinks waiting for us that I cannot take credit for ordering. Contact Club is clearly doing everything they can to make sure the future Mrs. Bennett is having a good time. The Bennetts are very well-known in Reed Point, a family of self-made billionaires who run the east coast's most successful boutique hotel chain. They attend countless charity functions and donate thousands of dollars each year to organizations that actually make the world a better place rather than elite causes that favor the rich. They are practically Reed Point royalty.

"Olivia, I'm proud of you. I bet Magic Mike had zero clue you were dying the entire time," I say, trying to gauge her response to the performance. It doesn't take a mind reader to know it's probably not going to be favorable.

"Save it, Ells." She shoots me another death glare. "He knew damn well I was praying for an earthquake so we would all have to evacuate the building. I think setting myself on fire would have been more enjoyable."

"Okay, you're right." I throw my hands in the air, admitting defeat. "It was pretty painful to watch."

Olivia's nose scrunches up and she playfully swats at my arm. "It was painful to have to sit through."

"Well, sorry, not sorry, Liv. I hardly think it was torture to have a hot-as-fuck guy show you a little attention. Did you not see what I was seeing? Did you not see his *eight*-pack?"

"Oh, I saw what you were seeing. I unfortunately *felt* what you were seeing. And now I need a shower." She shifts in her seat and looks me straight in the eye. "You know, I know someone with an eight-pack who I could re-introduce to you. If you weren't so damn stubborn, you would give him a chance." Olivia raises her brow and takes a long sip of her drink. She can be sneaky when she wants to be.

"I know who you are referring to and I already tried that. But apparently I'm forgettable," I snap back. "He's too serious for me anyways, he works too much."

Olivia is referring to Liam Bennett, Parker's older brother. I drunkenly made out with him in a washroom at a party a few months back. *I know, cringey.* We saw one another at a few Bennett events after that, but he's kept his distance. His face was buried in his phone most of the time, he barely even glanced up to even look at me. I got the message, loud and clear.

"You didn't try anything. You two haven't even been on a real date."

"That's because we wouldn't be able to stop arguing long enough to actually go on said date. We would probably kill each other and then you would be spending the next twenty-five Christmases visiting me in a women's correctional facility."

"You don't know him at all, Ells. Not like I do. Yes, Liam works a lot. Okay, more than a lot. But he's sweet and funny and charming and any woman would be really lucky to be with him. Once you get to know him, you'll see that I'm right. He was into you at my beach house party and I know you were feeling him. It's a mistake to not at least give it a shot and see where things could go."

"I'm not convinced, and anyways, are we really talking about this at your bachelorette party, Liv? Convo over. Come on, lets dance. This is your final wild night of freedom and we are not wasting another second of it talking about this."

To stop the conversation from going any further, I grab Olivia by the hand and yank her from the booth. I drag her to the dance floor and spin her around, both of us laughing in each other's arms. I have my best friend back in Reed Point for the next few weeks and life is good.

Without Liam Bennett.

Chapter Two

Liam

My morning is shot. It's barely 9 a.m. and I'm already in a mood. I missed my usual 6 a.m. workout and the quiet morning in my office I was banking on has been disrupted by my brother Parker. I chug back the rest of the green smoothie that I drink every single morning and try to telepathically will Parker out of my office.

"So, are you going to tell me the reason for the super fantastic mood you are in or do I have to guess?" Parker asks, his voice dripping in sarcasm. He sits in one of the dark brown leather armchairs across from me, one ankle resting on his other knee. He knows I'm working double time right now, partly due to his upcoming nuptials, but he is enjoying frustrating the shit out of me anyways.

"Are you going to tell me why you are here throwing off my day?" I respond, glancing at my Rolex to make my point.

"Gracing you with my presence is how I would look at it," he smirks.

"Right. Lucky me. Make it quick before I throw you out of here so I can get some work done." Parker is younger than me by two years and he's probably the brother I am the closest to, though at this particular moment I'm not convinced. Although I don't work directly for our father's Seaside Hotel chain where Parker is CEO, my law firm Brooks, Gamble and Bennett acts as their legal advisors. *Yes, that's right, I made partner last month.*

"Happily. Dropping these off to you per Dad's request and reminding you about this afternoon. Four thirty. Don't be late." Parker drops a thick Manila envelope onto my desk.

"How could I forget? The 'Parker and Livy's Wedding' group chat reminds me daily of all my groomsmen duties. I don't remember subscribing to that, by the way." I try, and fail, to hide my smirk. "I'll be there with bells on."

Parker is marrying his high school sweetheart in less than two weeks and all jokes aside, I couldn't be happier for him. I've never seen him like this. The guy is annoyingly happy all the fucking time. My entire family is over the moon. Tonight is our final tux fitting.

"Thanks. I thought since we'll have all the guys together we could grab drinks at Catch 21 afterwards. Sound good?"

"I can make that work. Speaking of… have you heard from Miles? Has he made it to Mom's yet?" I ask, leaning back in my chair.

Our youngest brother Miles is flying in today from Los Angeles for the two weeks of wedding events that have been planned. Miles Bennett is a household name across North America. Women go crazy over him. He's an actor who has starred in a string of A-list movies over the past four years and shows no signs of slowing down.

"Not yet. His flight is scheduled to arrive around noon. Jules is picking him up."

Juliette, or Jules as she prefers to be called, is our sister and the baby of the family. Jules also works for my father and the Seaside Hotel group, heading up the marketing team. She's based here in Reed Point with a large corner office next to our father's - I'm pretty sure he arranged that so he could keep an eye on her. Jules has been a firecracker since birth, always giving our parents a run for their money. People probably assume us boys would be the ones been keeping them up at night, but it was always Jules.

I reach for the envelope Parker set on my desk and remove the files that will require my attention. Jules landed a deal with one of the largest VR tour tech companies and she needs me to go over the contracts. If everything is in order, a go-ahead on the deal will mean the Seaside Hotel chain will be on its way to allowing potential guests to experience the properties right from their devices.

"Speaking of Jules, how's she doing with the breakup?" Parker asks. "Mom told Livy that she has been pretty worried about her." Jules had been dating Alex, a quiet, introverted med school student, for the last two years. "She said Jules actually thought Alex was the one. I can't be the only one who didn't see the connection between those two, right?" Parker asks, eyes on his phone. A slow smile curves his lips as his thumbs fly across the keyboard of his phone.

"Fuck no! I never could figure out what she saw in that guy. He has the personality of a shoe. She's better now, but she has her moments. I still can't believe *he* broke up with *her*."

Glancing across my desk, I'm not sure Parker has heard a word I said. He's still furiously typing something on his phone, his smile now replaced with a cheeky grin. Unable to hide my irritation, I ask, "Are you fucking sexting Livy right now in my office?"

His fingers continue to tap the screen of his iPhone at warp speed. He looks up at me for a split second. "I bet you'd like to know." He laughs, appearing amused, then drops his gaze back to his phone.

"I sure as hell would not. Why are you still here? Don't you have a wedding to plan?"

Parker stands and slides his phone into his pocket. "I hope the rest of your day is a pleasant as you are." He shakes his head and turns for the door. "See you this afternoon. Don't be late." As the door closes behind him, I instantly feel a shift in my mood. The silence that I love settles around me. I slip off my suit jacket, hang it on the back of my desk chair and roll my sleeves up my forearms. I ping Silvia, my assistant, and ask her to bring me my morning cup of coffee.

My mind wanders to the tux fitting this afternoon, then to the two weeks of wedding events I have scheduled in my calendar and then suddenly to one gorgeous, uninhibited brunette who is also in the wedding party. A woman with long, flowing hair, the deepest blue eyes you've ever seen, a bright smile that hints at playfulness and confidence and wit. A woman I'll be spending a lot of time with in the coming weeks, considering we are both in the wedding party.

Ellie.

I haven't seen her in months, but the distance between us hasn't been enough to make me forget about her. Every time I think she's finally out of my thoughts I remember the feel of her skin or the taste of her lips. Then I remember how her smart mouth gets on my last nerve. She's wild and impulsive and uncontrollable and everything I don't need wrapped up in a slender, just over five-foot frame. She drives me fucking crazy.

I'm. Beyond. Fucked.

Irritated with myself for allowing visions of Ellie to distract me, I lean forward in my chair and wake up my computer. I pinch the bridge of my nose and exhale.

A relationship is the last thing I need in my life right now. Sure, I believe in love, but I definitely don't have time for it. I have finally achieved my goal of making partner at my firm, a goal I set for myself in college. I've worked my ass off to become one of the East Coast's most illustrious attorneys. My record is impeccable. I'm determined, laser-focused and not afraid of putting in the hard work and long hours. So, when I say a relationship is low on my list of goals and exasperations, I'm not lying. Scratch that, a relationship doesn't even crack that list. I barely have enough time to get done in a day what needs to be.

That settles it.

I know what I need to do.

I need to stay *far* away from Ellie Reeves.

"I THINK THEY LOOK GOOD," Dylan, a friend of Parker's from college who is also a groomsman, deadpans. His eyes are on the navy suit pants I'm wearing that are approximately seven sizes too small.

"You're an asshole, Dylan."

"Whoa." Parker steps out from behind the change room curtain and stands next to me, eying me in the three-way mirror. He laughs hysterically. "Looks like someone has been indulging in too many late-night snacks."

"Funny, Parker," I say, rolling my eyes. "I'd like to know where you found this guy. Did you get a Groupon entitling you to half-price suits? I mean, what the hell? I obviously take up more room in the front section than you do," I say, gesturing to my favorite body part, which is currently crammed behind the zipper that is cutting off all circulation to my dick. "But this is ridiculous."

Miles jumps in, not wanting to miss an opportunity to give me the gears. "You need to stop skipping your workouts, Liam. Maybe lay off the gin and tonics too," he says with a burst of laughter.

"Fuck you, Miles. You don't have a clue what a real workout is. FYI, fetching beer bottles from the fridge doesn't count as one."

We are interrupted by the pint-size Italian tailor, Marco, who speaks with an accent so strong I have to struggle to understand a word he's saying.

"So, gentleman, how are we doing? How is everything fitting?" he asks. His eyes go wide when they land on me, and he covers his mouth with his hand.

Kill. Me. Now.

Parker, Miles and Dylan all double over in laughter, clearly enjoying seeing me in pants small enough for a toddler. *Dicks!*

"We have a problem with your pants, I see," Marco states, or at least I think that's what he says. He bends down in front of me, pulling at the seams that are struggling to remain intact.

"No shit we do," I mumble under my breath. Parker eyes me, fighting to keep his composure.

"Not to worry. I can fix this." Marco says, sliding the measuring tape from around his neck to my waist and cinching it.

"I say leave them," Miles suggests. "Liam likes his pants extra tight. He thinks it helps him land the ladies." I stare him down while he snaps a photo on his phone of the situation happening south of my midsection. I make a mental note to snatch his cell phone from him later and throw it into oncoming traffic.

"Have you forgotten I'm making a speech at your wedding, Parks? Payback is a bitch," I warn as Marco gets a little too handsy for my liking. Thankfully, he finishes up five minutes later and I'm able to take these things off. I get dressed behind the curtain and then meet the guys in the front of the shop. Parker finishes up with Marco while Miles, Dylan and I make our way outside.

My phone vibrates in my pocket seconds later and I dig it out to see a notification from the goddamn wedding group chat. I shove my phone back into my pocket.

I don't need to even look. My disaster of a tux fitting will be an endless source of entertainment for these idiots for years to come.

"Aren't you going to check that?" Miles side-eyes me, unable to hide the stupid smirk on his face.

"Seriously? You guys are assholes. You just couldn't resist, could you?"

"Nope. Not when it's that good," Miles laughs.

Chapter Three

Ellie

I'm jolted from my sleep by the sound of my phone. I curse to myself, trying to find it on my dresser. I'm still half asleep, but I'm awake enough to know it's nowhere near morning. My fingers finally grip my phone and I check the time on the screen. Four effing thirty in the morning and of course, it's from my parents. I rub my eyes in attempt to focus on their message.

My annoyance fades quickly because seeing a photo of my mom and dad makes my heart swell. They're standing in front of a huge sandstone canyon, my father's arm draped across my mother's shoulder. My dad is shirtless with layers upon layers of crystal healing necklaces around his neck, and he's gazing at my mom likes she's the best thing he's ever seen - even better than the impressive rock formations behind them. Half of my mother is cut off in this picture, which is not surprising. They haven't yet mastered the art of the selfie, so at least one of their heads is usually missing from photos. My mom is wearing a long, flowing, printed skirt with an embroidered halter top and her hair is tied up with a bandana. She looks beautiful.

The message reads, "not to worry ells bells your mother is still madly in love with me ;) antelope canyon is home for the next month we love you forever." Of course there is zero punctuation or capitals. I can't help but laugh as I read it.

I laugh and then I smile. I miss them so damn much. I haven't seen them in almost three years. I haven't even heard their voices in six months. There's no use calling them, they have one crappy drug store cell phone between the two of them and they can never remember to charge it. And when they do decide to charge it, they manage to plug it in the wrong way. It's a wonder those two survive. Or maybe it's just simple…they've always survived on love and each other.

It was the day after my eighteenth birthday when they left. They packed up the house and loaded up their RV and hit the highway as fast as they could. They said they were tired of living in the same zip code all their lives, and people needed them. I had no idea who the "people" were that they were referring to, but they said it was their calling. They kissed me goodbye. Little did I know then how infrequent their visits back home would be or how little we would speak, but I've never felt like they didn't love me. They are simply two free spirits living out their dreams.

But that doesn't make it easy. Watching them go was the hardest thing I've ever had to do. To this day I struggle with the realization that I'm alone. Being an only child only solidifies that.

My parents were high school sweethearts, having me shortly after graduation. I was a surprise - the best surprise of their lives, as they put it. My father, an artist among other spiritual things, owned a successful gallery that afforded us a very comfortable life. My mother, a born healer as she would refer to herself, grew berries and plants that she concocted into balms and edibles to heal people who were sick or wounded. I grew up an only child, in a two-story craftsmen home in the suburbs. My childhood felt so ordinary growing up. My parents were unconventional, but the love in my family always felt endless. They were madly in love with each other and still are. They never hid their affection for one another. Then, the year before I turned eighteen, my grandfather died, leaving my parents a substantial amount of money. The inheritance combined with the money from the sale of their home bought them the double wide and enough money to travel the nation. Enough money to give a lot of it away to those in need along their travels too.

I type a return message knowing they probably won't see it and make a mental note to print a copy of their canyon photo so I can add it to the collection on my refrigerator door. I never know when I will hear from them next, so I hold on tight to every photo they send me.

I set my iPhone back on the nightstand and roll over onto my side. A slideshow of childhood memories plays through my mind. My father teaching me how to ride a bike, family game night and picnic lunches in the yard. I miss my parents. I miss having family nearby. Most days now I am able to forget that I'm all alone, that I have no one here in Reed Point to call mine. But some days are harder.

I pull my duvet up to my chin and close my eyes, listening to the ticking of the clock on the bedroom wall. I let out a deep breath and eventually fall back into a deep sleep.

"DID you get the dick pic today?" Olivia asks, her eyes wide and twinkling. It's just the two of us, working together at Bloom. We're busy mock-creating her rehearsal dinner centerpieces – getting an idea of what she likes and doesn't. We're also creating the centerpieces for her rehearsal dinner tonight - a task she refused to hand over to anyone else. She insisted we do them together for old time's sake.

"Is this a joke?" I ask, my nose crinkled,

"Would I joke about something like that?"

We both answer at the same time: "No."

As I wait for her to fill in the blanks, I take a sip of coffee from my favorite mug, the one that says, "I'm not always this amazing. Sometimes I'm asleep."

"Didn't you check the group chat yesterday? Miles posted a picture of Liam in his suit for the wedding. His pants were way too tight and let's just say you could see *everything* south of the border. He is HUGE!"

"Oh that. Yes, I did." I bring my mug back to my lips to cover the grin that threatens to give me away. The picture was hot. Liam looked hot. I'm breaking a sweat just thinking about it again, but there's no way I'll admit to it.

"That's it? That's all you have to say about it?"

"Olivia, he's your fiancé's brother. I am not having this conversation with you. It feels all kinds of wrong." I am also not going there with her because I know where this line of questioning will lead. *You and Liam would be perfect together… blah blah blah.*

"You're zero fun today. Just make sure fun Ellie shows up at my rehearsal dinner tonight. That's all I ask." Olivia runs her hands down her work apron and reaches for another empty vase. I grab a handful of green stems and get back to work creating something I think Olivia will love. She insisted on pink, white and chartreuse green flowers just like the ones we created for her soon-to-be mother-in-law's anniversary party - the very same party where Parker and Olivia found each other again after years apart.

"You know it. I'm looking forward to celebrating with you. I'm just so freakin' happy for you, Liv. You are going to outshine every bride who has ever come before you."

"Thanks, Ells Bells," Olivia says as she shears the end of a peony and jabs it into the arrangement in front of her. "Now can we talk about Liam again?"

I glare at her and respond through a mouthful of coffee. "No."

"Come on. Is it going to be weird seeing him again tonight?"

"Only if he makes it weird. Honestly Olivia, I don't know why he would. We were drunk. We made out in a bathroom at your party. It was months ago. It's done. Besides, the guy hardly speaks."

Olivia ignores me, which means she disagrees. But I stand by what I said. Liam Bennett is moody, stubborn and a complete control freak. He's infuriating. Not even his piercing brown and gray irises or his deep gritty voice can sway me. Not even his "dick pic," which I'm having trouble erasing from my mind. Lord, he looked good. *Nope, not happening. Stop it, Ellie.*

By the time Olivia and I finish the last of the arrangements we have a clearer picture of the centerpieces for the wedding. We load the flowers one by one into our Bloom van. I'll drive them myself to the rehearsal dinner venue then head home to get ready for the party.

I give Olivia a hug goodbye as we leave, then lock up the doors to Bloom. I hop into the van and crank the engine to life. I rest my head against the cool leather seat and remind myself again that Liam is infuriating, that he drives me crazy.

So crazy.

Then why is my pulse racing at the thought of seeing him tonight?

Chapter Four

Ellie

There are a few ways this could go. Liam could opt for the silent treatment and pretend that I don't exist. Or he could go with the nothing-ever-happened routine and brush our whole washroom make-out session from a few months back under the rug. There are other possible scenarios, but I shake them from my head as I enter the upscale restaurant Parker and Olivia have chosen for tonight's rehearsal dinner.

I take in the scene. The restaurant is stunning. The walls are painted a pale gold and there are glass chandeliers resembling jellyfish dripping from the ceiling. A wall of glass windows are pushed open on the far side of the room to a patio and a breathtaking view of the ocean. The sun is still high in the sky, and it's unseasonably warm for April on the coast. The dining area is dimly lit with candles, casting a glow over the white linen tablecloths. Along one wall, there is a gold-veined marble bar that stretches longer than a runway. Guests are busy mingling, glittering crystal champagne glasses in their hands. We have the entire restaurant to ourselves.

I carefully make my way deeper into the restaurant, teetering on the new four-inch heels that I splurged on for tonight. My magenta, one-shoulder minidress is giving me life and the extra boost of confidence that I need. My hair is down in waves. I quickly scan the room, trying not to acknowledge the fact that I'm looking for one person in particular. *Why would I want to see that killjoy?*

"There you are, and holy crap Ells, you look *hot*!" Olivia greets me, handing me a glass of champagne. "That dress is everything." She takes me in her arms, and I squeeze my hands around her tiny waist.

"Thanks, babe. So do you. The restaurant looks beautiful," I gush. "I can't imagine what the wedding will look like if this is only the rehearsal dinner."

"I know, right? Especially with Mrs. Bennett hosting," Olivia says. Parker's mom is well known in Reed Point for throwing extravagant parties and charity dinners that rival any celebrity event. When Olivia asked if they could have the wedding at the Bennett estate, Grace Bennett practically jumped with joy. "I wonder sometimes if she is more excited about the wedding than I am."

"I would bet that's a yes. She really is the absolute sweetest. She would do anything for you and her kids. She is right up there with the Girl Scouts and Mother Theresa," I say, nervously glancing around the room wondering if Liam is here yet. It bothers me that I care. I shouldn't. *But I do.*

Kate finds the two of us and after a group hug, we follow Olivia to our assigned seats to set aside our handbags. I set down my purse on the chair at the place setting with my name card, then glance at the little white cards to the left and the right. My body stiffens as my eyes go wide.

"Don't kill me, Ells. Please don't kill me," Olivia begs, realizing I've figured out what she's done. Kate winces, looking at me guiltily. The trader must have been in on this too.

"Seriously Liv, I can't make any promises," I say through gritted teeth.

I stare at the card again, hoping that maybe I was hallucinating. No such luck. It still says Liam. I take a deep breath, gripping the chair rail in front of me. *Am I ready for this?* The answer is no.

"You're going to have to just trust me on this one. I know a lot more than you do about affairs of the heart."

"I'm not sure what old, low budget movie you stole that line from, Olivia, but please never repeat it." I lunge for his name card, but Olivia quickly grabs hold of my arm.

"Not so fast, Flo-Jo. If you move his place card it will throw my entire table off. You are just going to have to be a big girl about this." She bats her eyelashes, one hand on her hip. I finally exhale, realizing that I've been holding my breath. I guess I can tolerate him for one night.

We are interrupted by a server balancing a tray of hors d'oeuvres. "Can I offer you something to eat before dinner?"

"It might be easier if you just hand her the entire tray," Olivia deadpans, referring to our Cape May Bloom grand opening party and the unreal appies I overindulged in.

"Very funny," I say around a mouthful of gooey cheese puff.

I wash the phyllo baked goodness down with the last of my champagne, listening to Kate ramble on about some guy she met who likes to play bingo on Friday nights. Sounds like a real catch. She seems excited, so I resist the temptation to ask if she's visited his retirement home yet. The topic of conversation shifts to Club Eden, a brand-new upscale nightclub that Kate wants us to try. I'm about to tell her that sounds a hell of a lot better than bingo when I see him.

Our eyes lock and there's that crazy spark that zips through me every time we see each other. My stomach does a flip, my pulse races, and for several steamy seconds we maintain the kind of eye contact that you only hear about in movies and romance novels.

Liam is standing outside on the patio, Parker on his right, Miles on his left. It's a lot to take in when the three Bennett boys are together, they're all so gorgeous, but right now I can't take my eyes off of Liam. His suit clings to his muscular chest and strong shoulders. His dark brown hair is cut short and styled back and he has just the right amount of stubble on his face. His moody eyes on mine feel like he's touching my skin from across the room. My body heats. He raises the tumbler in his hand to his lips, tips back an amber liquid. His eyes never leaving mine. He somehow makes even the simple act of drinking from a glass look sexy. I look away. That's enough of that. He may be the best-looking man I've ever layed eyes on but he's still a stuck-up lawyer. I won't let him affect me. He had his chance.

Needing to move, and more importantly needing a new line of vision, I let the girls know I need a drink. I spot Jules at the bar and Kate and I decide to go say hello. We leave Olivia to mingle with her guests. I order myself a dirty martini, hoping it will take the edge off. It does.

Eventually, it's time for dinner so guests are asked to take their seats. I take my time, stopping to chat with a group of girls from the bachelorette party a few tables over. We reminisce about Jay, the sexy stripper, and all have a good laugh. Not able to stall any longer, I take a deep breath, making my way to my table. Seated at the round table are Kate, Jules, Miles, Dylan, Parker, Olivia and of course, Liam. I reluctantly take my seat next to *him.*

My stomach is one giant twisted knot when I sit down beside him, choosing not to make eye contact because I'm not sure what to say. I reach for the glass of water next to my place setting and when I do, my arm brushes against Liam's as he's adjusting his napkin on his lap. A jolt of electricity zips through me at just the faintest touch and I can't help but wonder if he felt it too. I try to focus on the small talk around the table. A cousin of Olivia's has wandered over and is busy fan-girling over Miles, while he happily eats it up. Jules and Parker are talking about something that happened at the office earlier while Kate is discussing the most recent episode of *Stranger Things* with Dylan. Meanwhile, I'm fighting the flush that is warming my cheeks and the tingling sensation covering my skin - my body's reaction to Liam's presence. This is going to be a long night.

Partway through the first course, I suddenly feel eyes on me and look up to find Kate and Olivia staring at me, eyebrows raised.

"Sorry… what? I think I missed something."

"Dancing!" Kate says, apparently repeating herself. "I need a headcount for the club we're going to next weekend. So far Miles, Jules, Parker, Olivia, Dylan and I are all in. You're coming right, Ellie?"

"Of course," I say, never one to miss a night out.

"I knew you would be down!" Kate practically squeals. "How fun is this going to be?"

She turns her attention to Liam, still sipping his scotch beside me. *He's such a Debbie Downer.*

"What about you, Liam? Is the nightclub scene your thing?" Kate asks him, and I can't help but snicker. I'm betting that's a hard no. If he notices, he doesn't show it.

"Nope," Liam answers. *Well, I called that one.* Of course he hates to have fun. He's too busy drinking his fancy top shelf scotch with his boring lawyer partners at some snooty country club that makes me want to gag with a bath towel.

"Don't be such a downer," Jules groans to her brother. "I promise I'll make it my job to make sure you have fun. You'll come with us, right?"

"And make sure you wear those pants. The really tight ones," Miles shouts across the table before Liam has time to respond. We all erupt into laughter at Liam's expense. If it was considered appropriate to high five Miles across the table, I would. Liam rolls his eyes, exuding annoyance like only he can, before answering with a clipped, "No."

I glance over at Olivia, making my point silently: *See? I told you he doesn't talk.* She shakes her head at me.

"Of course he's coming. Don't listen to him," Miles says, looking at Liam. "Think hot girls in too-tight-dresses. Sweaty bodies grinding all over you. Hot!"

This earns Miles a shove to the shoulder from Olivia and a chuckle from Liam. "Right, noted. My calendar is clear," he says. *Ugh, he's so annoying.* Everything feels awkward and I hate it. It's my best friend's rehearsal dinner and I hate that I wish I was anywhere but here.

Seconds later, waiters with white gloves place our meals in front of us. Beef tenderloin, roasted baby fingerling potatoes and grilled vegetables decorate the plate. It takes me a minute to unfold my napkin and remove the cutlery. That's a minute too long for Liam, apparently.

"Everything okay? Do you need me to cut up your meat?" he asks, flashing me a cocky smirk.

My shoulders tense. I blow out a breath. He finally decides to talk to me, and those are the eleven words he chooses to say? I shouldn't let him get to me. He knows exactly what he's doing. He's under my skin, where he likes to be. I retaliate, I can't help myself. "How sweet of you to offer. It really is a wonder you're still single."

Liam just smirks and goes back to eating his meal, looking completely unfazed. He's so hard to read. In that sense he's unlike all three of his siblings. They all wear their hearts on their sleeves, but Liam is guarded. He's so serious.

We finish our third course, doing a fantastic job of ignoring each other through the rest of dinner. Not able to take another second, I rise first from the table, excusing myself. At this point I'd rather be helping the kitchen staff wash dishes than sit next to *him.*

After dinner and a few speeches wrap up, guests are out of their seats and milling about. The guys have ventured outside for cigars and the girls are doing a round of shots at the bar - the latter organized by me, of course. Jules pulls Olivia away to introduce her to a cousin who's flown in for the wedding and Kate takes off for the restroom. I strike up a conversation with a tall attractive guy who introduces himself as Logan. He has blond hair to his shoulders that he clearly spends a lot of time on. He tells me he grew up with Olivia and that their families are close friends. He's a physiotherapist, so I assume he's good with his hands. But as handsome as he is, his hands aren't the ones that I find myself fantasizing about. He keeps on talking, but I've checked out. Seeing Liam again has reignited that spark in me that burns hot for him. It's so hot, I'm sizzling. My nerves are fried. He's all I've been able to think about tonight. And now I've gone from imagining Liam's hands brushing over my shoulder blades to running over the curve of my hips and down to... *speak of the devil.*

Liam stalks slowly towards me, but stops several feet away. Is it just me or does he look bothered? Maybe even jealous. His hands are clenched, and his lips are pressed together in a straight line. I instantly feel satisfied that seeing me with another man is affecting Liam this way. I turn my attention back to Logan, gazing into his eyes, giggling at his jokes. Putting on a show. All the while I feel Liam's stare blaze right through me.

Logan and I exchange numbers. I might not be feeling that connection I feel whenever I'm around Liam, but you never know. Maybe with a haircut and a little time, that could change. After a sweet kiss on the cheek, Logan politely leaves me to take a family photo on the patio. I eye the bartender for a glass of water.

I'm afraid to turn around because I can feel Liam's eyes on me before I actually see him. But there's no avoiding it. I turn to face him, my chest rising and falling, and his gray eyes instantly blaze into mine. It's a sexy, assured, *I don't give a fuck* look that excites me. My heart beats rapidly in my chest and a wave of heat tickles up my spine. He just watches me, his gaze sweeping over my entire body. And in this heart-pounding, spine-tingling moment, I forget how to breathe.

He moves closer and I can't help but feel like I'm his prey. He stands beside me at the bar while I fight the overwhelming urge to look at him. He motions to the bartender and orders himself a drink. My feet are planted firmly to the ground, unable to walk away. My back leans against the bar beside him.

What is happening?

With ice clinking in his glass, Liam swirls his drink. He leans in closer, so close I can feel his warm breath on my ear when he says, "Who's your date, Ellie?"

My skin prickles from the slightest touch of his breath on my skin, but I try my best to not show the effect his nearness has on me. I wish I knew why he sparks these sensations in me.

"Do you really think that's any of your business?" I answer him, finally getting the courage to turn my gaze his way and face him.

"He has nice hair. It looks a lot like my sister's. Was he asking for your number or hoping to borrow your hair-spray?" Liam is smiling. He's amused. I'm anything but. It feels like I'm a game to him. A game he's used to winning. I hate to break it to him, but two can play his stupid games.

"You're actually quite cute when you're jealous. Like an oversized Bichon Frise begging to be petted," I counter.

"Is that how Ellie Reeves flirts with a guy she's lusting over? If you would like to pet me, feel free."

"Compelling as that sounds, I'll pass."

"Are you sure about that?" Liam turns his body to face me, his eyebrow raised, a smirk tugging at the corner of his lips. His deep voice is the sexiest sound I've ever heard.

"You know what I really want?" I go for theatrics, really amping up the drama.

"To see me naked?" He cocks his head slightly to the side. His dark gray eyes are trained on me.

I roll my eyes. How do I even answer that? Hell yeah, I want to see him naked but there's no way I'm admitting that to him. Instead, I square my shoulders and move towards him until I'm so close I can smell his scent. Like cedar and fresh laundry. Being this close to Liam is intoxicating, I feel like I'm under his spell. There's a look in his eyes that I can't put my finger on but it's dizzying, it's electric. My heartbeat threatens to burst through my rib cage.

"I think you would like that," I answer him, my voice low and gravelly. I've never been so turned on in all my life, but I won't give him the satisfaction of knowing what he does to me. So, I add, "but no thanks."

"I don't think you really mean that, Ellie." He lifts his hand to my cheek, softly brushes his knuckles across my jaw towards my ear. He twists a loose strand of hair behind my ear and my body flames. I'm on fire. I feel alive. Everything and everyone around us fades to black, and it's just him and I at the party. He takes one small step closer until his chest is almost touching mine. My lips part. For a second I think he's going to kiss me. What's crazy is that I want him to. Let everyone watch him claim me.

I shouldn't be getting this close. I must be out of my mind. But I want him to stay and continue the banter that we've fallen into. I want him to touch me. Kiss me. Anything to ease this ache.

"I prefer men who are straight shooters, not ones who enjoy toying with me."

"Good to know. But do you wanna know what I think?" he asks as my temperature rises, the scent of his cologne going straight to my head.

"I think you are going to tell me regardless, so I might as well listen," I tease, holding his gaze, leaning in the slightest bit closer.

"I think you like it when I toy with you. Very much so." he says, his voice all low and sexy as hell. *Cocky bastard!*

His quick wit is the biggest turn-on. It feels like I'm drowning in this man and I'm not sure that I want to be saved. I'm at a loss for words, for once in my life, but I manage to string three together. "Is that so?"

My breath hitches.

The bartended appears in my peripheral vision, sliding a glass of water towards me, breaking the spell that Liam and I are under. *The guy has shit timing.* Liam notices too, suddenly blinking. We break apart. Liam takes a step back and turns and walks away.

I'm left breathless.

Chapter Five

Liam

She's infuriating. She's frustrating and maddening and stunning in every way. Everything about this girl turns me on.

I'm so fucked. Ellie Reeves is my kryptonite.

I'm standing with my mother, but my eyes are on Ellie. I don't know how she is able to drive me so crazy, but I haven't been able to shake her from my mind since Parker and Olivia's beach house party a few months ago. Her smile breathes life into any room. She knows just what to say in every social situation. Always the center of attention, always the most beautiful girl in the room with her long, caramel-colored hair and eyes as blue as a clear winter sky. Those damn eyes, a thousand hues of blue. The world seems to spin around her axis. Scratch that; the whole damn universe. I should look away, but I can't take my eyes off her.

I came *this* close to kissing her. Everything in me wanted to feel her mouth on mine again. Her sassy mouth that never stops talking. I wanted to press her up against the marble bar and put my mouth all over her. I could see in her eyes that she wanted it too. And then I remembered that a relationship is something I definitely don't have time for. Especially a relationship with an insane person. But I do enjoy getting under her skin. I get off on pushing her buttons. She's bossy and scrappy and never stops taunting me, and somehow she is everything I crave.

"You seem to be enjoying yourself tonight, sweetheart. Especially the view over here." My mom looks at me, then looks over at Ellie, like she's reading my mind. I'm silent. A vault. I put my hands in my pockets and set my gaze in a different direction.

I knew Ellie would be here tonight but for some reason I was still stunned to see her. She's shockingly beautiful in her tight pink dress with her light pink lips and rich brown hair. My eyes return to her and for a moment, it feels as though I'm standing on uneven ground. Ellie sips from a glass, unaware that I'm not the only one watching her right now. I've spotted men and woman all night long take notice of her because how could they not- she's heart-stoppingly, can't-look-away beautiful.

"I've been your mother for twenty-eight years. I'd like to think I know you better than most. And that look in your eyes, Liam, is lust." She winks.

"I love you, Mom, but you're wrong about that."

"I'm always right, Liam. You should know that by now. I know a connection when I see one. I think I proved that with your brother and Olivia."

"Do not make me your project, Mom. You are getting way ahead of yourself," I say, irritated that she's right. She's always been this way, able to see right through me. She sees right through all of us kids.

"What kind of mother would I be if I didn't offer my advice when I believe it's needed? I see the way you look at her. She looks at you the same way. She's a sweet girl and she'd be good for you, maybe loosen you up a little." My mother brings her palm to my cheek like she's done since I was a little boy. "I'll stay out of your way and let things happen on their own. I promise. But..." she says. "Don't wait too long. A girl like Ellie won't stay single forever. I'd hate to see you lose your chance."

I shake my head at my mom, who is wearing her *mother knows best* face, running her fingers across the pearls around her neck.

"I love you, Liam."

"Love you too, Mom." I kiss the top of her head.

She leaves me standing there. This is so typical of my mom. She tells you what's on her mind, then leaves you to think about it.

Desperate for some fresh air, I slip out the front doors and around to the side of the restaurant. It's quiet, with the only faint sounds coming from the party inside and the waves from the ocean in the near distance. When I tilt my head to the sky, I see a million bright stars against a jet-black backdrop.

What. The. Hell.

What just happened?

It took everything in me to walk away from Ellie tonight. I can't figure her out. What is it about her that always makes me want to come back for more? We've been taunting each other all night, the push and pull wearing on my last nerve. She's a challenge, but I'm not sure how much more fight I have in me. All I want to do is touch her, run my fingers through her long hair, drag my tongue across her skin.

I'm pacing the pavement, dragging my hands through my hair, when I feel a familiar energy coursing through my veins. I always sense her before I see her. *Ellie.*

I look in her direction and our eyes meet. She tilts her head, a look of annoyance crossing her face. And because I can't help myself or more because I love to get her riled up, I ask, "Missed me?"

The look on her face says *you've got to be fucking kidding me.* She rolls her eyes so hard her whole head moves with the motion. "What are you doing out here, Liam?"

My name falling off her lips goes straight to my dick. I cross my arms over my chest. My eyes drift down to her dress. I watch her body move in that damn dress as she comes closer to me. I have no words. I'm damn near drooling. That fucking pink dress should be illegal. It shows off her toned, tanned legs and her curvy body. Her long hair moves with the breeze off the ocean. She's fucking perfect. There's no other word to describe her. I suck in a breath, knowing I'm in trouble. Knowing that there's no way I should be alone with her.

"Did your date leave? Out past his curfew?" I ask with a smug tone to my voice because I know she'll enjoy hurling a witty remark right back to me.

"His name is Logan, and I can introduce you if you like. You seem to have a *thing* for him."

"If I'm ever in the mood to play Frisbee golf or shotgun beers, I'll give him a call," I say, with an amused smile.

"That all sounds like a good time to me. You should try rolling up the sleeves of your fancy dress shirts and having some fun for a change."

I smirk. This is one of my favorite sides of Ellie, the one where she pushes me back. There aren't too many people in my life who will go up against me. She enjoys it. She's good at it. I like how she challenges me and I'm aware of my heartbeat picking up, of the surge in my veins.

"Are you interested in that guy?" I ask her, needing to know. Curiosity getting the best of me.

"What guy?"

"The guy with the hair."

"He has a name, Liam. It's only two syllables. It can't be that hard to remember. Lo-gan." She enunciates each syllable to really drive her point home.

I'm pissed and it shows when I ask her, "Are you going out with him?"

"Would it matter if I was?" She looks me directly in the eye. Her posture stiffens. I do too. How does this girl have the ability to get me hard with just a look? The air between us is thick. This back-and-forth thing is grating on me, the push and pull is suffocating.

"I wouldn't have asked if it didn't," I admit.

"Wow, Liam, so many questions for a girl who seems to be completely forgettable." *What did she just say?* Does she think I could ever forget anything about her? "Is that what you really think?"

She looks away. She's fidgeting with the ends of her hair. Uncertainty passes over her face. It's an emotion I'm not used to seeing on her. She looks almost vulnerable. She looks afraid.

"Answer the question, Ellie. Do you really think you're forgettable? To me?" I push.

"It doesn't matter," she says finally.

"It does to me." I watch as her eyes narrow on mine. I keep going. "I remember everything about that night. Every single thing," I tell her, my voice low. How could I forget? The way her eyes, those fucking goddess eyes, looked at me, the way her skin felt against mine. And her mouth. That mouth that I couldn't get enough of. I wanted all of her that night, but I wasn't going to have sex with her in my brother's bathroom. Not with Ellie. There was something different about her. I knew it even then. I wanted to do things right.

For the first time, I bet, in her entire life, she's speechless. Her gaze softens with my admission, the energy between us sizzling. I look her right in the eye, my heart pounding. I nod, so she absolutely understands that I meant what I said.

"Liam, I'm not doing this with you. You give me an inch and then backtrack a mile. You're just like all the rest."

"What exactly is that supposed to mean?"

"It means exactly what I said." She straightens.

"Not fair, Ellie. You don't know me."

"How could I? You're closed off, you're surly," she says, answering me almost instantly, starting to gain her confidence back.

"I think you like my surly," I say. She furrows her brow.

"I hate to break it to you, but I don't. I don't know anyone that would."

"I bet you do. I'll even take it one step further. I bet you think about me all the time. Nonstop."

Her cheeks flush and there's a flicker in her blue eyes. "You're insane."

I smile. "You probably even dream about me."

"You really are crazy." Her eyes sparkle in the moonlight. They've come alive again, back to the bright, playful eyes I'm so used to seeing. I wish I could figure out what she's thinking.

"I'm not crazy, Ellie. I'm confident."

"I believe 'arrogant' is more accurate. So arrogant. That's what you are."

"Is that so?"

"Uh-huh."

I should shut her up with a kiss. I feel her gaze trail

down my chest. It gets me harder. Without thinking and without warning I move towards her, backing her up towards the brick wall of the restaurant. I cage her in, pressing her up against the cold stone with my hip and placing my hands on either side of her head. I lean in, feeling the heat of my body burn into hers. A slow burn that will quickly turn into a full-blown fucking inferno if we let it.

I run the tips of my fingers down the edge of her jaw and she stills. A shock lights through my body. *Does she feel it too?* Needing to touch her again, I gently tilt her chin up, giving me access to the soft skin of her throat. Her chest rises and falls and her lips part. I press my lips to one side of her neck then pull back. She gives me a look that tells me she doesn't want me to stop.

I smile and the corners of her lips tip up. Her eyes under her long thick eyelashes are glazed over. She's beautiful like this and I wonder what she would look like underneath me, screaming my name.

"Are you going to go out with him? With Lo-gan?" I ask her, my voice so deep I barely recognize it myself.

"Are you going to give me a reason not to?"

The question catches me off guard. It takes a few seconds to work its way through my brain. I'm not sure where to go with it. Am I willing to cross lines with Ellie? Because once I do, there's no turning back. I should pump the breaks. I'm not looking for a relationship and she's an all-in kind of girl. Logic tells me a one-night stand is a horrible idea.

But the chemistry between us is so damn hard to resist. I know I shouldn't break my golden rule – to never fall for a woman. The rule that keeps me focused on my career and keeps my judgement crystal clear. But I've never met a woman this difficult to walk away from. My body is telling me exactly what it wants. Her. Now.

My throat goes dry. I hesitate for a second too long. Her bright blue goddess eyes suddenly blink and when they open, that blurry look in them is gone.

"That's what I thought," she bites out, then pushes past me, her heels clicking on the pavement like a woman scorned.

Seconds later, she's gone.

Chapter Six

Ellie

"Double shot vanilla latte for Ellie."

I look up from my chair by the window and wonder how many times the barista has called my name. I am out of it this morning, exhausted thanks to a lack of sleep last night. I need this coffee like I need air to breathe.

"That's me. Thank you very much," I say, grabbing the cup from the bar. I take my seat again, sipping the vanilla bliss. I need a jolt to my system to get me going.

I tossed and turned all night, suffering from the worst case of pent-up sexual tension. I went back and forth between trying to remember how good it felt to have Liam's body so close to mine, to trying to forget it entirely. The former won out. I like the way Liam makes me feel way too much, which is why I needed to leave. I saw the look in his eyes when I asked him for a reason not to date Logan. His hesitation was all the answer I needed, so I left before he had the chance to crush me. I'm sick of his games.

Giving up on sleep, I got dressed and left my apartment at 8 a.m., hoping the three-mile walk to Dream Bean Café would help shake the memory of last night from my mind. The sun was already warm as I walked the sycamore-lined streets of Reed Point, past the shops and cafés of First Street to the boardwalk along the beach. I stopped when I got to White Harbor beach and sat on one of the many empty benches lining the boardwalk.

It was still early enough to be quiet at the beach, just a handful of people out jogging or walking. Looking out across the sand, my thoughts drifted back to my parents. It always happens when I visit White Harbor; the three of us spent so many summers here when I was a kid. I miss them more than usual these days. With Olivia in Cape May and my parents who knows where, sometimes I just feel all alone. I shake my head to clear my thoughts and tilt my face to the sun, feeling the warmth of its glow on my skin.

Twenty minutes later, I'm sitting in my usual window seat at Dream Bean trying again to drown out thoughts of Liam. Being around Liam feels like being on a roller coaster. Thrilling, exciting and slightly nauseating. I can't help but wonder if things could ever just be easy between us. I know deep down the answer is no, which is why I need to stay away. Falling for Liam Bennett would be way too easy, but he's made it pretty clear he's not looking for a relationship. And if I'm being totally honest, it's not something I could give him anyways. I'm still carrying around too much baggage of my own. An entire cargo plane of baggage from six years ago. Either way, I'm tired of the constant up and downs with him, and I need to put an end to this. My phone vibrates on the table, knocking me from my thoughts. Olivia.

Olivia: You disappeared last night. My friend Logan was asking about you... Did I miss some-

thing? You have some explaining to do! Call me when you're up ;)

Logan. He seemed like a nice enough guy, and maybe he's exactly the kind of distraction I need. It was eleven thirty when I left the rehearsal dinner last night. I called an Uber and slipped out without saying goodbye to anyone. There was no way I was hanging around after *almost* sticking my tongue down Liam's throat… twice.

I tap the screen to respond and am still trying to decide how much to tell her when I hear that low voice that sends shivers over my skin. I immediately look to the door.

Liam. What are the chances?

He's in the middle of a phone call when he walks in wearing faded jeans and a gray T-shirt that hugs his abs. I love the way he looks in his suits - nobody wears a suit like Liam Bennett - but I'm liking this casual look too. A lot. His hair is tousled like he's spent all morning running his hand through it and the stubble on his face is scruffier this morning than it was last night. I hate that I'm so attracted to him.

After ending his call, he greets the barista and I watch her blush as she takes his order. Of course she does. Just look at him. She obviously thinks Liam is hot. What woman with two eyes and a pulse wouldn't? He shouldn't be allowed out of the house looking like that. Or in the suit he was wearing last night. I can only imagine what he would look like in joggers. Jesus, I bet it's more than any woman could handle.

Liam reaches for his wallet from his back pocket. His eyes sweep the room but he hasn't seen me yet and I briefly consider rolling onto the floor and army crawling towards the door.

Too late. He turns and his eyes meet mine as he pays for his order. I look away, hoping maybe he'll just take his order and leave. It's not my lucky day. I look up again to find him strutting towards my table, coffee cup in hand.

"Hey." A small smile crosses his lips as he reaches the table I'm sitting at.

"Hey." *Breathe, Ellie, breathe.* I'm still feeling the sting of last night's rejection and am completely humiliated.

"Can I sit?" I'm not sure why he asks, because he lowers his tall, muscular body down into the chair across from me before I even have a chance to answer.

"Feel free. I was just about to leave." I push my chair back to stand when he stops me. He grasps my hand across the table, and I feel that now familiar jolt of electricity zip through me.

"Do you need to be somewhere?" he asks, flashing that cocky grin he has perfected. I shift in my chair and he releases my hand.

"Anywhere but here works for me right now."

"No plans then. So you won't mind staying here with me for five minutes." He's so bossy. Why do I like that he's so bossy?

"Being here with you doesn't even crack my top ten list of things I want to be doing today, Liam. But a root canal makes the list." A muscle in his jaw twitches. A giveaway. I'm under his skin.

"A little effort here, Ellie, would be nice. I'm pretty sure the two of us are capable of a civilized conversation."

I shrug as if I'm bored. "You think? I'm not convinced." This man is infuriating. I know I should be trying harder to be nice for Olivia's sake, but he makes it's so damn difficult.

"Five minutes, Ellie. I have to get to the office anyways to catch up on reading. I can make it quick. We need to talk." He swallows. "Okay?"

I don't answer him. I say nothing. Instead, I lean back

in my chair, fold my arms across my chest and wait to hear what he has to say. I'm sure it will be incredibly annoying.

"Thank you," he says, then sips from his to-go cup. He rests his elbows on the small table, leaning closer. "Look, the wedding is coming up-"

I interrupt him, my eyes glaring, "I'm well aware of that."

"So, it would be nice if we could be in the same room together. We are going to be spending a whole lot of time together."

"I agree. Good talk. So, I think we are done here. Have a great day, Liam." I start to push up from my chair, but he stops me again, reaching for my hand.

"Can I have my hand back?" He releases it, sitting up straighter in his chair.

His gaze is locked on mine and I refuse to look away, glaring at him like it's some sort of petulant staring competition.

"You said five minutes, Ellie. That means I still have three and a half left. Sit."

I've got to give it to him. He's persistent and for some reason I go along with it, when getting up and walking away is what I should be doing.

"Fine. I'm listening. You have three and half minutes, and then I'm leaving."

Liam knocks back some of his coffee. "Ellie, there are two things that can't happen at my brother's wedding. One, I can't be fighting with a bridesmaid. And two, I can't be throwing that same bridesmaid up against a wall and devouring her mouth." I nearly fall off my seat. My heart flip-flops behind my ribcage. Then I remember that feeling this way about Liam is trouble. I need to steer this conversation to safer ground. I banter back, "Then I suggest you stay far away from the bridesmaid in question all together if you can't handle yourself around her. Seems easy enough to me."

"That's the problem. I can't help myself." I stare at him, trying not to let my jaw drop. *What did he just say?* The temperature in the room skyrockets to a bazillion degrees.

"Well, you should try harder. I can't help myself around chocolate chip cookies. I see them and I can't say no. But they're not good for me and after I've had four, I regret it."

"I wouldn't regret it, Ellie." He looks me directly in the eye, pinning me with his steel-gray ones.

"Yes, you would, Liam. Trust me. I know better than anyone how regrets work."

"What is that supposed to mean?" His voice is softer, the fight in his eyes gone. He sets down his cup and rests his large, strong hands on the table. I'm a sucker for this particular body part so my eyes dip down to sneak a glance. His nails are perfectly manicured, his fingers wide and long.

I ignore the question because I've already said too much. There are things he will never know about me, things I keep under lock and key from everyone in my life. Including my best friend, Olivia.

"Look Liam, the truth is you could never keep up with me," I say, redirecting the conversation. "You work too much. You have no idea how to have fun. Do you even know the definition of spontaneous?" I sit up straighter in my chair, my willpower renewed. "You can't plan life down to the second. You can't expect things to go smoothly all the time. Especially if you want to be with me." I look at him, anticipating his reaction. The tension between us so thick, it's hard to breathe.

Liam chuckles, but something changes in his eyes. I can tell he has something to say. "Let's get out of here, Ellie."

He reaches for my hand across the table. "Spend the day with me."

"What happened to going into the office? I thought you said-"

"Fuck it. What's the matter, Ellie? Don't you know how to be spontaneous?" A wide grin spreads across his face and shows off the dimple in his left cheek. He should really smile more. My heart twists. He's so fucking handsome.

Something in me wants to go with him and see what it would be like to spend a day with him. There are at least a dozen reasons why this is a very bad idea, but I already know I'm going to ignore them. I want to spend the day with Liam.

I meet his eyes and nod, bringing the coffee cup to my lips to hide my smile.

"Is that a yes?"

"I must be crazy. It's a yes." My pulse races and I swear my heart skips a beat as Liam weaves his fingers in mine and pulls me out of my chair. I follow him out the door.

"Where's your car?" he asks.

"I don't have one."

"Why don't you have a car?"

"I hate to break it to you, Liam, but not everyone has a car. Reed Point is a small town. I walk or I ride my bike. Plus, there's this revolutionary app called Uber." He looks baffled. Of course he does. I shake my head, amused with him. He squeezes my hand a little tighter, leading me across the street. We stop in front of a shiny black sports car. Looking at the bumper, I see it's a Porsche Taycan. I don't have to know much about cars to tell it must have cost a fortune.

"Is this yours, Liam?" I ask, frowning at the ridiculously expensive car that looks like it barely has room for two people.

"I hope so. If not, the guy whose car we're about to steal is going to be pissed."

"Liam, I can't go to jail," I joke. "I would make a horrible prison wife."

Liam scoffs and rolls his eyes. "Get inside, Ellie."

Liam opens the door and I slip inside onto the warm leather seat. After closing the door behind me, he rounds the front of the car and slides in beside me. The engine roars to life and he quickly shifts the car into gear, pulling away from the curb. He's put on a pair of black Ray-Bans and somehow he looks even hotter than he usually does. I'm not sure how that's even possible. How the hell am I going to able to keep my hands to myself today?

"Are you going to tell me where you are taking me?" I ask. My window is down, the breeze cooling my skin. It's helping to ease the butterflies deep in my belly. Being this close to Liam, just the two of us – it's almost too much.

"Nope, but I promise it will be *fun*," he says dryly, emphasizing the last word, turning his head to face me. He flashes me his cocky smirk, and I laugh. I'm enjoying this playful side of Liam way too much.

We drive in almost complete silence the rest of the way, until Liam pulls his car onto a rural gravel road. It's lined with tall mature oak trees that seem to go on forever, with a rustic three-rail farm fence bordering the property. He slows right down, driving cautiously. I'm having an inner conniption that his Porsche is no longer on pavement, but if Liam is nervous he doesn't show it. He actually seems more relaxed than I've ever seen him. The winding driveway leads to a charming country-style home with a wraparound porch and peaked roofs. To the right of the home is a yellow barn, and a handful of horses are grazing in the field just beyond it. It looks straight out of a movie.

"Liam, are you taking me horseback riding?" I ask,

looking over at him and admiring the view. The sun casts a ray of light across his face.

"How would you feel about it if I was?"

"I would love it! My parents used to take me horseback riding when I was a kid. I haven't been in years, but I always loved it," I answer. "I might have underestimated you, Liam Bennett."

"Your first mistake." Liam's mouth tips up into a gentle smile and my heart seizes. I force myself to look anywhere but his lips. Thankfully, he shifts the car into park and motions to step out, striding around to my side, cooling the heat that was rolling down my spine. He helps me from my seat, his hand resting at the curve of my back as he guides me to the stables. The sun is shining bright in the sky and there are perfect, fluffy clouds scattered across the horizon. We are greeted by Grayson, our guide, who's tall and very attractive and looks to be around our age.

"You two looking to go for a ride?" Grayson asks. We both answer yes, and Liam steps forward to handle the details. He fills out the necessary paperwork and pays for our rides. Grayson walks us over to two Morgan horses, a breed meant for riders who are less experienced, and runs us through the dos and don'ts of riding. Minutes later, we are ready to get moving.

"Let's get you up on the horse first, Ellie," Grayson drawls, motioning for me to step beside the horse. He places his hands on my hips and with my right foot hooked into the stirrup, I reach up and grip the saddle. I haul myself up until I am straddling the horse's back and then settle myself onto the leather. I reach for the reigns and I'm ready to go. "Thanks for the push," I say with a smile.

"Anytime, Ellie," Grayson replies, his voice smooth. I look over at Liam and notice that his jaw is clenched and he's looking at Grayson with a pointed stare. *He's jealous.* I sneak another glance to make sure I'm not just imagining it. *He's really effing jealous.*

It's Liam's turn to mount the horse. He expertly hitches his foot into the saddle and throws one leg up and over the muscular black horse. His biceps flex under his short sleeve shirt, his flat stomach that I wish I could get a glimpse of is taunting me to reach out and touch it. He settles into the saddle, and he looks sexy as hell while he does it. He catches me eyeing him, a coy smile curving his lips. Our eyes hold just long enough to feel that unfamiliar tug in my chest again. He mouths the words, *You okay?* I nod with a smile. I am so way more than okay right now.

Grayson decides we are ready, so I gently give Shadow a kick with my heel and he jerks a few steps forward, then relaxes into a steady walk. His ears perk up, his head bobbing in time with his feet, his hooves clacking along the dirt path. I give him a pat on his mane, a gesture of gratitude for not tossing me straight onto my ass. I look over my shoulder to see Liam and his horse Whisper following a few yards behind. Whisper appears to be hungover or half asleep, walking at a pace slower than molasses. "Liam, your horse has the temperament of a Basset Hound." I joke. It doesn't seem to bother him, though. Liam is patient with the animal, rubbing his hand over the horse's neck, telling him he's a beautiful boy. It's endearing and sweet and is working my ovaries into overdrive. At well over six feet tall with a hard broad chest and chiseled jaw and piercing gray eyes, Liam always looks gruff and commanding so seeing this softer side is making me dizzy.

"You live on the property, Grayson?" I ask, making polite conversation. Liam and Whisper have somehow caught up to us by this point.

"I do. Born and raised. My parents live in the main house up by the road and I built the smaller one down by the lake for myself." He points to a beautiful new home down the hill with a porch swing and a postcard-worthy wraparound porch. You two live around here?"

"Not far. We live in Reed Point. I mean, not together… I… I mean *we're* not together," I say, choking on my words. "Sorry, never mind me." It's definitely not the most eloquent thing that has ever come out of my mouth, but Grayson doesn't seem to have noticed. "I'm a city girl, I live in an apartment around the size of a shoebox. But I can see how a big home on this much land with a view of a lake would be appealing."

"It's all I've ever known, and I wouldn't trade it for anything. It really is a lot of house for just me, but I'm hoping to find the right girl and settle down soon." He looks me straight in the eye when he says it. "Happy to give you a tour if you're ever back in the area, Ellie."

I sneak a glance at Liam. His jaw is clenched, his eyes are narrowed and there's a vein in his neck that's pulsing. My heart pounds. He looks like he's ready to knock Grayson right off his horse. He's clearly feeling territorial. And I like it.

Chapter Seven

Liam

Is this Grayson idiot for real? I'm two seconds away from knocking this asshole out. Saying I'm pissed watching him flirt with the girl I'm on a date with is the understatement of the year. I know technically it's not exactly a date but close the fuck enough. He looks like the Marlboro Man. I'm half expecting him to pull out a bottle of beer and crack it open with his teeth. And for some reason Ellie is eating it up. *You've got to be kidding me.*

I listen to this Lone Ranger wannabe tell Ellie how handy he is with a set of tools. The guy *is* a tool, so I'm not the least bit surprised. I've never hated anyone more in my life than I hate this guy right now. He's in the middle of trying to persuade Ellie to come back for a night ride under the stars when I decide I've had enough.

I steer Whisper alongside Ellie and Shadow. Leaning in as close as I can, I ask, "Are you really going to make me watch you and the cowboy flirt with each other all day?"

She laughs. "Green's not your color, Liam. Besides, we're just talking," she purrs, a challenge simmering in her eyes. I know I have no right to be jealous - hell, I've never been jealous a day in my life - but it's Ellie. Everything's different with her. She's not some random, nameless one night stand I met at a bar. She's real and raw in a way I've never known.

"I'm not sure Grayson thinks the same. You should think about letting him know you have your sights on a better man. I'm four seconds away from telling him myself and if that happens, trust me, Ellie, he won't like it."

"Would that make you feel better? I'd hate for you to feel insecure," she says, giving me a mock, sympathetic look.

"Ellie, don't fuck with me," I growl, pinning her with a stare. I watch her eyes drift down my chest, lingering there for a second then returning to my gaze.

"Or else what, Liam?" She has mischief in her eyes. She picks up her pace, trotting ahead of me on her horse. She's messing with me and if I'm honest, I'm into it.

We spend the next twenty minutes riding through the trails. At one point, we pass through a shallow stream, the sounds of the water and the wind in the trees providing the soundtrack to the picture-perfect scenery. It turns out getting away from the office isn't half bad. For a few hours, at least.

"You're looking pretty good up there, Ellie." Grayson is flirting again. I grind my molars together so hard I'm surprised they don't crack. "Should we get moving a little faster?" *I think you're moving fast enough, buddy.*

"Let's do it," Ellie replies, with a smile on her face. I'm trying to stay as calm as I can. She's clearly loving riding and even though I'd like to drop-kick Grayson to the farm next door, I'm enjoying it too. I haven't thought about the office once or the cases piled up on my desk waiting for me. I can't remember the last time I've forgotten about work, even for a couple of hours. I was probably twelve. Scratch that - "never" would be the correct answer.

We pick up the pace to a slow trot and I fall back a little so I can watch Ellie. She looks gorgeous, her long brown hair blowing in the wind, the lighter caramel strands catching the light from the sun. She's wearing a fitted pair of jeans that hug her ass perfectly and she's leaning forward on her horse, giving me an incredible view. Damn, I want to touch her. I want to kiss her. Fist her hair. I've spent endless hours remembering what her lips felt like on mine and there's nothing I want more than to act on that fantasy. Shit, I need to get myself together.

An hour later and not a minute too soon, we are back at the stables saying goodbye to Grayson. I've had enough of watching this moron flirt with Ellie, but I'm not ready for my time with her to end. All day, I've had the urge to reach out and touch her. Her arm. Her cheek. Her hair. Anywhere. Just to feel her skin, make a connection. But I haven't because I'm still unsure where this is leading.

"I had a great time, Liam. Thank you for taking me," Ellie says as I lead her back to my car. "On a scale of one to ten, that was a solid nine type of day." She looks at me with her bright blue twinkling eyes, a sheepish smile on her face.

I hold open her door and we both slip inside. "Really, Ellie, a nine? That was one hundred percent a ten," I argue.

"Think what you want," she says. "But it was a nine."

"Do you always have to be this difficult?" I ask her. She looks at me like she has no idea what I'm talking about, then grins. And for some crazy reason, I think it's cute. Her crazy usually drives me insane, but right now, I like it. I crank the keys in the ignition, reluctantly taking my gaze off of Ellie, shocked by the feelings I'm having for her.

"I'm just busting your balls, Liam. I'm really impressed that you thought of horseback riding. I didn't think you had *fun* in ya. You proved me wrong." I'm more than satisfied with her answer.

Her phone chimes, interrupting my thoughts, and she digs it out of her purse. She has a text message and I notice her swiping the screen to life to read it. Her face lights up. I can't help but wonder who's putting that smile on her face. Is it a guy? Did she and the cowboy exchange numbers when I wasn't looking?

"Will you be able to drop me at my house?" she asks. "I'm not too far from Dream Bean. Only about a four-minute drive."

"Our date's not over." I give her a hard look. "You have somewhere to be?"

"Looks like I need to get ready for my date tonight. Logan asked me for dinner. You know, the guy from last night whose hair you're strangely jealous of. And wait - who said this is a date, Liam?""

Just fucking fantastic. I swallow. The guy with the hippie hair wants to take her out for dinner. Not. Happening. Not if I have anything to say about it. My stomach tightens. I'm having a difficult time remembering why I shouldn't take things further with her.

"Did you say yes?"

"Not yet."

"Put your phone away, Ellie. You can text him later to tell him you have a headache. Like I said, our date's not over." Her big eyes go wide.

"But-"

"No buts." I narrow my eyes in her direction, reversing my car from its parking spot. "Spontaneous, remember? You wanted spontaneous. I'm giving you spontaneous."

She slides her cell phone into her purse and I silently

declare myself the winner. I don't dare say it out loud though. I value my life too much for that.

"Okay, where to next?" she asks. "Ziplining? Skydiving? Maybe we're going to ride bulls?" She's challenging me again and my pulse picks up in response. This is the side of Ellie that I like most. The push and pull is such a turn-on.

"I have somewhere I need to be. I'm bringing you with me."

"Ooh, errands. Sounds exciting!" she jokes while fiddling with a ring she wears on her right hand.

I laugh and shake my head.

A little while later we're back in the city, pulling into my driveway. I park in front of my forty-five hundred square foot contemporary home and shut off the engine, turning to face Ellie.

"Is this where you live?" she asks, removing her seatbelt. "It's not what I expected."

"What did you expect? Or dare I ask?"

"I'm not sure, but not this. Maybe an old castle with a moat around it? Gargoyle statues guarding the entrance. Oh, and obviously a bridge. You know, so you can cross the moat," she explains. "Just your run-of-the-mill fortress, that way you could bury yourself in your work without having to worry about people annoying you or getting all up in your personal space," she continues, amused with herself. She seems to be amused with herself often.

I shrug, trying my best to keep my expression neutral, not wanting to give away that I find her little fantasy about my home life pretty entertaining. "What goes on in that brain of yours, Ellie? It's terrifying."

I dip my eyes to my seatbelt and un-click it and when I look back up, Ellie is reaching to the floor in front of her to grab her purse. My eyes steal a quick glance and I take the time to stare at her shamelessly. I have the sudden urge to trail my hands softly over her thigh or take her hand in mine and thread our fingers together. I swallow hard, asking myself what it is about her that gets my heart rate to skyrocket. Why do I want to take her face in my hands and kiss her breathless?

I get out of the car and walk around to Ellie's side, opening her door. I'm happy she's here, but this feels strange. Whatever this is. I don't usually bring women back to my house. Elle may have been joking around, but in a sense she was right - my home is my sanctuary. I don't like having anyone else around. For what feels like the hundredth time today, it makes me realize that Ellie isn't just anyone. She's different.

When I open the door, we are immediately greeted by my golden retriever Murphy. Ellie drops to her knees in an instant, giving him a big hug and burying her face in the soft fur of his neck.

"This is Murphy, but it looks like you two are already acquainted," I laugh.

"Look at you, you handsome boy," Ellie coos at my favorite guy. "You are such a good boy, Murphy, yes you are." She's rewarded with an onslaught of slobbery kisses, not that she seems to mind. She gazes up at me through her long, dark lashes and giggles. My pulse races, and I wonder again how she can infuriate me one minute, then make me want to do dirty things to her the next.

She eventually stands and follows me further inside, Murphy padding along beside her. I look at Ellie, gauging her reaction as we make our way through the foyer, past the living room on the left and the staircase leading upstairs on the right, into the kitchen at the back of the house. Her eyes are wide, taking in the marble countertops, top-of-the line stainless steel appliances and high-end cabinetry. I purchased the house two years ago and, with the help of an interior designer, remodelled it to make it feel more like me.

"This is amazing, Liam," she says, removing her sweater, revealing a pale green tank top she's wearing tucked into her skinny jeans. And she looks smoking. I swallow down the moan that sits at the back of my throat as I take in her slim frame, the slight curve of her ass and her flat stomach.

"I'm happy you like it. Come here, Murph, time to go outside." I give the dog a scratch behind his ear, then slide open the glass door to the backyard needing some air. Needing my eyes on anything but Ellie. I follow Murphy outside, busying myself with the barbecue, planning on making the two of us lunch. Ellie follows after giving herself a tour of my living room. She steps outside to admire the pool, hot tub and grounds that cost me a small fortune every two weeks to maintain. Her jaw is slack as she takes in the view.

"Do you ever use your pool?" she asks.

"Not often."

"Right, too busy stickin' it to the bad guys," she teases, dipping her toe into the water. "Swimming is good for you. Exercise *and* stress relief."

"I'm sure. So is work. I enjoy what I do, Ellie. I have goals." And my goal right now is to keep my hands to myself. But she's making it so damn hard. I'm not sure what to make of the spine-tingling sensations rolling down my back. It's a feeling I've never felt before. But one thing *is* clear - the sexual tension between Ellie and I is stifling. I fist my hands into tight balls, doing what I can to relieve the tension wracking my muscles.

"If I remember correctly, you already made partner, Liam. You achieved the goal you set for yourself. Now you deserve to relax a little. Enjoy your accomplishments. Enjoy life. Enjoy the pool," she says, plopping herself onto a lounger.

"Says you." I raise my brows at her.

"Says any normal, sane person," she counters. "We have very different ideas of what balance looks like. You're always so serious."

"I'm not serious. I'm realistic. There's a difference."

"Ugh, you're impossible," she says, feigning annoyance. "And you are a heart attack waiting to happen."

I watch her as she reclines by the pool, taking in her toned, tanned arms and shoulders glowing in the sunlight. I force my eyes away from her. *I need to get as far as I fucking can from this girl.*

"Take your time out here," I tell her, turning back to the house. "I'm going to make us lunch." *And maybe take a cold shower.*

"You know how to cook? Don't you have someone hidden in a bedroom upstairs at your beck and call? Let me guess… you just ring a bell and they come running?" She reaches towards Murphy, taking the ball from his mouth and throwing it across the lawn. Murphy pounces after it, clearly happy to stick with Ellie rather than follow after me like he usually does. Traitor.

Shaking my head at her, I walk inside, subtly adjusting the semi I've been sporting for most of the afternoon. I search the fridge for what I need, thankful for Bernadette who stocks it for me twice a week. I pull out two chicken breasts, a head of romaine lettuce, a lemon, mayo and parmesan cheese. I season the chicken, then make my way outside to fire up the grill. Ellie is happy with Murphy, so I go back inside and grab us two bottles of water. When I return, I find Ellie on her back laughing, laying in the grass with Murphy on top of her. Everything suddenly feels different. And right. And something in me wants more. More of Ellie and more of whatever is happening here.

I get to grilling the chicken, while Ellie goes back and forth from lounging by the pool to entertaining Murphy. Every now and then, she lies back against the pool chair, stretching her legs out in front of her, and my pulse hammers though my veins at the sight. If only she knew that I'm envisioning my hands on the curve of her hips, my mouth on the sensitive skin behind her ear. My body flush with hers. I need to stop this, maybe douse myself with this bottle of cold water.

After I've fixed the salad, we sit at the table on the veranda overlooking the pool, where I've laid out our lunch along with two glasses of wine. Red for me and rosé for her. Murphy has chosen to sit at Ellie's feet. That dog is as loyal as they come, but he hasn't left her side since she walked in the door. Ellie not only has a way with people but seems to be a dog whisperer too.

"Liam, this looks really good. I love Caesar salad," she says, picking up her fork and stabbing at a piece of romaine. "Mmmm, it tastes as good as it looks." The "mmmm" sound she makes with her lips goes straight to my dick. *Fuck.* This would be a lot easier if she wasn't so damn sexy. If her jeans didn't hug her perfect heart-shaped ass just right or her tank didn't show off the freckle right below her collarbone that's quickly become my favorite. If she didn't smell like sugar and lemons. *Dammit.*

I keep shovelling chicken into my mouth because my brain seems to have short-circuited and stringing words together feels impossible. How could I ever have thought bringing her here was a good idea? I've told myself before I can't be alone with her. I should have known better. I did know better, I just figured I could control myself. I may have been wrong. I spend the rest of lunch with a raging hard on, going out of my mind wanting her.

"Done," she says, setting her knife and fork across her plate. "Incredible, Liam. Thank you."

I shrug. "It was just a chicken salad."

"It was one of the best I've had, and I appreciate that you took the time to cook for me. It's been a while since anyone has done that." The compliment is nice, but I need sassy Ellie back. I know what to do with that version of her. I'm also sensing there's something more behind that comment, but I won't press her today.

"You always look so serious, Liam. You should smile more. I love it when you smile." Her cheeks flush a pale shade of pink. She looks beautiful sitting under the sun, a light breeze moving through her long hair. I can't help myself. I reach for her, brushing a few loose strands from her face, tucking them behind her ear. She slowly closes her eyes, enjoying my touch. She blinks back at me with her deep, blue goddess eyes. Those fucking eyes. Heat charges down my spine.

"I smile, Ellie," I say, pushing back in my chair, gaining some distance. "I smile when I win a case. Believe me, that happens often."

"That's not enough," she says with a hint of sadness.

"It might be for me," I reply, struggling to resist her. Fighting the urge to keep my hands to myself.

"I don't believe you."

"You should believe me when I tell you something. I don't just speak to hear my own voice."

She takes a deep breath and then exhales, her chest rising and falling with it. My gaze dips to her collarbone and my favorite freckle. The one I've been dying to touch. I flick my gaze back to her eyes because dammit, I'm not sure how much longer I can resist her.

"I know how to have fun," I tell her again. "Maybe you'd believe me if I threw you in that pool. Would that meet your criteria of fun?"

"On any other day, it would make my list. But today, not so much. Can't get my hair wet. I have a date tonight, remember?" A wicked grin flashes over her face. She stares into my eyes it's reckless. It's her *try me, Liam* face. And just like that, any control I thought I had is gone.

I want to kiss her.

Kiss her senseless.

I want to touch her.

No, I *need* to touch her. Kiss her. Give her pleasure.

I want her so fucking bad.

I push back my chair, the metal legs screeching across the stone deck. I stand and with two long strides I'm standing in front of her chair. I lean over her, resting my hands on the arms of her chair, caging her in, hovering over her sugary lemon scent. There is only a hair's distance between us.

"Cancel the damn dinner with Logan, Ellie. Now," I growl. Her breath hitches. Her blue eyes peer up at me, never breaking eye contact. She sucks her bottom lip under her teeth. My dick is now a steel rod in my pants. I've never been harder.

She narrows her eyes at me. "Why would I do that? Answer me, Liam. Why would I cancel a date with a handsome man that-"

Her eyes on mine, challenging me, is all it takes. My pulse races. I shut her up with a kiss, owning her mouth. I kiss her like I can never get enough and it's the last time I'll ever have my mouth on hers. Her lips part and my tongue takes full advantage, sweeping in to find hers. I deepen the kiss as her warm hands grip my hips. I want her so bad I can barely think. This is so far beyond anything I've ever felt. My need for this girl is so strong I'm helpless to stop it.

I press her back against the chair with my mouth, kissing her harder, causing her head to fall back against the cushion from the force. My tongue slips deeper into her mouth and she moans. The sultry sound is enough to make my mind go hazy. The kiss is intoxicating. It's enough to make me want all of her. I need to be inside her once. Just once, to get her out of my system.

She rests a hand on my cheek, scratching my beard with her fingernails. Chills cover my skin and I smile against her lips, loving the feel of her fingertips on me.

But she breaks the kiss, pulling back, her eyes meeting mine, "What are we doing?"

"No more talking, Ellie," I say, dropping my forehead to hers. "Why do we need to fucking talk so much?"

She nods her head in agreement, breathing hard, her eyes ablaze. She drags her tongue lazily across her bottom lip. She is liking this as much as I am and that's all the reassurance I need. I slide my hand to the back of her neck, pulling her closer, needing her out of this chair. Needing more. She stands on shaky legs. I take her face in my hands, backing her up, walking her backwards into the house. She bites her bottom lip, never taking her eyes off mine.

The back of her legs hit the dining table as I push her against it with my hips, grinding my arousal into her center. She whimpers, bringing one hand to the back of my neck, pulling my mouth into hers. I wrap my hand around her throat, my thumb resting on her pulse, feeling it tick, feeling it race for me. Pushing her head back, I'm given full access to the smooth skin of her neck. My mouth sucks a path of slow, wet kisses from under her chin to her collarbone, while I drag my grip on her neck slowly down to her chest. She groans like she's drowning in lust and just that sound she makes winds me up in a haze of need. I'm slowly losing all control.

I whisper into her neck, "Do you have any idea what you do to me?" It's rhetorical. There's no need for her to answer but I want her to know how she turns me on.

I inhale her scent while my nose trails lower between her cleavage. Her chest is fucking amazing and I take extra time grabbing, licking and pinching her perfect breasts through her tank top while her hands fist the back of my head. When I look up at her, she's smoldering. She's loving every second, her body writhing under my touch.

"Liam." She whispers it, her head thrown back, her body begging mine to give it what it needs.

No one has ever felt like this. Not even close. I'm losing all control. "Fuck, Ellie. I've missed your mouth." Her arms snake around my neck, one hand grasping the back of my hair again. Her grip on me is so tight, her nails digging into my skin.

Sliding my hands up her thighs to her waist, I free her tank top from her jeans, working my fingers over her flat stomach to her chest. Her chest heaves when I find the underwire of her bra. I drag my fingers across her ribs to her spine and unhook the clasp of the lace.

Her gaze is on mine again, leveling me with a look in her eyes that's laced with heat and desire. I want to remember that look in her eyes for later, when she's gone and I'm replaying these moments in my mind.

Finding the hem of her tank, I haul it over her head. I keep going. I need to see more of her, tearing her pink lace bra from her chest. It's so Ellie to wear hot pink lace and I love it.

Needing to see her, I take two steps backward to look at her. She's perfect. Better than perfect. Her olive skin is smooth, her stomach is toned, and her breasts are just the right size, not big and not small. Perfect. She's fucking gorgeous. My eyes moves up her stomach to her chest to that freckle on her collarbone that I've been dying to touch. I rip my T-shirt over my head, her gaze stopping on my chest for a second before I close the distance between us, pressing an open mouth kiss directly on her freckle. I moan and hum into the kiss then run the tips of my fingers over the mark on her skin and kiss it again. Her hands squeeze the sides of my face as she presses a kiss to the top of my head. "God, Liam," she says, her voice breathy as I press my mouth deeper into her skin. "More. I need more."

"I'll give you more, Ellie. I promise I'm going to make you feel so good." I'll give her anything she wants, but I'm not rushing this. I want to remember every single second of what we're doing right now. It's too good to not take my time, worshiping every inch of the body that has consumed my every thought over the last few months.

I cup her breasts in my hands, massaging and kneading them as I trail kisses across her chest. She's watching me through hooded eyes as my mouth finds the soft peak, pulling it into my mouth. Her eyes slam shut when I start to suck and lick, closing my mouth over the sensitive skin. She groans and arches her body into my mouth as I continue to devour her. To worship her. To lavish her with my tongue. I move to the other one, giving it the same hungry attention. From under my lashes, I look up at her. She's watching me with hazy eyes again and a shock of heat shoots straight to my groin. She's hot. So hot I can barely breathe. This all feels different. She feels like mine, if only for today.

"Cancel the date, Ellie or I'll do it for you," I demand, then tease her nipple with my tongue, my eyes on hers.

"Ahhh," she groans. Her breathing is shaky, her eyes laser-focused on mine.

"Answer me, Ellie," I demand again, kissing my way up her body to her mouth. I nip her lip, then follow with a slow, heated kiss. Her goddess eyes slam closed, then open again slowly; blue as the deepest part of the ocean.

"I already cancelled it," she pants, her breathing shallow and labored. "While you were grilling our lunch."

"You let me sit though lunch..." I kiss her with force. "Without…" I kiss her again, harder this time. "Telling me?" I slip my tongue into her mouth. Her hands move lower to my ass, palming and squeezing.

"Yes," she breathes.

"You will pay for that, Ellie," I hiss, reaching for the button of her jeans. I rip it open, then get to work on lowering the zipper.

"Hmm," she breathes into my neck, her breath on my skin warm and lingering. I want more. I need her out of these jeans. I need her body under mine.

I couldn't care less that this might be the biggest mistake of my life. The biggest mistake of my career.

I want her. I need her. I have to have her.

Take it all.

Chapter Eight

Ellie

Holy mother of hotness! Liam's big, strong hands are roaming my body. His bare chest is the best thing I've ever seen. *In my life*. It's chiselled and lean, with a dusting of chest hair. He's all hard lines, and that glorious V of muscle that trails down beneath his jeans into the promised land. And it's all mine for the taking. The view from where I'm currently trapped by Liam's pelvis is mind blowing. It's circuit overload. I can feel his size against my belly. *Je-sus!*

I slide my hand between us until I find what I'm looking for and palm him with my hand over his jeans. The dick pic that circulated through our group chat didn't do him justice. He's hard and huge behind the zipper of his jeans. I rub the outline of him up and down over the fabric and he groans against my mouth, causing me to smile. He kisses my smiling lips.

Pulling back, he watches me. His gray eyes are dark, three shades darker than they usually are, and I can feel his heated stare on my skin. I'm not sure how this happened, but right now I really don't care. I'm supposed to hate him, but I want him. He wants me too.

Liam flicks open the button of my jeans, then my zipper. It's frantic and feral, he's driving me mad. I know I should be stopping this. I know how this will end. Liam doesn't do relationships, and I can't either until I straighten out my life. I should end this now, but I won't. It all feels too good to stop. Maybe this could be nothing more than a one-time deal. Scratch an itch. Get him out of my system. Nobody gets hurt.

"Ellie," he rasps. My name on his tongue makes my heart pound, and I instantly forget the doubts floating through my mind. I open my mouth to answer him when he kisses me. He bites down on my bottom lip, gently tugging at it with his teeth. It's such a turn-on. My pulse thunders in my ears.

I continue rubbing the bulge in his pants, giving it a gentle squeeze. He grips my hip tighter at the contact, I'm sure leaving a mark on my skin. "Feel good?" I ask, my voice full of lust.

"Fuck, yeah. It does," he rumbles, his lips all over me, travelling from my jaw, down the column of my neck to my collarbone. The scruff of his beard scratches over my skin, driving me out of my mind.

My hands fly to the waist of his jeans. With steady hands, I undo the button and unzip him. I pull him out, curling my fingers around him. He groans something under his breath that I can't make out, the sound muffled by the flesh of my neck in his mouth. I fist my hand around his length and stroke him, up and down, then again. He pulls back and his mouth falls open and his eyes squeeze shut.

"Holy shit," he groans. "I love the way you make me feel. That feels so good."

Then his mouth crashes into mine. He yanks down my jeans with his hands as he kisses me. He can multitask. I'm good with this. He kneels down, tearing my pants from my legs, leaving me in only in my pink lace thong.

Liam stands back up. I'm suddenly dizzy, taking him in. I've never seen anything sexier. His bare chest with hard planes of muscle, his jeans slung low on his hips, the fly of his jeans undone and a happy trail that I can't wait to get my hands on. He's every girl's late-night fantasy. *What did I do to deserve this?*

"Jesus, Ellie. You're body's incredible." His eyes sear over me from my toes to my lips.

"I was just thinking the same about you," I say, leaning back, resting my hands flat against the table on either side of me. Liam's eyes rest on my mouth and before I know it, he's kissing me again. His hands find my ass, lifting me onto the table, our mouths still locked in a deep, lustful kiss. With his knee, he nudges my legs open wide for him, his hard length grinding into me. My eyes fall closed as he lays me out on the table, taking my hands in his, stretching them up above my head, his hard, warm body stretched out over mine.

I. Die.

Then I die again.

He's demanding and confident, taking complete control. Liam definitely knows what he's doing.

My pulse races when his hands and his mouth head south, trailing wet kisses over my skin. When his lips make contact with my ribcage, I arch my back off the table. His warm mouth causes a ripple of goosebumps over my skin. "Yes, Liam. So good." It feels like an out-of-body experience. My skin feels too tight for my body.

"I'm going to make you feel good, Ellie. So fucking

good." He makes good on his promise, trailing the tips of his fingers like a feather down my stomach, finding the edge of the only piece of fabric on my body. He dips his hand inside of my thong. "I want you so bad, Ells." He shortens my name, and my breath stops in my throat. There are only a handful of people who call me anything but Ellie. It feels intimate. Terrifying. A lot more than the hookups I'm used to, the only intimacy I've ever allowed myself.

I still, and Liam notices.

"Are you okay?" he pulls back, his hand frozen on my pelvis inside my panties. The look in his eyes has softened. It's thoughtful and sweet. It's steady.

"Fine. More than fine. Don't stop, Liam."

"You sure?"

"Never been more."

That's all the assurance he needs to kiss me senseless. The hand that was so close to giving me the release I needed moves from inside my thong, up my torso to my cheek. His chest flattens flush over top of mine and my fingers wind tight through his thick brown hair. My hips rise off the table, needing contact with the giant package he's packing behind his briefs. And as good as he looks in those, I really need them in a puddle on the floor.

Liam traces his thumb over my bottom lip, his gaze so intense my body shudders. His mouth replaces his thumb, and he forcefully slips his tongue inside when, *shit no*, the doorbell interrupts us. *No. No. No.*

"Ignore it, Ellie. I'm not stopping," he says, continuing the hungry kiss.

The doorbell chimes again. This time it's accompanied by the high-pitched voice of a child calling Liam's name. I freeze like a deer in headlights.

Liam blows out a big breath, dropping his forehead

against mine. "I'm sorry, Ellie. Fuck, you have no idea how sorry."

Liam starts picking up our clothing from the polished hardwood floor, handing me my bra, my tank top and jeans. He throws on his T-shirt and tucks himself back into his jeans, then waits until I'm fully dressed before stalking to the door. He opens it to a little boy in the doorway wearing a ball cap on his head, clutching a leather baseball glove.

"Hey buddy. What's up?" Liam lifts the boy's cap from his head and flips it around so it's backwards. My stomach does a cartwheel it's so stinking cute.

"Hi Liam. Wondering if you wanted to play ball with me? I've been practising my fastball so much just like you taught me." The boy's eyebrows shoot up when he spots me behind Liam.

"Who's your buddy, Liam?" I ask, padding my way to the door, my hair I'm sure a wild mess from Liam's hands. The kid looks to be around eight years old, with light blond hair and two missing front teeth. There's a splatter of freckles across his nose.

"This is Kip. Kip meet Ellie." Liam goes on to tell me that Kip lives next door and that he's been helping him amp up his softball skills. This sweet boy is beaming, his little face tipped up high, looking at Liam with awe in his eyes.

"Hey Ellie! You know Liam is the best coach in all the world and I'm his very favorite player." Kip greets me in the cutest little voice. "You can play with us too if you like? Or maybe you're busy and I should go home. I know girls like softball too. There are three girls on my team. But I can come back another time if you're busy." His face drops to his shoes, making me immediately want to hug him. Liam catches my gaze, his eyes full of warmth and something else, something I've never seen in him before. The person staring at me seems nothing like the moody, standoffish man I thought I knew. This kid obviously means a lot to him and seeing that makes it easier for me to set my steamy thoughts aside. For now. Liam's lips part to answer, but I beat him to it.

"No way, little slugger. Liam needs to see your mad softball skills. Don't let me stop you." Kip's face lights up like fireworks on the Fourth of July. Liam turns to me, pulling his bottom lip under his teeth with a half-smile. His eyes linger on mine as he starts to walk Kip towards the front lawn. I'd be lying if I said it wasn't hot as hell. So much for putting those thoughts aside.

"Alright little buddy, show me what you got! You comin', Ells?" Liam asks me, peering over his shoulder with a gorgeous smile, the dimple in his cheek on full display. He takes it one step further, following his question up with a wink. I feel my heart skip a beat.

"I wouldn't miss it." I shoot him a wink back, following the sexiest man I've ever seen as he clasps a hand on the shoulder of the cutest little guy at his side. My ovaries might not survive the sight.

The next half an hour is spent sitting in the grass under the sun watching the two of them throw a ball. My heart beats a little faster watching Liam help Kip with his windup with incredible patience, and another one when I see Kip practically bursting at the seams with happiness. Dammit, if the sight of Liam helping this towheaded little boy with his fastball isn't the hottest thing I've seen in my life. He's more gorgeous than anyone has a right to be.

Not only is he ridiculously handsome - not to mention unbelievable with his tongue - but he has this softer side that I had no idea existed. Up until now I had been convinced that Liam was incapable of any real emotion besides being surly. Watching him high five Kip after he throws a near perfect pitch, I realize I may have gotten him all wrong. After this afternoon, Liam has a few more ticks in the pro column of my why-is-Liam-such-a-moody-jerk list than he did yesterday.

"You're a natural! You've definitely been practising," Liam calls to Kip, hyping him up.

"You noticed, Liam? Because it's true. I listen real good to what you tell me."

"How could I not? Your arm is killer. Keep up the practising, big guy."

Butterflies flutter wildly in my belly, but I do my best to calm them. I don't want to overthink this. I don't want to start envisioning a future with Liam that doesn't exist. I will not repeat the mistakes I made when I was young and stupid and reckless. As the boys continue tossing the ball back and forth, my thoughts drift to six years ago, to the tangled mess I got myself into back then.

I could never have predicted the way my life would unravel in the months after my parents left. Maybe I thought I'd be okay, that I had the smarts and the strength I needed to navigate life on my own. Boy, was I wrong. It felt like everything changed overnight. My parents were gone, Olivia was busy dealing with her own problems. There were no siblings or grandparents to lean on. I still remember how lost and alone I felt, how desperate I was for affection, for someone to love me. A familiar weight settles on my shoulders, the same one I feel whenever I think back to that time in my life, and to the damage I've yet to repair.

Kip hollers my name and I'm thankful for the interruption, for any excuse to push those memories from my mind.

"Ellie, last one and it's going to be my very best! Watch this."

"Watching, little dude," I say.

Liam crouches down to the ground, readying his glove to catch what turns out to be Kip's very best throw of the day. I stand up with my arms in the air, giving him a fist pump. "You are ready for the big leagues! Better start practising your autograph for when you turn pro!" I say, giving him my own giant high five. Liam is next in line, scooping Kip up off the ground and onto his shoulders. My heart swells and for a second I forget about all the reasons I shouldn't let him get too close.

When the excitement subsides, Kip says a reluctant goodbye. "I better get home. Thanks, Liam. It was nice to meet you, Ellie. I hope I get to see you again soon." Liam pulls him in for a side hug, then Kip runs to me and wraps his arms around my waist before leaving.

"He's the cutest. You are really good with kids," I say, rocking back and forth on my heels with my hands in my pockets. "You also have a great arm. Pretty impressive."

"I'm pretty good at everything I do. It's ridiculous, really." He says it with that cocky smile that does me in every time. My mind goes straight to the gutter and I have an overwhelming urge to find out just *how* good he is. *Pull yourself together, Ellie.*

"You gotta go and ruin a good day, don't you? Just when I was starting to change my mind about you, your huge ego makes a comeback." I turn towards the front door to grab my shoes. I need to get out of here. Now that it's just the two of us again, things are starting to feel a little awkward and tense. Leaving now would definitely be for the best. Before Liam and I take things too far. If we end this now, we can be friends, and nobody will get hurt. Maybe we'll even be able to handle being in the same room together without wanting to kill each other. Most importantly, there will be no risk of secrets being uncovered. Those will stay hidden, like they're supposed to.

I discreetly order an Uber.

THREE HOURS later I can still taste him on my mouth. I can still feel his touch all over me. The game of cat and mouse Liam and I have been playing caught up with us today and I'm still not sure how I feel about it. I'm still not sure what to think of *him*. He's prickly but soft, serious but playful, arrogant but kind. In other words, he's everything I want in a man and nothing I can have.

But his lips. The way he kisses. My God, the way he kisses.

He takes control, consumes, devours and owns my mouth. His big hands are strong when he grabs me, his body controlling me expertly. And there's no doubt that if we ever did take things all the way, it would be the best sex I could ever imagine.

The easy banter we had fallen into throughout the day became uncomfortable almost as soon as Kip left. We looked everywhere but at each other; he grew quiet and I went back and forth between struggling to find words and talking one hundred miles a minute to fill the silence. He didn't fight me when I told him I should get home but was pissed that I called an Uber. He made me hand over my phone, then cancelled the booking, most likely ruining my five-star rating and screwing me over for future rides - as I was happy to point out to him. He drove me home, my body humming the entire way, remembering what he looked like bare-chested and in briefs. Majorly tented briefs.

One thing I know for sure amidst all the uncertainty: I liked spending time with Liam today. Never would I have imagined having so much fun with him, he's usually so busy being brooding and testy. But today Liam was funny and quick-witted, thoughtful and sweet. Gentle, even. An actual smile replaced his typical serious "work mode" face.

Sitting up from the couch, I reach for the wine bottle on my coffee table and pour myself a little more. I take a sip, sit back and pull my knees into my chest. I reach for my crossword puzzle book to get my mind off Liam. Some people meditate, I do crossword puzzles. My dad got me hooked when I was a kid. We'd sit together for hours trying to figure out the grids of squares and blank spaces. My dad used to say puzzles push our brains to the next level, increasing vocabulary and fluency. I think they were secretly his way of connecting with me, a reason for just the two of us to spend time together. Whatever it was, I loved that time with him and in the process became a cruciverbalist. It's kind of hard to believe, though, considering my ongoing love affair with my favorite four-letter words.

Opening to my page and grabbing my pen, I search the grid for where I left off. Finding my spot, I read the clue. *Falling in love observation.* I stare at the black and white print on the page like the answer will telepathically come to me. And when it does, I smile. It's a seven-letter answer. I write out each letter in capitals.

ITS SO EZ

Is it?

Maybe it can be.

Chapter Nine

Liam

I set my pen down, leaning back in my office chair, slowly closing my eyes. I'm distracted. My focus is shot. I keep telling myself it's the case I'm working on but it's painfully obvious to me it's not. It's Ellie. It's been twelve hours since Ellie was underneath me, and she is all I can think about. How good she felt in my arms and how badly I want more of her. I'm so lost in my thoughts, I'm barely aware that there are people in the room with me. Unfortunately, they seem to have noticed that I haven't heard a word they've said.

"Liam," Jules snaps, levelling me with a *what the fuck* stare when I look her way.

My sister and my father are sitting across from me in my office. They are here to meet with me about the VR tour contracts, to get my opinion on the terms. What I say goes when my family asks me for my opinion on Seaside business deals. With a yes or a no, I can cause massive deals to move forward or to crash and burn.

"It's a go," I say convincingly. "The contracts look

good. Great work on this, Jules," I add, sitting back in my chair and crossing my left ankle over my knee.

Jules straightens her spine, sitting up in her chair with a confident grin. It's the same grin she's worn since childhood, the one that screams *I'm just that good.* She exchanges glances with our dad. I wasn't sure how seriously she would take the position at the Seaside Corp when our father first offered her a spot in his company, but she has proven herself time and time again. Ever since we were kids, Jules has never taken life too seriously, intent on living in the moment, making her own rules. We're basically exact opposites in that way. I have to admit, though, that I admire her and what she has accomplished at the family business. She has a distinct vision of taking the Seaside brand worldwide, and she's killing it.

"Thanks, Liam. I can't wait to get started on this. 'Try it before you buy it' will be huge for us."

Expanding into a VR booking process will not only allow potential guests to tour our properties through virtual reality, but it will also let them compare hotel prices and book rooms directly. It's a no-brainer deal.

"Great work, Jules. I am proud of you. This will put us a step above all the rest," my dad adds, reaching over to give her forearm a gentle squeeze. Our father is a genius when it comes to business dealings, so his stamp of approval says a lot.

"Thanks, Dad. I've got this. It's going to be great. I'll keep you in the loop once filming starts. They said they could be ready as early as next month."

"That's great, sweetheart. Now to a different matter: your brother's wedding. Your mother has been very busy getting the house ready for Parker and Olivia's big day. I would appreciate it if you could both check in with her and help out in any way necessary. You know she won't ask, and I don't need her putting out her back or breaking a leg."

"Not a problem, Dad. I'll stop by today after work,"

"Thank you, Liam." He nods with approval in his eyes. It's an approval I've worked very hard to earn for most of my life, from a man I've always looked up to. My dad has an abundance of charm and wit, but he's a hard-ass in business – we have that in common. But when it comes to looks, I'm told most often that I resemble my mother. I'm an inch or so taller than my father, broader chested with lighter features. His dark eyes to my gray, his hair once almost black where mine is a dark brown. Like me, Miles takes after our mom while Jules and Parker look more like our dad.

"I'm out tonight with Olivia and the girls, but I'll give her a call. I still can't believe they're getting married at the house. I think it's so cool. They are like a living, breathing fairy tale," Jules adds. "I just wish they would move back home already. I miss having them here."

My curiosity is piqued, I can't help myself from asking: "What's going on tonight? Who are you going out with?"

"Since when do you give a flying f- flapjack who I'm hanging out with?" She looks at my dad, remembering to censor her language. My dad had always preached to us kids that if you wouldn't say the word in church, you shouldn't say it at all. *So much for that piece of advice.* Her eyes narrow at me. "Ah, I get it - you care since there's a big, big possibility that my plans might include Ellie," my sister teases, a knowing glint in her eyes. "Why didn't you just come out and ask if Ellie was going to be there? I would have been happy to let you know that yes, she will be there."

This gets my attention. I find myself wondering, at different points in my day, what Ellie could be doing or where she is. I'm embarrassed to say I even drove past Bloom this morning to see if I could catch a glimpse of her in the shop window. *What the hell is wrong with me?*

I try to play It cool when I answer. "Wasn't asking about Ellie."

"Oh, you weren't, were you?"

"Nope."

"Interesting," she says, arching her brow. "I saw the way you were looking at her at the rehearsal dinner. Everybody saw the way you two were looking at each other. You were practically trying to procreate with your eyes all night. Cut the crap, Liam. What's the story with you and her?"

What did they see? Were we that obvious? There was no denying the smolder between us, and damn right, I wanted to have sex with her, but I thought I was at least a little discreet about it. I lean back in my chair, folding my arms across my chest, making it clear I am stopping this conversation before it starts. My stare shifts to my dad, but thankfully I can see that he's going to leave this one alone for now. My look tells him I'm not in the mood for talking.

"That's fine, Liam. I'll drop it… for now," Jules says. "But for the record, I like Ellie. I like her a lot and it's obvious you like her too. Don't be an idiot. Ask the girl out."

I shake my head, ignoring what she just said. "Don't you have work to do?"

She stands, reaching across my desk for the contracts, but I don't miss the twinkle in her eyes and the confident grin that spreads across her face. This conversation may have been put on pause, but I can see it's not over as far as my sister is concerned.

My dad follows, rising from the chair and offering his hand.

"Liam, always good to see you, son." I shake his hand

with a firm grip. "If you need to talk, you know where to find me. I'm always here to listen."

"I know, Dad. Thanks. I'll see you later tonight at your house." He nods, then follows my sister towards the door. Jules opens the door for our dad, but before she follows him out, she turns back to look at me. "Ask her out, Liam. I'm serious. I'd give anything to have someone look at me the way she looks at you. Ellie's the real deal. Don't miss your chance."

Before I have the chance to respond, she's gone. I make a mental note to check in with her more often. I know she's still heartbroken over her split with Alex.

I stand and pace my office, rubbing the back of my neck. I walk towards the window, shoving my hands in my pockets. My mind wanders back to Ellie. *Did I take things a little too far? Okay, fine, maybe I did.* I made a mistake that day, and I'm making an even bigger one by considering taking things further. I didn't make partner to be distracted by a beautiful woman. Years of commitment and hard work got me to where I am today. I have a reputation in Reed Point as a fearless attorney - serious, restrained, unrelenting. If you're looking for understanding and a soft touch, I'm not the attorney for you. I'm a shark in and out of the courtroom, and that's just how I like it. I've spent my twenties perfecting the art of self-discipline – daily 5 a.m. workouts, green smoothies every morning on my way to the office, then work, work and more work. Letting a woman get in the way of my career is never going to happen.

But this woman has gotten under my skin with her smart mouth and sexy curves. The playful banter and innuendo between us have become an obsession. It's the sexiest form of foreplay I've ever experienced. It makes it hard, pun intended, not to think about what she'd be like in bed. Is she as wild as I think she might be? Would she like it fast and hard or slow and soft? I hate that I want her so badly.

Threading my hands through my hair, I ask myself why I'm still thinking about her when I have a million other things I need to be working on. Instead, I'm wondering where she is and what she's doing. Is she making somebody smile with her crazy jokes, is she thinking of me? I resolve to push all thoughts of Ellie out of my mind. I have a long day ahead of me and I need to get some work done.

I try to return my attention to the case on the desk in front of me. It's just one of many. I currently have more clients than I can handle, and my workload just keeps on piling up. Straightening in my chair, I open the file. A junior assistant catches the corner of my eye passing my door, nodding her head in hello. Her long brown hair is down and about the same length as Ellie's. My thoughts wander to Ellie on my dining table looking hot as fuck, to the feel of her soft hair running through my fingers. Already it seems like it was a futile attempt to concentrate on the work I should be doing. *Just fucking great.*

Shaking memories once again from my mind, I get to work.

I can do this.

I can go an afternoon without thinking about Ellie.

I hope.

IT'S seven o'clock when I pull up in front of my parents' house, cut the engine and head towards their front door. I open the door to the 10,000 square foot estate I grew up in, greeted by the sounds of chatter coming from inside. I recognize the voices - Jules, Olivia, Olivia's sister Kate. And Ellie. *WTF.*

I walk through the foyer and head for the kitchen at the back of the house where my mom typically spends most of her time. Sunlight streams through the wall of glass windows, and there's country music playing lightly through the surround sound speakers. It's Mom's new favorite genre of music, thanks to my soon-to-be sister-in-law, Olivia.

My mother greets me in the hallway with a hug and a kiss on the cheek, always happy when one of her kids comes over to visit. "Hey, honey. Your dad told me you might stop by tonight. How's my baby?"

"I'm good, Mom. What's going on in there?" I nod in the direction of the laughter coming from the back of the house.

"The girls are in the kitchen. They met Olivia here, and I talked them into staying for a drink before they head out on the town. You should go say hello. Parker is here too."

I nod. No, this isn't going to be awkward at all. I've thought about Ellie all damn day long, but I haven't tried to contact her. Instead, I fantasized about all the ways I would take her if I ever got another chance, my personal favorite being the on-the-kitchen-counter scenario. Up-against-a-wall is a close second. On-my-lap-in-the-back-seat-of-my-Porsche also made it into the highlight reel spinning through my mind today.

"Did you eat? Knowing you, you worked right though dinner. Am I right?" My mom cocks her head to the side, her eyes meeting mine. Smiling, I shake my head, both in answer to her question and to shake the dirty thoughts from my mind.

"I ate, but nothing as good as your cooking. I'll eat whatever you're offering."

"Good." She pats my cheek, then turns towards the kitchen. I follow behind. "Liam's here," she announces to the room. The four girls are perched around the large marble island in the center of the kitchen, drinking wine and nibbling on cheese and olives from a charcuterie board.

Olivia slips off her stool and wraps her arms around me in a hug. I've learned over the last year that Olivia is a hugger and although I'm not one for touchy-feely stuff, I like her too much to not return the embrace. There's no doubt my brother found "the one" in Olivia and seeing them so happy has made me start to wonder if there might one day be room for a relationship in my life too. Jules doesn't get up, but mumbles a hello through a mouthful of finger food, while Kate smiles and tosses a hello my way. And Ellie, well, she avoids eye contact all together. Her lips are curved in an awkward smile, and she seems pensive. Or maybe just annoyed? I can't read her expression, and it frustrates the fuck out of me. This is a woman who typically wears her emotions on her sleeve, but right now I can't tell what she's thinking. Her big blue eyes drift around the room, looking at nothing in particular. Definitely not looking at me, which I think is the point.

"Have a seat, honey," Mom says, standing in front of the stove, preparing me a plate of something that smells of garlic. "I made homemade sauce this morning. You're in luck."

I take a seat on a barstool at the opposite end of the island from the girls, and my mom hands me a beer and slides a bowl of steaming hot pasta on the counter in front of me. It's Bolognese, and nobody makes a sauce like my mom. I twist the noodles around my fork and blow before taking a heaping bite. Meanwhile, the girls are talking about *The Bachelor* and who they decided is the king of last night's episode. Their conversation makes absolutely no sense to me, but they seem totally engrossed in it. They all burst out in laughter at something Ellie said, but it's her laugh that fills the room. It's her smile that makes me never want to tear my eyes off of her.

I watch her. I can't look away. Everything about Ellie is a massive turn-on. She feels like danger, like lust. I take a long pull of my beer and try to clear my head. I can be in a room with Ellie Reeves and control myself.

"Where's Parks?" I ask, winding my fork thorough my pasta.

"He's watching football with Dad in the living room," Jules answers. I nod, my mouth too full to respond. It's official: My mom makes the best damn sauce on the planet.

"Speaking of Parker," Olivia says through a playful grin. "I should quickly go say goodbye to him. We should probably get going, hey girls?"

"Yes, we should. We all need dates for the wedding, and we aren't going to find them here in Mrs. B's kitchen," Kate says. *That* is enough to get me to stop eating, my fork hovering in mid-air over the bowl. A jolt of jealousy pounds its way through my chest. I can feel my mom's stare burning a hole through the side of my face, but I refuse to meet her eyes. I steady my gaze into the pasta dish, intent on looking anywhere but in Ellie's direction. I feel like a ticking time bomb. We haven't talked about what happened yesterday or where things between us stand. And I know that she's not mine and I'd be a dick to tell her what she can and can't do. But the thought of someone else with Ellie? I'm not okay with it. Not at all.

The girls get up from their stools and make their way to the door. Ellie rounds the edge of the island giving me, for the first time, a full view of her outfit. She's wearing fitted jeans and a low-cut, tight white sleeveless top. There is a sliver of her tanned, toned stomach on display. I have a perfect view of her cleavage: not too much, but just enough to make me wonder what she's wearing under that fabric. Is it the bright pink bra I saw yesterday? Shit, I'm practically drooling as I look at her because I'm a man, and Jesus… tits.

She lifts her goddess eyes to meet mine for a split second before looking away. That's all I can take. I'm out of my chair so fast, the motion catches her eye. I mouth the words "we need to talk" and when her eyes go wide, I add, "now" so she knows I'm dead serious. She tells the girls she needs to quickly use the washroom and she'll meet them outside. Her voice raspy, but convincing.

She hurries down the hall and when everyone else is out of the room, I follow close behind her. *What the hell am I doing?* I should be keeping her at arm's length but instead I'm chasing her down. She stops in front of the washroom at the far end of the hall, turns, and shoots me a confused look. Lowering my voice, I come right out and say it.

"Are we really not going to talk about this? Are we just going to fucking pretend nothing ever happened?" The air is so hot between us it crackles. A riot that feels impossible to quiet rages in my chest. I want to run my fingers over the exposed skin above her jeans. Drag my tongue down the dip of her cleavage. I want her so badly right now I think I might actually die.

"Do we really need to do this now? Jesus, Liam. We are in your parents' home and I'm leaving right now to go out with your sister and your sister-in-law," she hisses, keeping her voice quiet. "Now is not the time."

"Where are you going tonight?"

"That's none of your business, is it?"

She's right. It isn't my business. But I need to know. I feel like I'm losing it. My entire life is planned, controlled. But right now, I'm spinning. This has never happened to me before. No matter how hard I try to forget her, to resist her, I can't.

Every part of me wants her.

Craves her.

I know with complete certainty that I want another night with her.

"Ellie, we need to talk." I take a step closer and her citrus scent slams into me. Dammit, she smells fantastic. Her slow, measured breaths are the only tell that she's struggling to regain her composure. She backs up.

Her breath hitches. "Liam," she breathes. "Don't do this. Please, not now." She closes her eyes, swallowing hard. "Stop messing with me."

My pulse throbs. Her chest rises and falls. It feels like a game of chess. Each of us waiting for the first move. I make mine.

"I don't want to wait until the wedding to see you again," I tell her. My stomach is one giant knot. I'm wound so tight it feels hard to breathe.

There's a sparkle in her eyes and my skin heats all over.

"Me neither," she says in a quiet voice. "What are we going to do about it?"

"Go out with me tomorrow night. I'll pick you up at seven." I try to read her. Does she want me as badly as I want her? Her eyes squeeze shut, and she blows out a deep breath. She's thinking. I wait.

"Okay. I'll go out with you. I'll be ready at seven."

A slow, deliberate smile crosses my face. "See you tomorrow, Ellie."

"See you tomorrow, Liam." She walks towards the

front door, the roundest, tightest, sexiest ass rocking back and forth in time with her steps.

At the door, she pauses and turns back to look at me. She smiles, and just the sight of it knocks me off balance for a second. And then she's gone. In a way, I am too.

Parker walks into the foyer seconds before the door slams shut. He looks in Ellie's direction, then shifts his eyes to me with a grin.

"I see what's going on here," he says, waving his hand from Ellie's direction to mine.

"There's nothing to see."

Parker claps a hand on my shoulder while passing me on his way to the bathroom. "You keep on telling yourself that."

Chapter Ten

Ellie

It's girls' night so the obvious choice is Cocina Caliente. It's our ace-in-the-hole restaurant that never disappoints. It's where Olivia, Kate and I have always gone to celebrate life's milestones and achievements, and now that Jules and Olivia are about to be family we include Jule's too. Jules is great, and we're all happy that she's joined our little group. It's never felt awkward… until now. Sitting across from Liam's younger sister while the highlight reel of hot AF images of her older brother spin through my mind is not uncomfortable in the least. *I'm being sarcastic, if it wasn't already obvious.*

Each of us are two spicy margaritas in when the waiter arrives with our orders. He sets my enchiladas with extra guacamole - obviously - in front of me. My go-to order. I'm a one-trick pony when it comes to Mexican food. I grab my fork and dive into the pulled chicken and cheesy goodness, chasing it with a forkful of rice.

Olivia nudges my arm with her elbow. "He is *so* your type."

"Who's my type?" I ask her, wondering how much of the conversation I've missed while I've been busy taking a virtual ride in Liam-land.

She shoots me a concerned look. "Our waiter. He looks like he's fresh off the pages of Spanish *Vogue*. Where did they find him?"

"Hmm. I didn't notice," I say, bringing my spicy Marg to my lips and downing a gulp. It's lime, not too strong, and doing its job taking the edge off. To say I'm hot and extremely bothered after my run-in with Liam earlier tonight is the understatement of the year.

"What is the matter with you? You would never miss ogling a guy that looks like that." Olivia's suspicious voice cuts across the table. "Are you sick or something?"

I shrug. "Not that I'm aware of. I'll check him out when he comes back." I quickly help myself to another forkful of my enchilada. Can't answer questions with a full mouth, that's my strategy. I chew slowly, hoping they'll forget about me.

Lingering stares from all three of my friends are directed my way. Jules raises her eyebrow in my direction, and Kate tilts her head to one side quizzically. Olivia squints her eyes at me with an I-have-no-clue-what-is-wrong-with-her look.

"Olivia is right. You haven't been yourself all night," Kate agrees. "The Ellie we all know and love would have called dibs on our hunky waiter as soon as she sat down."

For a second, I consider filling them in on Liam and me. But I'm not sure what I would even say. I don't even know what's going on between us, and the last thing I need is Jules taking what I've said back to her brother. I decide to keep my mouth shut for now.

"Hate to disappoint you guys, but I'm fine. I'm not sick. I'm one hundred percent A-okay," I answer quickly, trying my best to sound persuasive. I immediately feel guilty. Olivia and Kate are the closest thing I have to family in Reed Point, I don't like not being honest with them. It's not like I told a bold-faced lie, I just didn't open myself up to them. It still makes me feel like a crappy friend.

It's times like this I miss my mom. She always knew all the right things to say. She would tell me exactly what I needed to hear. I know that she would tell me to listen to my heart, that the heart always knows the right path to take. If only it were that simple.

Luckily for me, hot waiter re-appears at our table to top up our water glasses and I do my best to gawk at him for the girls' sake. It really isn't that hard to do considering he looks like Orlando Bloom. Olivia's right, he is my type. But I feel nothing. Nada. Zilch. There's a six-foot-two reason for that, and I have a date with him tomorrow night.

Our Orlando Bloom look-a-like leaves to help the table beside us, and we continue on with dinner. Olivia and I make plans for tomorrow since she is stopping by to organize the order for the flowers for her wedding. No matter how many times I tell her I've got it, that she doesn't need to help with her own nuptial centerpieces, she refuses to listen. Which I guess is fine by me considering it gives me more time with my best friend. The wedding is just eleven days away and then Parker will be whisking her away to Bora Bora for their honeymoon. When they return they'll be heading back to Cape May.

"So, how was Bloom today, Ells?" Olivia asks, setting her fork down. We typically check in with each other to see how business is going every couple of weeks.

"It was uneventful until after lunch," I say through a laugh.

That gets the table's attention. "What happened?" Jules asks. "I love tales from Bloom."

I set my fork down and get right to it. "I got a call from a guy named Daniel. He actually seemed really nice. I had a hard time hearing his order, so he apologized for the noise and told me his son plays hockey and that he was at the ice rink watching him skate. He wanted to send his wife roses, so I took his order and billed his credit card." I pause the story, taking a sip of my drink. The salt from the rim of the glass tingles my lips.

Olivia rubs her palms on the table in a tell-us-more way. "And then?"

I set down my drink and cover my mouth with my napkin as I start to laugh again. "Then I asked him what he wanted written on the card." A laughing fit starts so I cover my entire face with my napkin.

"The shit people write on those damn little cards. What did he make you write?" Kate asks, grinning so wide her cheeks must hurt.

I get myself under control, sort of, then I tell them about one of the best cards I've ever written. "In his words… Dear Sadie, the ice at the rink isn't the only thing getting plowed tonight. Be ready. Love Daniel."

Kate nearly spits out her drink. The table erupts in laughter.

"That reminds me of the guy you told me about," Jules giggles, pointing to Olivia with her pastel pink manicured nail. "The guy who asked you to send flowers to his wife with a card that read 'Sorry, I slept with your sister. She looks just like you.'" That sends us into another fit of laughter.

Olivia raises her Margarita glass. "I tell ya, it takes all kinds of kinds on this planet." The truth is, Olivia and I have seen and heard a lot of crazy shit over the almost five years of owning Bloom. There was the guy who wanted his card to read, "These roses are as black as your heart, bitch." That was sweet. Then the one that said, "This felt like the best way for me to tell you that you might come down with Chlamydia." And let's not forget when some dipshit asked me to write a card for his girlfriend saying, "Welcome to Dumpsville. Population You."

We are finished our meals and our waiter is back to clear the plates when my phone buzzes in my clutch beside me. I dig it out of my purse to read the screen. My belly does a circus style trapeze flip. It's from Liam. He must have gotten my number from the wedding group chat. I discreetly open the message and read it, trying not to let my face give me away.

LIAM: I can't stop thinking about how good you looked tonight.

I switch my ringer to silent and lower my phone to my lap, discreetly typing out my response.

ME: Who? Me? :)

I watch the three little dots bounce across my screen. It feels like those same three dots are bouncing up and down in my stomach as I wait for his reply.

LIAM: Yes, you. You can't dress like that around me unless you want my hands all over you.

Holy hell. My mouth falls open. Is he really doing this now? He thinks *now* is a good time to send me spine tingling, racy texts? Thankfully, sexually charged banter is kind of my specialty. I take a giant sip of my Margarita and get to typing.

ME: Who says that I don't...

LIAM: Tell me what you're wearing under your clothes. Is it the hot pink lace you wore yesterday?

I swallow hard. My heartbeat races. A flash of heat bursts up my spine. Liam is bold, he's not afraid to say what's on his mind. I love that about him. I have no problem telling him what I want in return.

Me: Mmm, you're a man who appreciates lingerie.

LIAM: Very much. Now, answer me. Is it the hot pink one?

ME: No, it's not. The one I'm wearing tonight is purple lace and covers much, much less. I think you would really like it.

LIAM: Purple is my new favorite colour. Do you have any idea how badly I wanted to rip your clothes off tonight to see what was underneath?

I peek up from my screen, nervous I'm going to get caught. Thankfully, Olivia is in deep conversation with Jules about the wedding and Kate is busy texting someone. I look back to my phone, lust zipping through me. I should stop, but I can't. This thing with Liam is a fix that I'm totally and completely addicted to.

ME: I wish you would have. I've never had anyone rip my clothes off before.

LIAM: Noted. I'll have to change that. What are you doing right now?

ME: Struggling to keep my composure. Did you plan on texting me to rile me up?

LIAM: I want you as riled up as I am right now.

My. God.

I pull my knees together to ease the ache.

ME: Mission accomplished.

LIAM: Leave the girls, Ellie and come to my place. I want to finish what we started yesterday.

ME: That would be rude, Liam. My mother taught me manners. Besides, you can't always get what you want.

LIAM: I thought I was being spontaneous. You know, your favorite four syllable word.

He's not happy, I'm sure, that I turned him down. I, on the other hand like knowing that I affect him in this way. I sit forward in my chair and continue typing, wanting to take things a little farther.

ME: You didn't forget... and I'm impressed.

My fingers waver over the screen, as I try to decide if I'm really going to go there. Of course, I'm going to. This feels way too good.

ME: After yesterday afternoon, that's not the only thing about you that impresses me.

LIAM: I fucking love it when you talk to me like that.

ME: Same, Liam. Same for me.

LIAM: See you at 7 tomorrow, Ells. Text me your address....and wear the purple lace bra.

I contemplate sending him one more text. Something sexy. Something to let him know I can't wait to see him tomorrow night. But when I look up, I quickly realize it's time to put an end to my hot-as-fuck text chain. Kate fixes her stare at me as I quickly stuff my phone back into my clutch. "What is going on with you tonight, Ellie?" This gets the attention of Olivia and Jules, who stop mid-conversation and turn to look at me. I reach for my glass, needing something to do with my hands before I give myself away.

"Don't think I didn't notice you on your phone typing like your fingers were on fire." Kate says, her elbows resting on the table. "Dish, now. Who were you texting?"

I almost choke on my Margarita. I could lie but that feels so wrong. These girls have been better friends to me than I probably deserve. They know me better than anyone. They always have. They know the deepest depths of my heart, my fears and my insecurities. And I should feel like I can tell them about Liam. I'm also reminded of the only other part of my life they know nothing about. The secret I've kept since college. It's starting to feel like a 1,000-pound weight on my shoulders. I take a deep breath.

I could start by telling them about Liam. How good he makes me feel. How much he turns me on. How he makes me laugh and drives me crazy all at the same time. How something is happening between us and I don't know what to do about it. He makes me feel things I've never felt before. He makes me want things I never knew I wanted. But the words don't come.

"I'm not texting anyone."

Kate scoffs. "Pull-ease. What are you hiding from us?" She raises one eyebrow, her eyes filled with doubt.

"Should we order another round?" I ask the group, stalling, thinking of the right way to tell them about the man who has invaded my brain morning, noon and night.

Olivia gives me a look that makes it clear she's not ready to give up. "Only if you tell us who you were texting."

And because I must have saved an old folk's home from going up in flames in a past life, I am rescued by Kate's water glass tumbling over and shattering against the tile floor. The Orlando doppelganger is at her side in a flash, helping to mop up the spill. Kate apologizes profusely while she and Jules use their napkins to help the clean-up effort.

And just like that, the question of *who is Ellie texting?* is dropped.

Phew!

Chapter Eleven

Ellie

Today isn't my day. I spilt coffee down my favorite dress, just about got hit by a car on my bike ride into Bloom and arrived fifteen minutes late to work as a result.

Did I mention I'm also deadass tired from tossing and turning for hours, thinking about Liam and all the reasons I shouldn't go on this date with him tonight? I tried everything I could to wipe Liam from my mind, but then I would remember the way he kissed me and how good I felt in his arms. Or those gray eyes of his, the ones that look at me like he's imagining all the ways he wants to take me. So much for sleep. Day and night, all I can think about is Liam and how badly I want him.

I take a much-needed sip of coffee from my mug - this one reads "Coffee makes me feel less murdery" - and take a look at the arrangement that Leah is currently working on. Leah works full time with me here in Reed Point. I needed the help after Olivia left for Cape May, where we opened our second Bloom location. I was thankful that

Leah accepted the promotion and agreed to take on more hours. Having her here to handle the day-to-day has allowed me more time to focus on marketing and social media, and a little more freedom to come and go. And there's no doubt, we make a great team. We're constantly running new ideas and trends past one another. Leah works hard and most importantly, she's great with people. To work as a florist you have to actually like people, be patient and have a certain level of empathy. I like to think we both have these qualities in spades.

I've known since I was small that I enjoyed making other people feel good. I was the kid who picked an endless amount of dandelions, twining them together to make tiny bouquets, and gifting them to family and friends. I spent hours creating homemade greeting cards for every possible occasion and always baked treats for the seniors at my grandfather's care facility. Taking care of others has always made me happy. That's why I truly believe Bloom is my destiny. And yes, I believe in destiny.

"Is that the order for Mr. Stephens?" I ask.

Leah looks up from her perch at the worktable across the room, where she's arranging a bouquet of pale pink ranunculus, lilies and white gardenias into a bouquet. "It is. How does it look?"

"Beyond beautiful," I say, admiring her choice of blooms for Mr. Stephen's anniversary gift for his wife. He is one of dozens of repeat clients we work with on an ongoing basis. It's the part of the job I love most: building relationships, getting to know people. I love what I do.

"Thanks! When I finish this, I'll start potting the orchids."

"That would be great," I say, digging around in my purse for my pouch pharmacy. Every couple of months I'll receive a package from my mom containing a new batch of her latest herbal remedies and salves. What started as a hobby in our kitchen· years ago has turned into a small business with cult classic items that people pay good money to get their hands on. I unzip the small bag, reaching for my Ginseng supplement and peppermint balm. In need of a pick me up, I squeeze a few Ginseng drops into my coffee and roll the peppermint onto my pressure points. Leah looks up from the ribbon she is tying, noticing me with my peppermint roller.

"I used the oils you gave me the other day. I'm telling you… your mom is a miracle worker. I felt like I could scale a ten-storey building in high heels while reading my favourite book. I need to put in an order."

"I'll hook you up, but you might be waiting a while. It all depends if I talk to my mom in this century." I adjust my ponytail, tightening the velvet scrunchie in my hair, thinking of how pretty my mom looked next to my dad in the most recent photo they sent.

Leah shakes her head. "It still blows my mind that your parents travel the country in a van, giving their money away to strangers."

"It's not a *van*, Leah. You make it sound like they roam rural roads looking to kidnap small children. It's a motorhome. It has a kitchen and a queen-size bed and a bathroom with a stand-up shower."

"Ooh, it sounds as good as the Four Seasons Hotel," Leah jokes, rubbing her palms together in mock excitement. "Does it have a pool and a spa too?"

I roll my eyes. I make it a point not to tell too many people about my parents. It's not that I'm embarrassed, it's just that most people can't understand why they'd leave everything and everyone behind for "road life." It doesn't make sense to most, but if you ask me this is the life they were destined for. They love the community of people they meet along the way - free spirits, minimalists, adventure lovers. People just like them. Nine-to-five was never for them. And although it means I rarely see or speak to the two people I love most in this world, I can't help but be happy for them. Happy Ellie, that's me. It's genuine, but it also serves a purpose. Happiness has become my armor. It's how I've been able to forget that I'm alone.

"You know I'm just teasing," Leah says, interrupting my stroll down memory lane. "I think your parents could teach a few of the Reed Point elite a thing or two about being satisfied with what you've got." She's not wrong there.

"So, do they have any plans for a visit back home?"

"Nothing definite, but I'm sure it will be soon," I say, turning my gaze back to my computer in hopes of hiding my disappointment. Soon? Probably not. It's just my way of ending the conversation before it starts. A conversation that will surely crack my heart in two all over again.

A half hour later, I power down my computer and say goodbye to Leah.

"You good to close up here? I have a few errands to run."

"You bet. It's not too long until closing time anyways. I gotcha girl," she says. "I'll see you tomorrow."

I head out of Bloom and hop on my bike, inhaling the fresh ocean air. Butterflies dance in my belly at the thought of seeing Liam in a few short hours.

I turn down First Street, passing some of my favorite shops. Reed Point is beautiful this time of year, with stores boasting shutter boxes full of brightly colored springtime flowers and striped awnings. The streets are a little quieter too with tourist season not quite in full force.

After a couple of errands, I'm back at home running a bath. When the tub is full, I slip into the water - it's so hot it makes my skin tingle. I rest my head on the edge of the tub, closing my eyes and inhaling the mango bubble bath I added.

As I sink deeper into the tub, I feel some of the stress I've been carrying start to melt away. The harsh reality of my past looms heavily over my head these days. I've learned the hard way that feeling all alone can make you desperate, it can cloud your judgment and make you do crazy things. Sometimes those things come with consequences - the kind you regret for years to come.

I finally make the decision I should have made a long time ago. I can't keep up the lies. The pretending has to end. Tomorrow I will figure out how I'm going to get myself out of this mess.

But for tonight, I just want to enjoy Liam.

LIAM IS WEARING a white collared dress shirt and perfectly tailored navy blue dress pants, casually leaning against the side of his car. His left leg crossed over his right at the ankle, he looks totally at ease. He is the hottest thing I've ever laid eyes on.

He smiles my way, then his eyes stroll up and down my body. He takes in the form-fitted black dress I'm wearing that ends at the knee. His eyes then roam to the three-inch heels that I bring out on only special occasions, the ones that buckle with a slim strap around my ankle. Lastly, his gaze completes its saunter of my body at my hair, which is pulled back in a long, wavy ponytail. A wave shoots through me from the way his eyes appraise me. It feels like it's lighting a fire straight to my soul. He likes what he sees. And I like that he does.

"Hey," he says. His dark hair is styled tonight, short on

the sides and pushed back off his face like he came straight from the barber - just the way I like it. His jaw is covered with a five o'clock shadow that my fingers are aching to touch.

"Hi," I say, hoping it's not obvious that I'm desperately trying to catch my breath.

He holds open the car door and I slide inside, watching him round the front of the car and slip in beside me. He is taking me to Catch 21, a hotspot restaurant which is always impossible to get into, unless you know people. Liam knows people.

The place is packed with Reed Point's elite. We are seated at a table near the back of the restaurant- secluded, dark, private. I'm not sure it would matter anyways; when I'm with Liam, it feels as though we are the only two people in the universe. Everything else around us seems to evaporate.

Our waiter greets us at our table, taking our drink order. Liam orders a scotch for himself and a glass of rosé for me.

"You look beautiful, Ellie," he says from across the candlelit table.

I feel my cheeks heat at the compliment. "Thank you," I say, enjoying my view as well. The flicker of the candle on the table is casting a glow across Liam's strong features. "And you look really handsome tonight."

"Just tonight?" A devilish smirk crosses over his face.

"You want to know the truth?" I decide to give it to him straight, dropping the teasing banter that typically consumes our conversations. He nods.

"Always. You always look handsome. Sometimes it's too much."

"Is that so?" he asks, with a playful smile. I watch his

eyes darken to resemble onyx as he stares at me. I swallow hard.

I bite my lip to cover my smile. "Very much so."

"Good to know." Our waiter interrupts us with our drinks, sliding Liam's scotch to him, and then placing a wine glass in front of me before walking away. The heat between us cools, for now.

"How was your day?" Liam asks, laying the white cloth napkin across his lap.

"It was fine. Uneventful. How was yours? You seem happier than usual."

"I had an exemplary day in court today. I'm expecting the rest of the trial to go the same way."

"You really love your job, don't you?" I ask him.

"I do. I like the challenge." His eyes turn serious and I get the feeling that the courtroom isn't the only challenge he's up for. My pulse races beneath my skin. He's always so intense. Being with him makes me feel more alive than I've ever felt before. I don't want that feeling to end.

I decide to have a little fun with him. Raising my glass to my lips, I sip the rosé then set the glass back down. "I've wondered what it would be like to go on a date with you," I tell him. The sounds of the restaurant - cutlery tapping against plates, guests chatting amongst each other, footsteps on the tile floor - all fade into nothing.

"You have?"

"For a long time," I admit, then watch Liam's serious face switch to a grin. He pins me with his dark eyes, causing tingles to sprint over my skin.

"Well then I hope our date is meeting your expectations. Is it, Ellie?"

"It is. You are, too." I blush.

"Good, I'm happy because the feeling is mutual. I've

had a really hard time getting you off my mind since the beach house. You left a lasting impression."

I might combust. I might just die here right on the spot. I've been attracted to Liam for so long and it seems he's felt the same way about me. The look in his eyes confirms it. And dammit all to hell, this feels too good to be true.

The air between the two of us is charged. I take a deep breath to even my breathing. I'm silently wishing he would kiss me senseless, but we have a dinner to get through, so I pull myself together.

Our meals arrive; Liam ordered the sablefish while I went with the linguine in cream sauce. Figures Liam gets the heart smart meal while I'm twirling my way through a 7,500-calorie noodle dish.

"Mmmm," I say, finishing a forkful of pasta. "This is so good. You really need to try this."

Liam laughs.

"What?" I giggle, looking across at him.

"I'm not sure I've ever met anyone who appreciates their food as much as you."

"I like my food. I know a good pasta dish when I taste one. Seriously, you've got to try this." Liam leans in closer, twisting the pasta on my plate around with his fork. He takes a mouthful. I can tell by the sated look on his face that he agrees with me. The pasta dish is exceptional.

"So, tell me about your family," he says, reaching for his glass. The ice clinks as he turns the tumbler in his hand.

"What do you want to know?"

"I want to know everything."

"Well, I'm an only child, the daughter of two free spirits. And I've lived in Reed Point all my life."

"Free spirits? I'm intrigued. Tell me about them."

I hesitate. It's bittersweet talking about my mom and

dad, but telling him a little about my family feels important. "They're amazing. We are very close. Well, as close as we can be without living in the same city."

Liam tips his head to one side. He looks interested in hearing more. "Where do they live?"

"Good question." I shrug and he raises an eyebrow quizzically in response.

I fill him in on my parents' nomad lifestyle and share a few stories they've told me about their travels through the years. I tell him about afternoons spent at my dad's art gallery and how my mother used to throw me the most incredible birthday parties with homemade cakes and decorations she crafted herself. Liam seems genuinely interested, asking me a bunch of questions about my childhood and my family. We sit together in the dimly lit restaurant, me opening up to him, and it feels easy. It makes me wonder why I never do this, why I hesitate to talk about myself with my friends. Maybe it's just Liam who makes it feel easy. I decide I like talking to him. I exhale.

"It can't be easy for you. You must really miss them." Liam's eyes are on mine, and he's looking at me like he wants to get me. Like he wants to understand me. He's not looking at me with pity in his eyes. He's not judging my parents for leaving. He's simply trying to be supportive.

"I'm fine," I say simply, because I try very hard each and every day to be. I've never said I'm not fine out loud. I'm not sure what would happen if I did.

He drops the conversation when our waiter approaches the table to ask if he can get us another round of drinks. I order a second glass of wine.

"I'm good for now," Liam says to our waiter, who has left us alone for most of the night. It makes me wonder if Liam asked him to give us some privacy.

"Only one drink?"

"I never have more than one," he says, lifting his fork to his mouth, enjoying his meal.

"You don't get drunk? Ever?"

"Never."

It's so Liam to never risk losing control.

After we've finished our meals, Liam orders us a dessert to share, a coconut panna cotta with fresh berries. I end up eating the entire thing, of course, while Liam indulges in a strawberry and a cold glass of sparkling water. It makes me silently laugh.

At some point between my first and my last spoonful, I can feel the tip of his dress shoe against mine beneath the table. I can smell the cedar and fresh laundry scent of his cologne. I can feel the chemistry between us that is impossible to ignore.

In this moment it feels like Liam and I could be so much more. Like "Liam and Ellie" could belong in the same sentence. On the same Christmas card.

And if I'm not careful, it feels like what started out as wanting Liam just once could turn into so much more than one hot night of sex.

Chapter Twelve

Liam

I scoop a berry onto my spoon, wishing I was eating it off of Ellie instead. Those sexy-as-hell heels - I have plans for those later tonight. And Jesus - that black dress. I don't know a guy on this earth that can resist a woman in one of those dresses. Her lips are a darker hue of red than I'm used to seeing on her and her eyes are smoky. The knee-length hem of her dress shows off her long, incredible legs and her hair is swept up in a ponytail, revealing her neck that I am itching to trace with my mouth.

She looks deliciously incredible. I watch her as she brings a raspberry up to her soft, pillowy lips and her eyes close as she chews it. There is nothing better than watching this girl eat. Well, I can think of a few things that are better. They all seem to include her.

"This dessert is my new favorite thing," she declares, taking another spoonful of the creamy Italian custard.

"I'm happy you like it. I thought you would."

After a couple more bites, she sets down her fork and

glances at me playfully. "You know, you could have gotten me into trouble last night. The girls were all over me at dinner. They wanted to know who I was texting." I watch her run the tip of her finger along the edge of her wine glass. *Does this girl have any idea what she does to me?*

I arch an eyebrow, curious to know more. "And what did you tell them?"

"I didn't tell them a thing. I wasn't sure what to say." She sips from her wine glass, then licks her lips. My eyes can't help but linger on her mouth for a few seconds too long and wonder if her lips taste like the sweet wine. I inwardly sigh.

"Not even Olivia?"

She shakes her head. "Not even Olivia." This surprises me, but I like that she kept us all to herself. Our little secret. "What about you? Did you mention to Parker you were taking me out to dinner tonight?"

"I did not, but Jules is on to us. She suggested to me it would be a good idea if I asked you out."

"Thus, the reason we are here tonight?"

I lean in closer. She looks up from our dessert, her eyes meeting mine. "Definitely not. The reason I asked you to come to dinner with me is I can't stop thinking about you."

Her eyes light up. She smiles, a sweet, sexy grin that makes my heart race. Unable to resist her, I move closer and press my lips to hers like I've been dying to do all night. She tastes like strawberries and rosé, and it makes me want nothing more than to get out of here early and get her alone.

"I like it when you kiss me," she says.

I lean in a little closer, my voice low and raspy. "Right here is where I'm dying to kiss you." I run the pad of my finger softly along her collarbone and over my favorite freckle.

Her lips part. Her eyes go hazy. I feel her skin pebble under my touch. She wants me to kiss her there, but I've never been one for PDA. Instead, my hand finds the edge of her jaw and I run my fingers up towards a loose strand of hair that has slipped from her ponytail, tucking it gently behind her ear. Any excuse to touch her.

"I also like it when you touch me, Liam. Or hold my hand. I like being near you."

"Same, Ellie. Same for me," I say, relaxing my shoulders, enjoying the exhilaration of flirting with Ellie.

It feels good.

It's thrilling.

And I like how I feel when I'm around her.

While she finishes her wine and I enjoy an espresso, we glide into a discussion about our favorite things. She likes yoga and spicy foods. She tells me about the time she went skydiving in college, and I tell her about the ski trips my parents took us on every winter to Vail. She tells me she's never tried skiing and I offer to teach her one day. And soon, an hour has past that felt like ten minutes.

I pay our bill and we leave the restaurant hand-in-hand, because I listen, and I know she likes it. I help her into my car then round the bumper and slip in beside her. We're alone and I have her all to myself. All bets are off. I reach for her hand across the console, lacing her fingers through mine. My thumb traces lazy circles on the back of her hand.

Her full, soft, kissable lips form a smile. It gets my pulse racing. I reach for her face, taking it in one hand, and kiss her fiercely. It's heated, passionate and it feels different than all the rest. It's laced with promises of more to come. So much more than I've ever felt for anyone else.

I can feel her smiling again through the kiss.

"You can't kiss me like that, Liam, and expect me not to want more."

Her blue eyes sparkle an even more vivid shade of aqua than usual. I have a thing for girls with bright blue eyes and Ellie's are slaying me right now. I might not know exactly what is happening between the two of us, but for a moment everything feels as it should. It feels right.

"I want more too, Ellie," I tell her, my voice low, sexy. And I mean it. I'm not ready to say goodnight. I want more of her. "It's still early. Come back to my place?"

Her face melts into the prettiest smile as she nods. I slide my hand to the back of her neck, watching her lips part. She's breathtaking. I brush my lips gently against hers, teasing her, then pull back, narrowing my eyes on hers. Her tongue glides across her bottom lip, her eyes provoking me, hard and sensual at the same time. My dick likes it. Very much. It's straining against the fabric of my pants, wanting more of her attention.

"As much as I want to keep kissing you, I need to have you all to myself. Just mine." Our mouths so close, but not touching, just painfully on the edge of wanting to attack her lips.

"Tonight, I'm yours," she whispers, then leans in to kiss me. "You have me all to yourself. Anywhere you want me."

"Anywhere?"

"Anywhere."

"My dining table again? Or the counter?" I kiss her again, and she lets out a desperate little moan.

"How about up against the wall?" she suggests, smiling. And I'm a goner because fuck, what guy wouldn't die to hear those words? A spark shoots right through me. I need to get her back to my house as fast as possible.

And that's exactly what I do.

Fifteen minutes later, in Formula One record speed, I

have her in my living room. My hands are in her hair. Her mouth is on mine. Her hands stroking and scratching my arms and my back over the fabric of my shirt.

We barely made it through the front door, flicking on only one light in the living room, when our bodies collided together knowing just how good it was going to be. The tension crackling between us all night at dinner had been like a live wire.

"This doesn't happen, Ellie," I tell her honestly, because what can it hurt?

"What doesn't happen?"

"I never feel this out of control. I can't stop thinking about you."

"Same, Liam," she says, fisting the collar of my dress shirt. I want her now like I've never wanted anyone else. This is not a familiar feeling. I've passed the time with other women, never catching feelings. I've always been able to compartmentalize sex and emotion.

Until now.

"This dress, Ellie. God, this dress." The need to feel her is so intense. "You fucking kill me in this dress, but I need you out of it. Now."

She takes two small steps away from me and begins to slowly lower the straps of her dress down over her slim shoulders. She slowly turns around, never breaking eye contact, displaying her back to me, watching me over her shoulder.

I'm about to combust. I feel like a cannon ready to fire. She's teasing me, watching me from under her long, dark lashes. She's putting on a show and I'll happily watch it all night long.

"Help me with the zipper?"

"Is that even a question?" In one stride, my fingers find

the zipper, slowly drawing it down the center of her back to her tailbone. She shivers.

"Fuck, Ellie. The purple bra."

She turns to face me, then presses her palm flat to my chest with challenge in her eyes. "Let me," she says, forcing me two strides backwards. My eyes follow the fabric of her dress as she strips it from her body. Standing in front of me, she lets the dress fall to the floor leaving her in the purple lace bra she tormented me with last night. Thank fuck she never mentioned the matching purple lace panties in our text exchange, or I would have driven to the restaurant and taken her back home with me.

She bends to remove her heels, but I stop her. "Leave them on, Ellie. Leave the heels where they are." She stops, straightening to her full height, kicking her dress to the side. I can't hold back a second longer. I close the distance between us, reaching one hand to her shoulder, hooking my finger through the purple bra strap.

"Never in my life have I ever seen anything hotter. I need you, Ellie. So bad," I say. She looks up at me and her eyes match mine, full of want and need.

My hands find their way to the curve of her hip, gripping her hard, yanking her into me. I press her body against my rock-hard erection, wanting her to feel it. I want her to know what just the sight of her does to me. She fists my hair, panting. Her shallow breath tickles my neck, lighting every nerve ending in my body on fire. Her pelvis rocks into the outline of my length, searching for friction. Grabbing her ass, I give her what she wants, rocking into her faster.

We stumble into the bedroom. Somehow I manage to flick on the light. I want to see every bit of her body, laid out naked for me for the first time.

Standing at the foot of my bed, I palm her face in my

hands and kiss her long and slow. She's still in nothing but the purple lace bra and panties and her heels, making the difference in height between us less than usual. I take advantage, kissing her long and slow while her hands drift down my rib cage. Freeing my dress shirt from my pants, her fingers slip between the fabric and my skin, finding the grid of my abs and dragging her hands across them. Her warm hands move lower, rubbing the outline of my dick through my pants. I growl into her hair, feeling it thicken against my zipper.

My hands get busy working on the buttons of my shirt, working the top three open. Impatient with the rest of the tiny round discs, I grab the hem of my shirt and tug it over my head, then unfasten my belt buckle, pop the snap and unzip my suit pants in three seconds flat. I kick them to the floor. I can't get to her fast enough. "I want you naked and in my bed."

I hook my finger under the satin ribbon strap of her bra. "I love you in this set, Ellie, but I want to see what's under it more."

A quiet sigh slips from her mouth. "I want you to take them off of me."

"Happy to." I'm like a kid on Christmas morning. This feels better than taking that first sip of a 60-year-old bottle of scotch. Better than a puff of the finest Arturo Fuente cigar. I do what I'm told, reaching around her, unhooking the clasp, stripping it from her torso. Next I shimmy her lace thong to the floor, removing her heels while I'm perched at her feet, kissing my way back up her body like a treasure map.

"You are perfect, Ellie," I murmur into her calf. "Every," I kiss her there. "Single," I kiss the inside of her knee. "Inch," I taste her smooth skin of her thigh. "Of you," I say, dragging my tongue up the silky skin of her leg. "I want to be inside of you."

"Yes, Liam. Yes,'" she says, her voice full of lust, her hands clutching at my hair as my hands roam her thighs, her hips and the curve of her ass. I want my mouth everywhere on her body, kissing her, tasting her, making her come undone.

I lay her down on my bed, my eyes touring her tan skin. Seeing her naked, laying in the middle of my king-size bed, is what dreams are made of. My dreams especially. She's been the star of all my fantasies for months. I've envisioned her naked on top of me in my bed, in the shower doing wicked things, but here right now, in the flesh, this is even better than what I've dreamt up.

She continues to blow my mind, dragging the elastic from her ponytail, freeing her thick caramel hair. It spills down all around her over my pillow. Her eyes are full of lust. She's stunning.

"Take off your briefs, Liam. I want to see all of you," she says, sitting up, leaning on the backs of her forearms.

I slide them down my legs and my hard-on springs free. Her goddess eyes go wide, shamelessly staring at my goods, appearing to be happy with what she sees.

Her voice trembles as I crawl over her, widening her knees to make room for me. I dip my face along the center of her chest, kissing and sucking and licking her sensitive flesh, my stubble tickling her skin as I go. She arches her neck, silently asking me to kiss her there too, so I do. My mouth finds the hollow of her delicate throat.

"I love it when you kiss me there. Mmmm. Do it again."

"Happy to," I say, trailing a delicious line of open mouth kisses down her throat, inhaling her, making her groan. I taste her citrusy, sugary scent, wanting more and more. I graze her flesh with my teeth, marking her, wanting to make her mine. She shudders, arching her breasts against my mouth. "Your mouth, Liam, it feels so good."

I am barely able to keep it together. I've wanted this for so long. Ellie is finally naked in my arms, in my bed, and it feels better than I ever imagined it would.

My mouth finds her perfect breasts, moving between them, sucking and licking and massaging each one with my hands.

"God, Ells. You make it so hard to go slow."

"I don't want to go slow. We can take our time with each other later. I want you now."

My lips move back up her body until they're on hers again. She slips her tongue into my mouth, while her hand travels down my body between us. I groan into her mouth when she fists my erection in her hand, and it takes every ounce in me to not go off like a rocket. It feels incredible. Her soft hands slide up and down my length, stroking and squeezing. Her hands begin to move faster and harder and I know I need to stop her before it's too late.

"Ellie, it feels too good. I'm not going to last if you keep doing that," I say, breaking the kiss, pushing back off her. Reaching towards my nightstand, I dig out a foil package, break it open with my teeth and roll on the condom while she watches. I settle between her legs.

"You want this, Ellie?"

"I want *you*. Now, Liam. Please."

My pulse pounds through my body. She knows what she wants and she's not afraid to ask for it. She gives as good as she takes, and it's such a massive turn-on.

Her deep blue goddess eyes never leave mine as I push into her slowly, taking my time, savoring the incredible feel of her body hugging mine. She's warm and tight, gripping me as I push in further. It's so good I can barely breathe. We fit perfectly together.

Her hands find my ass, squeezing and forcing me deeper. We find a rhythm, speeding up and then slowing down again, bringing us so close to the glorious edge but stopping before we go over. I listen to her cues, her sounds, giving it to her how she needs it.

"Oh my God, it feels so good," she gasps. "I never knew it could feel this good."

"So good. So damn good. You're not going anywhere tonight. I'm going to make you feel so good, again and again."

Her breath is shuddering, and I push deeper and deeper until we're both shaking.

She grabs me, pulling me down onto her chest. Her hands roam my pecs, my abs, my arms, clawing at my skin. She's unravelling beneath me, chasing her release and it's beautiful in every way. I love that I can make her feel this way.

I change the angle, pushing into her in a faster rhythm, dizzy with how good she feels. I'm light-headed and on the verge of coming apart. But there's no fucking way that's happening before I get her there.

I reach down between her legs and give her exactly what she needs. In seconds, my name falls from her lips and her whole body trembles. I follow right after, moaning and groaning as I soar into a blissful ecstasy.

"Ellie," I shudder through my release as my entire body trembles. Waves of pleasure shoot up my spine.

"That was incredible," she whispers back.

When I collapse onto her chest, she kisses me softly. I'm breathing hard as she runs her fingers through my hair and down my shoulders.

"You are incredible," I tell her, brushing my lips against

her cheek, not ready to break our connection, wishing I could stay inside her forever.

I had no clue sex could be that good. That phenomenal. Beyond belief.

Eventually I pull out, tie the condom and wrap it in a tissue beside my bed. I turn her so that her back is against my chest and nestle in behind her, pressing my lips to her shoulder. Our breathing slows.

"Stay the night with me, Ellie."

She says yes.

So I pull her closer into my chest.

Lying in bed with her, I'm left to wonder how it's possible to feel this way after just a couple of days with her. We lay sleepy and sated, tangled in each other's arms, when it occurs to me that she's the first woman I've ever shared my bed with. The first woman I've ever wanted to stay.

Maybe, just maybe, Ellie Reeves is the girl for me.

Chapter Thirteen

Ellie

These sheets must be 600 thread count. Or maybe 800. Is there such a thing as 2,000? I'm going with that. I assume these are the kind of sheets the queen sleeps on, they're that incredible. It also helps that the rich scent of coffee is floating through the air.

I woke up in Liam's bed, the morning sun casting a ray across the lush down comforter. The mattress is so heavenly it feels like I'm floating on clouds. My attention drifts to his dresser and my clothes from last night, the ones I remember stripping to the floor. They are folded neatly, piled on top of each other in a stack. It's so Liam. Not only a control freak but apparently a neat freak too.

The bed feels a lot bigger because Liam is not nestled in beside me. But I can hear him downstairs, making breakfast. I sit up, pulling the silky cotton sheet over my bare chest, and consider following the delicious, rich aroma, but think twice, not totally sure how to navigate this situation. Instead, I slip into Liam's en suite bathroom and after dealing with the morning necessities I hunt around for some toothpaste. After a quick rinse with mouth wash, I check my phone then fall back into the bed, draping my arm across my eyes and remember last night.

It was pure frickin' magic. My stomach flip-flops just thinking about it. It was the best sex of my life; back-arching, sheet-gripping sex that I never knew existed. He's ruined me for all others.

The way he kissed me, consuming and carnal. The way his hands gripped my flesh, so possessive and sexy. The way he took complete control of my body, knowing exactly what I needed. Then, to top it all off, we fell asleep naked in each other's arms, our arms and legs tangled up in each other, his big, strong body cuddling me into sleep. Like I said before… *it was pure frickin' magic.*

There's nothing about last night that feels one-night-standish. Everything about it feels like a heck of a lot more. I am so tempted to let myself believe that the off-the-charts chemistry I feel with Liam is real, but I have to remind myself that I can't get lost in it all. I've known from the start I don't belong in Liam's world. If ever two people were opposites, it's the two of us. Besides, this is not what either of us do, and I need to remember that. We needed to get it out of our systems, and now we have. One night, and one night only, of giving into temptation. Nothing more.

But why does he have to have such a great dick?

"Good morning," Liam says, appearing in the doorway with a lazy smile on his gorgeous face. He's bare-chested, rocking sex-tousled hair. He's wearing only a pair of thin black joggers slung low on his hips, revealing that V of muscle that I've decided is my favorite part of Liam's body. Or maybe it's the corded muscles of his arms? Nope, has to be his abs and that faint trail of hair that leads to my *other* favorite body part. This man is a work of art.

With two cups of coffee in his hands, he pads to my side of the bed. I try to read him. Is he feeling weird after what happened last night? Is he regretting asking me to stay the night with him? I need to say something funny, defuse the situation, but I can't focus. His gray eyes are on me, but I can't read what's in them.

"Morning," I manage to say, suddenly struggling from a severe case of I-forgot-how-to-form-a-fucking-sentence.

"I made you coffee," he says, offering me one of the white mugs in his hand.

"Thank you." I smile, sitting up in bed and pulling the crisp, white sheet over my chest, suddenly feeling very naked. Does he iron these things? He probably pays someone to do it for him. I can't remember the last time I ironed my dress pants, never mind bedsheets. I wrap my hands around the warm mug. "A smart move considering I can be an evil villain without my morning cuppa."

He laughs while I get to thinking of how I'm going to pull off my exit plan. I cringe, realizing I will be committing the ultimate walk of shame in my cocktail dress and four-inch heels. Olivia would have a field day with this. *What a total nightmare!*

Shaking that image aside, I ask, "What time is it? It feels really early, which I guess is a good thing considering we both need to get to work."

"It's six thirty. You have plenty of time. My body is just wired to get up at sunrise. I didn't mean to wake you."

"You didn't."

"I made you breakfast."

"You didn't have to do that."

"I know, but I wanted to," he says, reaching for the loose strands of hair that have fallen over my face, pushing them back with the tips of his fingers. I think on that for a second, then take a sip of my coffee.

"Thank you."

An awkward silence descends on us, which is thankfully interrupted by Liam's cell phone vibrating on the nightstand. He moves around to his side of the bed, sets his coffee mug down and picks up his phone. Crawling back under the covers, he checks his message.

"This damn wedding group chat. How do people deal with these? Every time I look at it, I have 500 missed messages. Who has time for this?" He absently pushes his hand through his hair, his bicep flexing with the motion. My mouth literally waters. *I might be drooling.*

I shoot him a side-eye stare. "What's the latest, Mr. Grumpy Pants?"

He fires me his own side-eye stare. "Clubbing. Kate has reserved a table this Saturday for the group at that bar she was talking about. Club Eden. I'm guessing you are excited about this?"

"Who wouldn't be?"

Liam just shakes his head, the corners of his lips curving up in a smile. His dimple is on full display, doing crazy things to my brain. He stares at me as if he's studying me.

"What?" I ask him.

"You, is what." Liam rolls on top of me, his corded arms on either side of me, pinning me in place. He brushes his lips softly over mine then pulls back with an up-to-no-good grin. *My God.*

"What about breakfast?" I ask him.

"I'd rather have you."

I PULL the heavy wood door to Lola's open and follow the girls inside. I take a seat beside Olivia at a high-top table near the bar, with Kate and Jules taking the seats across from us. Drinks and appies post-yoga have become our weekly routine after I talked the girls into getting their namaste on with me a few years ago. Lola's is one of the restaurants we have on rotation of approved girls' night spots. They make world-class lemon drop martinis and it's removed from the beach, keeping the clientele mostly local.

We're all showered and changed after a challenging class and are looking forward to some girl chat. Our waiter takes our order, four Super Sunshine lemon drop martinis as usual, and leaves us to catch up.

"How was everyone's day?" Kate asks, slinging her purse over the corner of her stool.

My day? If they knew about my day – and the night leading up to it – I'm pretty sure they would lose their minds. After breakfast in bed, me being the "breakfast," Liam drove me home to get ready for work. After a busy day at the shop with renewed vigor, taking breaks only to salivate over a few flirty texts from Liam, I'm feeling like I've won the Heisman. The mother-flipping Superbowl. I know I need to stop this. I need to reel it in and not allow myself to fall for him. I just haven't figured out how to do that when it feels so good.

"How about you, Ells?" Jules questions me, resting her chin in the palm of her hand.

"Enjoying the calm before wedding season kicks my ass," I reply innocently because it's the truth. "Olivia, your wedding feels like the kick-off to our busiest time of year."

"It really is," Olivia says, "You guys, I can't wait to marry that man."

A pang of envy batters my chest. Olivia has found her person, her one true love. She deserves all the happiness Parker brings her. I hadn't thought I wanted that kind of love, the forever kind, until recently. Or maybe I've always wanted what my parents have but just got lost along the way. Either way, I'm happy for my best friend.

"My brother is the lucky one," Jules jumps in. "Speaking of…what needs to be done before the wedding? We are at your beck and call."

"I think it's mostly under control. The night before is when I'll need you the most: setting out seating cards, helping with décor, things like that."

I squeeze Olivia's arm. "I'll be there. Whatever you need. I can't wait to see you in your dress. Parker is going to lose his mind when he sees you." And it's true. Parker is beyond in love with Olivia. One look at her in her form-fitted mermaid gown and he'll be a goner.

"Nine more days, Olivia," Kate says to her sister. "Can you believe it?"

"Barely." Olivia smiles. "I can't wait to be Olivia Bennett."

"I think that deserves a toast," Jules announces, reaching for her drink. We raise our glasses to the center of the table. "To my soon-to-be sister and her blissful, perfect happy ending."

I point at Jules, "Can we keep their sex life out of the toast please? Eww!"

We laugh and then knock back our drinks. I sit back in my chair, taking in the scene around me. The four of us share a friendship that not many are able to find and I feel lucky. And maybe a little bit icky that I slept with Jules' brother last night. But mostly just lucky.

The warm, fuzzy feeling in my chest turns red hot when out of the corner of my eye I spot Liam striding into the restaurant. He shakes the hands of two older gentlemen I don't recognize before taking a seat at their table. I take the opportunity to really look at him before he notices me. He's in the same expensive gray suit he put on when he got out of bed this morning, the one that matches his eyes. And the way that suit fits his body he looks like sex on a stick. For the love of all things mighty, that man was inside of me less than twelve hours ago. *Ho-ly.*

A minute later we make eye contact and as soon as we do it's like we're the only two people in the place. It feels as though silence has descended on the entire restaurant. All I can hear is the hum of the current that instantly connects us, running from his soul to mine. There is no controlling this.

He shoots me a steamy grin that makes my insides light up. I return the smile, then force myself to look away.

After another round of sugary sweet drinks, with Liam and I stealing glances across the room, Olivia spots him. "Hey, Liam is here." She waves her arm in the air, catching his eye. "He must be with his partners from the firm."

Liam nods and waves our way, his gaze lingering on me just a little too long.

"Um, what was *that* look all about, Ells?" Kate leans across the table, pinning me with a stare.

I try to keep my tone even. "I don't know what you're talking about."

"Are you smoking the flower-food packets you stuff into bouquets? Liam just looked at you like he was picturing you naked."

"Okay fine, it was something," I admit, deciding to come clean. "But I don't know what kind of something. Therefor I don't know what to tell you. But we hooked up." I cover my eyes with my palms, shaking my head. "Twice."

"What?!" Olivia whisper yells, stretching the word out into five syllables. "And you didn't tell me? Were you ever going to tell me?" Her voice escalates with every word, clearly hurt that I didn't spill the beans.

"I'm sorry, Liv. It just happened. I didn't think it would happen again, but then he asked me to dinner last night… and it happened again." It all comes out in a rambling mess of a way and I inwardly cringe.

"What?" Olivia repeats herself, digging her fingertips into the sides of her forehead, her eyes wide in an *oh-my-gosh* expression. "You went on a date with my fiancé's brother, the guy I've been trying to sell you on for months, hooked up with him last night, and we're just hearing about it now?"

"Yes, last night. Now, can we stop talking about this while he's sitting twenty feet away? Where's your chill?" I exhale, leaning into her, doing what I can to stop this before Liam hears us.

"We'll stop for now, but we are nowhere near being done with this topic. I have a lot of questions that you can answer over coffee tomorrow."

"Fine."

"But can I just add, the man's hot. Look at him over there oozing confidence and class," Kate adds, not helping in the least. She glances over at Liam's sister. "Sorry, Jules."

Poor Jules is going to be scarred for life. She mimes throwing up, while looking in the opposite direction of her brother.

"Doesn't he look handsome in his suit?" Olivia adds. "Men of the world could learn something from the Bennett brothers. There are way too many clueless guys out there wearing black socks with runners."

Olivia is right. Liam looks like pure sex in that suit. His crisp white shirt is open at the collar, the cuffs rolled up his forearms. He is breathtaking.

"Don't forget the guys wearing cargo shorts," Kate adds. "Ugh, or those hideous baggy dad jeans."

"And the polyester polo shirts and boat shoes," Jules chimes in.

"What about tank tops?" I add, because it needs to be said.

"Men should never wear tank tops," Olivia answers. The rest of us add, practically in unison: "*Never.*"

"The guy to Liam's left is cute, too," Kate says, taking a sip of her drink.

"He looks like he's sixty, Kate," I point out, shooting her a look. "Stop perving on the DILF."

Kate raises her shoulders in a think-what-you-want shrug, reminding me why I love that girl so gosh darn much. She's never given a fuck, she just is exactly who she is. She'll happily ogle the "dad-she'd-like-to-fuck" without a care in the world. And she is constantly putting herself out there, trying to find the guy for her. She's done it all: speed dating, blind dates, online dating. You name it, she's tried it. You've got to give her credit for putting herself out there.

An hour or so later, I knock back the last of my martini just as I notice Liam getting up from his seat and heading straight for our table. I feel his eyes on me. I swear my face must be the shade of a stop sign.

"You ladies look like you're having a good night. Much better than mine, talking business deals and negotiations," he says in his swoony, low voice.

"We always do," Kate says. "We're warming up for Saturday night when we all sling back beers and dance our brains out."

"That's right, the club. I don't know how I will get through the next two days with all the anticipation. Dancing my brains out is very high up on my list of favorite things." Liam smirks. With his height and broad shoulders, he fills up the room. He stands inches away from me, so close I can barely think straight. His scent floods my brain. Goosebumps cover my skin.

"I'm taking off. Can I give anyone a drive home?" he offers. His eyes casually peruse the table then land on me.

"I'm late to get home to Parker, but I said I'd drive Ellie home. You wouldn't mind giving her a ride home for me, would you?" Olivia's smile turns into a devilish grin.

Subtle, Olivia. Real subtle. My first instinct is to kick her under the table, but I can't lose my cool. Barely able to meet Liam's eyes, I stay quiet in hopes someone else will start talking.

"Not a problem. I'd be happy to," Liam replies.

My face on fire, I slip my phone out of my purse. "It's fine, honestly. I'm happy to call an Uber."

"Put your phone away, Ellie. I'm not letting you take an Uber," Liam states. It's a command, not a question and it's sexy as hell. My mouth goes dry. Maybe I owe Olivia a thank you after all. No, I definitely do. I'll do one better and send her a gift package from Sephora.

Stuffing my phone back in my purse, I reach for my wallet. "Thank you. I need to pay the bill and then we can go."

Liam clears his throat. "It's been paid."

"What do you mean it's been paid?" Olivia asks him, leaning across the table.

"It means exactly that. Parker wouldn't let me hear the end of it if he knew I was dining in the same restaurant as you four and I didn't pay your bill."

Olivia looks at me. I can see the devilish smirk on her face rise to the surface. She's thinking what I'm thinking - this man is too good to be true.

We all thank him, then grab our things and head outside to say our goodbyes.

Sitting in Liam's car a few minutes later, I steal a glance

in his direction as he cranks the engine and shifts gears into traffic. He cracks a sly smile when he catches my gaze on him.

"They know, I assume?"

"It was that obvious?"

"Couldn't have been more. Between Olivia offering you up to me like a party favor and your face turning the shade of a firetruck - I wish my opposing council had tells as obvious as the four of you do."

I cover my face with my hands. "That bad, huh?"

Liam just shakes his head with a laugh.

"What are the chances we ran into each other tonight? We seem to be doing that a lot lately," Liam notes coyly, stopped at a red light.

"It must be pure coincidence," I answer. "Definitely not anything more than that."

"Definitely not the universe working in mysterious ways. Not possible. Couldn't be."

"Most definitely not a sign. No way. No how," I say playfully.

He meets my eyes again seconds before the light turns green.

"I want you to know my intentions right now, Ellie. I'm going to take you back to my house and have you tonight. I'm going to make you feel so good."

I try to hide my grin. "Please, Liam, drive faster."

Chapter Fourteen

Ellie

Taking a deep breath, I follow Liam into Club Eden off First Street, his hand pressed firmly against the arch of my back. He called me this afternoon and asked if he could pick me up and drive me to the club. To say I'm a little nervous about arriving together - our first public appearance - would be a bold-faced lie. I'm a boatload of nervous.

I'm still unsure of what we are - if anything. We haven't had "the talk." We seem to be too busy doing other things. Much more fun things, therefor I'm not complaining.

Liam leads me past the dance floor and the large bar in the center of the space. There's top 40 music playing through the sound system and deep purple velvet booths beckoning patrons to lounge with a drink. The dance floor isn't large, and the music not too loud, making it an ideal spot to talk to people and have a good time.

Wading our way through the crowd to the back of the nightclub, we scan the room for our friends and find them gathered around a private table on plush couches and chairs. Parker spots us first, flashing us his usual megawatt smile. That's what I love most about the man who is about to marry my best friend. He's always happy and in the moment, always ready for a good time. That, and the fact that he makes my best friend stupidly happy.

"Hey, you two," he says, clapping Liam on the shoulder and pulling me in for a hug. "It's good to see you."

"It's good to see you too," I say, just as Olivia makes her way over to us, looking gorgeous as always. She hugs us both, then links her arm through Parker's.

"We know Ellie's ready for a good night. We can always count on that. How's this guy?" Parker asks. He's referring to Liam, but the question is directed at me. I'm not sure how to answer that because it feels like a couple-y kind of question, so I go with what I know best. Light-hearted humor.

"This guy is dealing with it. With any luck, I think he just might survive it."

"Maybe, maybe not. I'm not convinced just yet," Parker says, arching a brow. "I'm not sure how great the Wi-Fi is here, how's he going to check his email? This might be worse than a colonoscopy for my big bro."

"Thanks, Parker. I appreciate your earnest opinion. I can live without Wi-Fi for at least an hour before throwing a fit." Liam claps back in true Liam fashion with a witty, dry comeback.

"Never mind Parker," Olivia says, shooting a playful glare her fiancé's way. He raises his hands in surrender. "Parker, I love you madly, but you are wrong about your brother. He has no problem having a good time. He's also bigger than you and could kick your ass, so I'd be careful."

Olivia goes up on her toes and takes Parker's face in

her hands, pressing a kiss to the side of his mouth. Our cue to say hello to the others.

We greet the rest of the group, all clearly ready for a good time. Miles, Kate, Jules and Dylan are here, everyone excited to celebrate tonight in anticipation of Parker and Olivia's wedding, which is exactly one week away.

Liam orders himself a whiskey neat and a glass of wine for me. Once we've taken a seat with the rest of the group, settling in on a couch, Miles raises a beer. "Let's drink to a good night and to Parks and Olivia."

We all raise our glasses in cheers. I take a sip of my wine, set it down and welcome the warmth it brings to my chest.

Watching my best friend gush over the man she's about to marry does something to me. They're so in love, it's almost too much. And I mean that in a good way. It causes me to wonder…

Could a relationship, a commitment or even marriage make me happy?

This is what I could have.

This is what it could look like.

Could this be what I want, too?

Turning my attention to Liam, I watch him banter with his siblings and can't help but feel envious at their close family dynamic. I've always wondered what it would be like to have a sister to borrow clothes from or a brother to be my fiercest protector. These days I'd settle for having a mom and a dad to meet me for coffee or share Sunday dinners with.

I will myself to stop looking at Liam, who's too damn good-looking than anyone has a right to be. His thigh is pressed up against mine, his hand resting on his knee. Lucky knee. I shake my head, laughing at myself. I'm now jealous of a knee.

Miles is talking to his brothers now, pulling my attention away from Liam's leg. "A run tomorrow? It's been a while since I've schooled you two."

"That can be arranged, but school *me*? A group of toddlers could out-run you," Liam says, taking up his brother's challenge.

"I will destroy you. And you, too," Miles says, pointing his finger at Parker then miming his finger slashing across his throat. "On a scale of non-existent to sucks hard, your stamina, I'm betting, barely registers."

Parker leans across the table. "I recall that the last time we ran together you complained the entire time about a hamstring injury and shin splints. So, when I tell you I'm going to shatter you, you should believe it."

"Never going to happen." Miles flicks up his middle finger then leans back in his seat, knocking back the rest of his beer.

It's hilarious watching the three of them take jabs at one another. They could star in their own sitcom and I would watch every episode.

"I'm happy you three have each other," Olivia chimes in. "How would you ever keep yourselves entertained otherwise?"

"It's my party trick. Irritating the fuck out of my brothers," Miles jokes.

"Don't forget about me," Jules pipes up, joining the conversation. "No one should forget about me. I've been tortured by the three of you for twenty-four years."

"We're persistent, Jules. It's a quality one should admire," Parker deadpans.

A minute later, the DJ plays a Lady Gaga song and Olivia, Kate and I take it as a personal invitation to hit the dance floor. We excuse ourselves from the table, dragging Jules along with us.

The dance floor is absolutely packed with people, but the four of us manage to slip in amongst the crowd. We sway to the music, feeling the drum of the bass vibrate through our bodies.

Before long, Olivia is in my ear, shouting over the music. "Can't take it, Ells. You and Liam are giving me major vibes. What is going on with the two of you?"

"We are just having fun. That's it."

She slaps her hands on her waist, tilting her head to one side. "Fun? Seriously? He picked you up. That makes it a date. And that also makes it at least the third time you have been together. Liam doesn't do repeats, so this," she dramatically waves her hand in the air, "is more than fun and you know it."

Could it be? Could she be right?

I'm not ready to admit just how into Liam I actually am, so I wave off her comment instead. "I'm fine with a little fun with someone I know and trust. It doesn't have to be a big deal. You know how I feel about commitment."

"I don't understand why. I wish you would open your heart to falling in love. Life is ten times better when you're in love."

"For some, Liv. For you - and believe me, I couldn't be happier for you. You are deliriously happy. Watching you with Parker is like watching one of those YouTube videos of puppies wearing tiny, adorable sweaters."

"Ellie, really? You are comparing my relationship with Parker to puppies in sweaters?"

"Yes! Because I feel an immense joy when I watch both."

She stares at me. "Mmmkay. I'll go with it because it kinda makes sense on a very weird level. Anyways, promise me you'll at least be open to where you and Liam could go. That's it. Can you do that?"

I don't know. Can I? Once upon a time I thought I could. And that ended like an atomic bomb. I'm still living with the aftermath of it. But I am aware of how Liam makes me feel so I answer her with my heart.

"I can."

We keep dancing until Olivia spots someone she knows and leaves us to say hi. As we hear the opening notes of 'U Can't Touch This' come over the speakers, Jules heads to the bar for a drink. Before I can follow her, Kate grabs my hand, declaring this is her favorite song ever. She yanks my hand and pulls me further onto the dance floor into the center of the crowd. Trust me when I say you have not lived until you've seen Kate shaking her ass while yelling, "STOP! Hammertime!"

A few minutes later - and not a minute too soon - the upbeat song changes to a slower one and Liam strides over to me looking hot as hell. I pull him into me, not caring who's watching. We're all friends, and friends dance with friends. *At least that's what I'm telling myself.*

Liam's arms circle my waist. We dance like this for a few minutes before he takes my hand, twirling me around. He wraps his arms possessively around me from behind, pulling my back against his hard chest, his lips brushing over the shell of my ear. It feels good. No - it feels unbelievably good. He tightens his hold on me, sending a flutter of tiny lightning bolts through my belly. "I like watching you dance, Ellie."

My skin heats. "You were watching me?"

"Are you surprised?"

"A little," I say, as he spins me in his arms to face him. I slide my hands up the front of his chest and he wraps his arms tight around my waist. "I like dancing with you."

His mouth is against my ear when he says, "I like it too." I shudder. Full body shudders. *How does this man do that to me?* Every touch feels like my body is a live wire. Like a spark to a flame I can't wait to destroy me.

"I hadn't pegged you for a dancer, Liam. You continue to surprise me. What's next? Will I find out you make jam on Sunday mornings and package it in pretty little jars with ribbons? If so, I'll expect a care package at my door."

"I wouldn't hold your breath. That sounds messy and you know how I feel about messes," he jokes. "And dancing? I don't, unless I'm only required to sway to a slow song with my arms wrapped around a sexy brunette. That is my limit."

His tone is light, soft. My heart squeezes because something feels different. But I remind myself that this is just fun and games and the walls that I've erected over the years to protect my heart are there for a reason.

I need to remember that.

This is just fun for Liam

Enjoy it while it lasts.

I repeat the words *this is just fun* in my mind, fighting the feelings that make me wish it was more.

A couple of dances later, we walk back to our table, finding our friends.

Liam tightens his hold on me. He hasn't left my side all night, except for the few dances I spent with the girls. He hasn't gone more than ten minutes without his hand on my thigh or his arm around my waist. And if his hand isn't placed somewhere on my body, his lips or his eyes are, making me feel as though I am his, and he is mine.

"Can't you wait until after you leave to hump his leg?" Olivia jokes, leaning into my side. "I'm going to force you to say I was right when you two get married and have babies."

Every muscle in me tenses. Olivia has no way of knowing the nerve she's hit. Yesterday I sent an email that I should've sent years ago. Now I am waiting for answers so I can put the mess I created behind me and finally move on with my life. I swallow the lump in my throat. "I guess we will see."

She winks, and mouths *Oh, it's happening* as she walks backwards in her nude-colored heels away from me.

I laugh, which catches Liam's attention. "What's so funny?" he asks.

"Nothing," I tell him, shaking my head. He squeezes my hip, pulling me closer

"My fault. I could have sworn I heard you say 'let's get out of here so you can do dirty things to me.'"

"You are so bad," I tell him, lightly tapping his stomach with my palm.

"What? Are you saying you don't want me to?"

"Don't put words in my mouth."

He raises his eyebrows. "I can think of something else you could put-"

I don't let him finish, playfully nudging him with my hip. "Bad again, Liam Bennett. So bad."

Somehow we manage to stay another hour before Liam drives me home, parks in front of my building and follows me to my front door. Nerves whirl through me as I unlock the door to my tiny apartment that is nothing like Liam's million-dollar mansion.

He follows me inside. His eyes quickly scan his surroundings then land back on me. His gaze is so intense my breath hitches and my legs feel wobbly. Any insecurities I had about showing him where I live have vanished.

I'm pretty sure he can see the affect he is having on me. I'm breathless, shaky - my body betraying me as I fight to keep myself together. He inches closer. I remember to breathe.

"I've waited all night for this. I want you so bad," he

says in a gravelly voice. The need to have his body pressed up to mine so strong I'm coming undone.

I trace my bottom lip with my tongue and then he kisses me, long and slow before deepening it. His tongue searches my mouth, finding mine in long, lazy strokes. Sparks crackle down my spine.

This time it's soft and slow. His hands tangle in my hair. My fingertips lightly skim over the planes of his body underneath his shirt. He backs us up onto my couch, grabbing my hips, and tugs me onto his lap so I straddle him. Grasping my ass, he pushes me over his rock-hard erection. It feels so good.

He takes his time with me, undressing me carefully, savoring every bit. His kisses aren't like the last time, when they were harder, demanding, rough. Tonight, they're soft and gentle, slow and tender. My mind goes hazy, my body vibrating with desire and lust.

"I want you in my bed, Liam," I gasp. He picks me up like I weigh nothing, and my legs wrap around his waist, my arms around his neck. He carries me to my bedroom and gently lays me on my bed, removes his clothes and crawls over my naked body.

"I'm still not used to seeing you naked. Your body is fucking incredible," I tell him, almost drooling at the sight of his chiseled abs. His hard pecs. His strong, toned arms. They're all mine, all night long.

"Yours too. Don't you get what you do to me? You are driving me crazy. I can't concentrate when I'm around you. I'm never like this," he says, cupping my breast in his hand then dipping his head down to suck the firm peak into his mouth.

"I'm serious. I can't concentrate, Ells. I can't get you out of my head."

"Me too," I say. "I fought it for so long. I tried not to want you."

He growls as his mouth pops off of my breast then moves across my skin, gently biting my flesh. "Not. Possible. Our chemistry is too strong. We need to give in to each other. Give in with me, Ells."

"Yes, Liam. I'll give you whatever you want," I breathe as he presses a wet kiss to my collarbone followed by a nip from his teeth. I'll expect to find a mark there tomorrow and I'll love knowing it's there under my clothes.

"I love this spot right here." He kisses and sucks and licks a path from my chest to the sensitive skin of my neck.

"Liam." I arch my back under the weight of him, shivering at his touch. The lust and vulnerability are almost too much. His hand grasps my jaw, pushing my head further back, my back completely arched and my fingernails dragging down his back. He kisses the hollow of my throat, my neck, then the edge of my jaw while his hand slowly grazes over the curve of my hip. I know where his fingers are going and my skin heats at the thought. My legs are pressed open and his fingers find my most sensitive spot.

"That feels so good. Don't stop," I pant, as he traces tiny circles over and over.

He explores my body with his mouth, slowly sweeping over my breasts with feather soft kisses, down the center of my torso, below my belly button until he reaches where I want him most. He goes down on me and groans. My hips shoot up, searching for more as he kisses and sucks and licks me into a spine-tingling O. The pleasure so strong, my body goes limp underneath his.

He rises to his knees. "Feel good?" I nod in post-orgasm bliss.

"Good, but I'm not done with you yet."

"Maybe I'm not done with you," I smirk, rising up on an elbow, taking him in my hand. He moans as I slide my hand around his length. "…killing me, Ellie," he mutters. "Too good."

I work my hands up and down his hard flesh until he can't take it. "Condom, Ellie. Give me a second," he says, shifting to the end of the bed to search for his pants until I stop him.

"I'm on protection. I'm okay if you are?"

"You sure?"

"Stop talking, Liam, and make me feel good."

Crawling back on the bed, he nudges my legs open, gliding himself slowly into me. There's nothing between us. His heated moody irises never leave mine.

"I think about doing this to see you every damn night," he confesses, moving inside of me, our bodies joined. "Tell me what you like and how you like it, Ellie."

He wants this to be so good for me. He wants to make me feel good. "It's perfect. You're perfect. Just don't stop." And it's true. Liam knows exactly how to get me there. He knows exactly what I like. Nothing has ever felt this good in my entire life.

My eyes close briefly then they're back on his in the most intimate moment I've ever experienced. This is more than just sex. So much more. And I wonder if he feels it too. I wrap my legs around his back a little tighter, needing all of him. His skin on mine, my face now buried in his neck. My nails press tiny moons into his shoulders as he speeds up the pace

"You're mine, Ellie. I want you to say it. Tell me you're mine." My heart soars, realizing at that very second that those are the words I've been wanting to hear. It all becomes clear that I want him to choose me. I want him to be mine.

"I'm yours, Liam. I'm yours."

He goes harder. Faster. His eyes burning into mine again, moaning and shuddering and I can tell he's almost there. "Let go, baby. I've got you," he says, as pleasure builds and my skin tingles all over.

I cry out his name as ecstasy like I've never felt before ripples through my body. My body trembles as he follows me over the edge, pulsing, moaning, breathing my name.

"It's always this way with you. Nothing has ever felt better," he says, sliding his hand over the edge of my jaw. I am in a post-sex haze, spent and tired but somehow, I still want more. He drops his chest to mine, holding me close, and I know I've never been happier.

"I want you to stay, Liam. I don't want you to go."

And he does, until the Reed Point sun breaks through the morning sky.

Chapter Fifteen

Liam

If Ellie is wearing my dress shirt to torture me, it's working. It's buttoned only halfway, hitting her just above her knees, which are stretched out across my lap as we sit together talking over coffee and toast at her kitchen table. My hand lightly draws lines up and down her feet to her ankles. Taking a sip of my coffee, I admire her high cheekbones and her full, pink lips. Without a stitch of makeup, her hair ruffled and messy from last night, she is breathtaking.

Noticing her coffee cup is empty, I reach for it, begrudgingly slide her bare legs from my lap, and walk across her tiny kitchen to her coffee maker. I pour her another cup. Setting it down in front of her, I rest my hands on her shoulders and kiss her neck. "Tell me about your fridge," I say, looking at the small Polaroid pictures covering the refrigerator door.

She rests her head back against my stomach. "Every now and then, my parents will send me a photo of themselves from wherever they are. I like to print them and stick them up there so I can look at them whenever I want," she says, looking up at me with her turquoise eyes. "I know it probably seems silly, but they make me feel good. It sort of makes me feel like they aren't that far away."

"It's not silly at all," I assure her. I like this softer, vulnerable side of Ellie, who is always so strong and independent. "They've really seen some sights, huh?"

She turns her face to the fridge, and I notice the smile that curves her lips. "They have. It's pretty incredible. They've been to places I've only ever dreamed of." Her face lights up when she talks about them. Her love for her parents is undeniable.

"I take it you haven't travelled much?"

"No. The first time I flew anywhere I was in college and went to Vegas. It was a fly-by-the-seat-of-my pants trip that I basically booked on the way to the airport." I flinch remembering that time in my life but recover quickly when Liam re-routes the conversation.

"You didn't travel with your parents when you were a kid?"

"We did, but they were more local ones. We travelled along the coast, we camped on beaches and stayed in quaint little towns with pretty bed and breakfasts. My dad was never able to go for long because he had the gallery and never trusted anyone to run it for him. But I loved every second of those trips. I never felt like I was missing out. Would you believe I've never been to Manhattan? I realize how absurd that sounds but it's true."

"It sounds like your parents wouldn't have been big on the Big Apple." She nods in agreement then turns to glance at the fridge decorated with magnets again. "The vacations they did take you on sound like they were pretty great."

"They were, but now I would like to see more of the

world. I'd be happy with anywhere in the U.S for that matter."

"Yeah? Like where?"

"Well, for starters I'd like to see the Golden Gate Bridge, the Florida Keys, Hawaii... the Grand Canyon looks pretty spectacular. But I'd settle for New York City and a Broadway show."

"Hence the crazy *Cats* magnets?"

"Who says they're crazy?"

"I do. Definitely."

There must be 20 fridge magnets mixed in with her family photos, all something to do with that God-awful musical *Cats*. I will never understand the appeal - grown men and women dancing around a stage in furry feline costumes, licking themselves and coughing up hairballs. And people pay to watch it? People like Ellie, apparently.

"What's with the obsession? Please tell me there isn't a cat costume somewhere in this house because I won't role play. Unless it's Cat Woman, and you're doing the dressing up," I tease her.

She laughs, leaning her head against my stomach, her eyes meeting mine. "Jealous? I know you wish you had a Cats magnet collection too."

I laugh at the absolute ridiculousness of that. "I'm serious, what's your compulsion with a 1980s theatre production about a bunch of singing cats?"

"You wouldn't get it."

"Try me."

"Okay, fine. I've loved cats since before I can remember. It started with the actual animals, then went on to the musical. I loved them so much I dressed up like one for six straight Halloweens," she admits, laughing at the memory. "Told you you wouldn't get it."

I smile because as crazy as it is, it's incredibly cute. "Go on."

She sighs like she can't bear to tell me the history of her devotion to *Cats*, but continues anyways. "I rescued cats, I volunteered at a cat shelter bottle-feeding orphaned newborn kittens, I wore ridiculously ugly cat sweatshirts and then in high school, the best thing to ever happen to me happened."

"What happened? The suspense… I can't take it," I tell her, kneading her shoulders with my hands then moving towards the table to grab my mug.

She rolls her eyes. "The high school musical my senior year was - wait for it, yup you guessed it - *Cats*! And yours truly won the lead roll of Grizabella." Her eyes are bright as she mimes taking a bow. "And of course, I nailed it."

"There's no doubt in my mind that you did. You definitely have the whole theatrics things down pat," I say with a laugh.

"I should have won some sort of an award if I'm being honest."

I can't help it - I start laughing. Then suddenly she's laughing too.

"What's happening between the two of us?" she asks when we finally regain our composure. "We haven't argued in days." I sit down and lift her legs back onto my lap, finding any excuse to get as close to her as I can.

"That can't be true. We must have had at least a tiny argument at some point," I say.

Her eyes draw me in. They do every time. She's right, though. Neither of us has thrown any cheap shots or provoked any fights. But it's still fun to play the game with her.

"Right. You must be right," she says, narrowing her

eyes at me with a smile. "I'm sure we must have had a quarrel."

Lifting her legs from my lap, I lean towards her, pulling her chair between my open thighs. the legs screeching against the tile floor. I rest my hands on her knees and brush my lips over hers. Kissing Ellie has become my new favorite pastime. Her lips are pillowy soft and taste like strawberries. Her smooth skin smells like the freshest scent of citrus. I settle my hand on her neck, loving the feel of her skin beneath my fingertips. I love everything about this girl. I love her strength, I love her free spirit, which she obviously inherited from her parents, I love her goddess eyes and the way they sear right through me to my core. In short, I love how she makes me feel.

It's clear now, what's happening. What that feeling deep in my gut has been trying to tell me. I'm falling for her. I'm so far past falling, I'm already there, drowning in the depths of Ellie, so I decide to tell her exactly what I want. Tell her exactly how I feel.

"You know… I never mind it when we bicker," I say as I lean my face into the dip of her neck. "And I also really like it when we agree."

"Really?" she hums, tugging me closer, her hands winding around my neck. "What are you saying, Liam? You're going to need to spell it out for me."

"I'm saying that I really like you. I like being with you and I'd like to be with you more. Just us," I say, pulling back to meet her gaze. "I want it to be just us. No one else." Her bright blue eyes fade to a look that resembles sadness. "What's wrong?" I ask.

"Nothing, Liam," she says, but I'm not sure whether to believe her.

I lower my voice and drop my hands to her knees. "Tell me, Ells. What's bugging you?"

She shifts her gaze to my hand as it runs circles on her thigh then back up to meet my eyes. "Nothing, Liam. Nothing at all. I want that too. I want it to be just us. Yes."

Then why does it feel like there's something standing in our way? Like there's something between us, stopping her from being with me. I choose to ignore this sinking feeling that's set in and just take things one day at a time. One moment at a time because Ellie is worth it. *She said yes, didn't she? It's a start.*

"Hey, Ellie," I say.

She looks up at me. "Yes?"

"Don't make plans this afternoon. You're mine."

IT'S 6:30 a.m. when my brother Parker strolls into the gym, looking like he spent thirty minutes picking out his workout clothes. He takes a seat on the weight bench next to me, studying me as I run on a treadmill.

I'm in the zone, earbuds blasting 9 Inch Nails. A gruelling workout is exactly what I need today. I need to feel my muscles ache and my lungs burn and get my mind off of one sexy brunette.

But nothing is working. No matter how hard I run or how much I sweat, Ellie continues to consume my every thought.

I slow the machine to a jog, then to a fast-paced walk, and pop out my earbuds. I take a few deep breaths, feeling the air pump through my lungs. I wipe my face with a towel.

"Morning. Thought I'd find you here."

"Surprised to see *you* here. Shouldn't you be with Olivia choosing chair covers or something? Searching for the perfect shade of lilac tablecloths? Purple, but not *too* purple, Parks."

My younger brother watches me step off the treadmill and pick up a pair of weights. In a split stance, I start with a rep of bicep curls.

He arches his brow. "You realize you look like you want to murder those dumbbells, right? What's up with you this morning?"

"Nothing. This is how I work out." I blow out, followed by a deep breath in.

Parker laughs and rolls his eyes. "Level with me. What's going on with you? I'm pretty sure I can guess, or you could just be a man and tell me."

I give him a hard stare. "I don't know what you're talking about."

"Ah," he says, through his cocky grin. "I see how this is going to go. I'm talking about this thing between you and Ellie. We all saw it. We all knew you were crazy about her way back at our barbeque at the beach house months ago. You seem to be the only one who hasn't figured it out."

My brow wrinkles as emotions swirl through me because my brother is right. I am crazy for her. I broke my own rule. What was supposed to be one night with Ellie turned into wanting another. And another. And then telling her I wanted an *us*, which all felt exactly right. Until it didn't when Ellie looked at me with uncertainty in her eyes. And I'm left wondering if I've got it all wrong? This is exactly why I don't do relationships. I'm confused and distracted as fuck.

It's making me wonder if falling for Ellie is something I'm willing to put myself through.

Is it worth the risk?

"Ellis's a great girl. Of course I like her. Who wouldn't?" I say, because it's all true.

"I'm calling your bluff, bro. You more than like her. You're happier when you're around her. It's in your eyes, man. You're falling for her. It's obvious in the way you look at her."

I don't say anything. I just stand there, continuing my bicep curls, chest heaving, sweat dripping.

"News flash, Liam," Parker says, walking to the treadmill I just finished running on. He starts with slow strides. "You can be in love with her and not lose focus on your work if that's what's bugging you. I'm the perfect example of that. I'm in love, and business has never been better in Cape May. It's possible to have both."

"Who said I was in love?"

"Me, you dumbass." There's amusement in his voice. "You can deny it all you want. You can ignore the shit out of it, but it's not going to change. You're in love with her."

"And what makes you think that?" I ask. I'm not that guy who wears his heart on his sleeve. I don't do emotions. Besides, I really like the girl but *in love*? I think I would know if I was in love with her.

"Little known fact, Liam. You can't keep your eyes off her. Like I said, it's all in the eyes. The way you look at Ellie tells me everything I need to know. It's love."

"You know what I'm in love with? Seeing the look of fear in my opponent's eye. I'm in love with the high I get when I win a case. I'm in love with knowing I crushed the district attorney I'm up against," I tell him in one long breath. And it's true. I love all the things that make me happy. I have a great life indulging in the finest restaurants, the priciest bottles of wine. Women, cars, travel. I have all the things I love and more.

Parker rolls his eyes. "Good luck with all of that keeping you warm at night. You really need to get your head out of your ass and see things for what they can be."

"You're not going to stop, are you?" I say, dropping the dumbbells to the ground and grabbing my towel, dragging it over my face.

"You're lucky it's me trying to knock some sense into you and not Olivia. I'm much easier to deal with."

I grit my teeth. My brother is one of only a handful of people who really, truly know me. Who get me and are able to give it to me like it is.

"There's a lot more to life than work. You are obsessive over your job. You need balance. Balance is the key to life," he goes on. I wish he would stop.

"Balance? What I need is focus. Without focus, you're left with distractions."

"Are you listening to yourself? You sound like a nimrod. Falling for someone doesn't have to be a distraction."

I run both hands down my face. I can't figure out how this is happening. I've spent the last three nights with Ellie in my bed and I liked it. Correction. I fucking loved it. I can't stop the thoughts of Ellie that linger in my mind all day long. The way her breath hitches when I tease her, the way my body tingles under her challenging gaze. And the sex. It's never been better with anyone.

And here I go again, mind wandering to thoughts of Ellie. I should be thinking of my caseload, not Ellie's mouth, or Ellie's legs or the dirty things I want to do to her. I can't lose focus on my practise because I don't know how to make this work.

Thirty minutes later, Parker flicks his gym towel at the back of my thigh like a rubber band and tips his head to the door.

"My fiancé awaits me. Gotta jet," he says, grabbing his gym bag, heading for the door. He tosses one last look my way, "Figure things out with Ellie. Either way, I'm here if you need me."

The girl I slept with last night flashes through my mind again. Can I balance both my career and a relationship? Am I ready for that level of commitment? Is she? Am I willing to take that chance?

But by the time I've finished my workout, I'm seeing things a little clearer. Ellie Reeves is the first girl I've ever wanted more of. More lunches by the pool, more early morning Sunday coffee chats around her kitchen table. More dinner dates, even more dancing.

I know I want more.

The question is… does she want the same?

Chapter Sixteen

Ellie

To: Ellie Reeves
From: Darlene Reeves

SUBJECT: **Wedding.**

Hi ells bells. Had to tell you the most wonderful story. I met a psychic last night who told me I was a snake charmer in a former life…isn't that wonderful? She also told me you are going to get married this year. I better be the first to know. I love you.

--Mom

I'M STANDING at the worktable at Bloom surrounded by a mountain of eucalyptus stems, thinking about the email I received from my mom this morning. I'm not sure whether to laugh, cry or take this as a sign. My mother has visited psychics for years. She's spoken to dead relatives through them, sought advice, treated them like her own personal therapist. I take it all with a grain of salt. It's not that I'm a naysayer, exactly. I can appreciate that they help my mom make sense of her life, and every now and then she finds a psychic who gets it right, hits the nail on the head. It's just not my jam to believe anyone can foresee the future. And *me*, getting married this year… the chances are nil.

I turn my attention back to what I should be doing, shearing the ends of eucalyptus stems then placing them in a bucket of water. Leah is standing in front of the coolers helping an older gentleman with salt and pepper hair choose a bouquet of flowers for his wife. I overhear the man tell Leah that he needs just the right amount of tulips. And an equal amount of freesia. And the tulips need to be pink. Not fuchsia or pale pink, just pink. I chuckle, catching Leah's eyes from across the room, mouthing *good luck with that*. Leah will be just fine, though. This is the kind of challenge she thrives on. Mr. It-needs-to-be-exactly-perfect will leave Bloom a very satisfied customer.

I'm up to my eyeballs in eucalyptus when my phone lights up on the table, catching my eye. My heart sinks. It's the email response I've been waiting for. With trembling hands, I quickly swipe the screen to read it.

TO: Ellie Reeves

From: Simon Pearce

Subject: Re: We need to talk.

Ms. Reeves,

We are unable to help you with your request. A meeting, at this time, is out of the question.

Best, Simon Pearce

. . .

DAMMIT. He's such an asshole. Why won't they let me see him? Adrenaline pumps through my veins. This isn't good enough. This needs to happen. I need to see him, and I refuse to be pushed around. Slipping into the back office, I scroll my phone for his number and make the call.

"Simon Pearce," he answers in an overly confident, arrogant tone. *Fuck, I can't stand this man.*

Pacing the floor of the back office, I straighten my shoulders. I'm immediately on the defensive after hearing his voice. "Mr. Pearce, this is Ellie Reeves. I need to speak to you."

"Ellie. Did you not receive my email? There's nothing I can help you with. A meeting is not happening. It's not a good time."

And here we fucking go.

"I can appreciate that, but I just want to see him. It won't take long. Surely he wants to see me too," I explain, annoyed but trying to keep my cool.

"Like I said. It's not good timing. Now, I really have to go."

"No. *Wait!*"

"Look, Ms. Reeves, do I need to speak slower? I'm not sure how else to get through to you. We're done here. Goodbye."

He ends the call.

It takes everything in me not to hurl my phone against the wall. I lean against a chair, unsure of what to do next. For the first time in years, I know what I need to do but I'm not sure how to go about doing it. I consider telling Liam because he would know exactly what steps I should take. He could even help me. But how can I tell Liam what I did when I still can't face it myself? Am I crazy to think I could tell him the truth and it would all be okay?

No. I can handle this on my own. I will somehow find a way to see him.

I can do this.

I can do this.

I swear I can do this.

"What's going on back here?" Leah asks, walking towards the fridge and grabbing a bottle of water.

"Nothing." I tuck my phone into the back pocket of my jeans. "Were you able to find the ideal shade of pink tulips?" My tone is laced in sarcasm.

Leah rolls her eyes, twisting the top back onto her water bottle. "Was there ever any doubt?"

I just laugh, walking past her to the front of the store. I have work to do and I could use the distraction. Orders need to be placed, social media needs my attention and arrangements need to be made for tomorrow. I spend the next hour crossing each item from my to-do list, until my phone vibrates in my pocket. *Liam.*

Liam: Lunch? It's been a day. My office? I'll order in whatever you're craving. (I'm not on the menu :))

A smile overtakes my face as I type my response.

Ellie: Shame, but I'll settle for lunch. I'll do the ordering. I'll pick up something I think you'll like.

Liam: Looking forward to it.

Ellie: See you soon, Liam.

Liam: And if I wasn't clear, I'm looking forward to both lunch and seeing you.

My silly little heart beats a little faster. My response is clear and easy.

Ellie: Me too xx

. . .

I ARRIVE forty-five minutes later in front of Brooks, Gamble and Bennett. The elevator doors open to the fourth floor and I step out, making my way to reception. The woman behind the desk appears to be in her late forties with sandy blonde hair styled neatly in a bun. She is on a call, gesturing with her finger that she will be with me in a second.

"Can I help you?" she asks a moment later in a warm, pleasant tone.

After I tell her that Liam is expecting me, she makes a quick call, then says, "Follow me." She leads me down a hallway past several offices on either side. She turns a corner and stops in front of a door with the name Liam Bennett etched into a shiny silver name plate. "Go on in, Ms. Reeves. Liam is expecting you."

I thank her, then knock gently. "Come in." His voice is low and rumbly. I push the door open to find Liam sitting behind his desk, a stack of paperwork laid out before him. He looks impressive here, in his element. His hair is perfectly styled. His piercing eyes sweep over me. He radiates power and control, his stormy energy coursing through the room.

I smile as I take him in. It's impossible not to. He's so damn easy on the eyes. He returns the smile in my direction, his dimple catching my eye like it always does.

"Close the door behind you," he says coolly, pushing up from his seat and walking around to the front of his desk. I shut the door like he asked me to as he takes a seat on the edge of his desk. "Get over here."

He's wearing another one of his Liam-y suits. This one also looks like it cost a fortune. It fits him just right. Liam in a suit is my absolute weakness.

I stand in front of him, lunch in my hands. "How's your day going?"

"It's better now," he smiles, taking the lunch bag from my hands, placing it on the desk beside him. He studies my face.

"You seem tense," I tell him. "It doesn't look like your day has been easy."

"That might be because I've been busy all morning sticking it to the bad guys." He smirks. "I think that was your perception of what happens in this office, if my memory serves me correct."

"Well, isn't it true?"

"Of course."

"You don't fool me."

"I don't?" he asks with a smile that shows off his perfect white teeth.

"I'm getting to know the real you. You aren't the intense, cantankerous man you like people to believe you are," I say, fiddling with the collar of his crisp white shirt. Our chests are so close they're almost touching.

"Huh," he says, looking amused. He reaches for a loose strand of my hair and tucks it behind my ear. It's not enough. I want him to touch me. Liam knows how to touch a woman.

"I like this the most, you know," I say, running the tips of my fingers over the buttons of his dress shirt

Liam tips his head to the side just slightly and crinkles his brow. "You like what the most? I'm not following."

"You in a suit. I love the way you look in a suit," I tell him, watching his lips turn up in a devastating smile. My body reacts with a tickle of what feels like Champagne bubbles floating through my belly.

"Is that so?"

"It is. You look so good," I say, splaying my palms flat across both of his pecs.

"Give me a second," he says, holding up a finger, and

all of a sudden this feels dangerous. *Are we really going to do what I think we are?* Anyone could walk in. Like he's read my mind, Liam reaches for his office phone, lifts the receiver and presses a button.

"Please hold my calls, Silvia. I'm not to be interrupted during my working lunch with Ms. Reeves," he says in his typical take-charge way. It's broody. It's hot. It turns me on. I haven't decided which version of him I enjoy more: the kinder, gentler Liam who notices I need more coffee or the self-assured, always in control, commanding Liam who has the whole sexy arrogant thing down to a science. He sets down the receiver, then sets his gaze on me.

I swallow. "This is a lunch date. We should eat lunch. I brought you tomato soup and a turkey croissant."

"We should, but we aren't going to. Lunch can wait."

I open my mouth, not sure what to say in response. But it doesn't matter. His lips are on mine before I get the chance to string even a few words together. The kiss is incredible. His lips move over mine with skill and control, leaving me helpless to the intense desire mounting between my thighs. This man makes me feel so damn good.

I grasp the fabric of his shirt and he pulls my body into his by my hips. His mouth finds mine and the intensity shifts. He's kissing me wild and fierce now. My hands are on his neck. His tongue tangles with mine. The kiss owns me, like only Liam's lips can.

"I thought you said you weren't on the menu?" I tease him, breaking the heated kiss.

His answer is simple and straight to the point. "I lied."

He turns us, pushing me against his desk. It's only just begun and it's already incredible. I'm caged in Liam's strong arms, the scent of him driving me mad.

"I had to see you," he growls, against my neck. "I can't stop thinking about how good it is with you." The heat of his breath tickles my skin. Then his mouth closes over the column of my neck, sucking and kissing and sliding his tongue over my flesh. The sensations his mouth elicits are like fireworks, my core lit up like fire. Warm shivers and pulses travel all over my body, the deep sounds he makes when my hands find his ass spark a flame right through me.

Quickly his hands find my hips, lifting my ass onto his desk. The stack of papers that were there when I arrived are pushed to the side. So unlike Liam, which makes me realize how badly he wants me. My fingers curl over the edge of the mahogany desk as he nudges my legs open. His hands roughly move up my skirt, pushing the flimsy fabric up to my waist, before ripping my underwear down my legs.

Every single nerve in my body is reacting to him and the way his hands are touching me. I'm dizzy with lust and desire. I'm so far past caring who could walk in. There's nothing that could make me stop this.

My hands find the buckle of his belt, then the zipper of his dress pants and when I cup him over his boxer briefs with my hand, he groans into my mouth. He kisses me with an earth-shattering, mind-tingling kiss that sends desire spiralling and my head spinning.

"Fuck," he grunts, as I stroke his arousal. His pelvis rocks into my hand in short, controlled thrusts.

"Need you, Liam," I breathe, taking control, pushing his pants and his briefs down his thighs.

He goes slow as he pushes his way into me. "Liam." His name falls from my lips in a desperate plea to give me more.

"Please," I groan.

He just smirks as he withdraws his length from me in a titillating torture then pushes back in. I bite my lip to stop my moans from escaping. *My God, he's driving me crazy.* It feels incredible. He moves in and out of me, slow and smooth at first and then it changes to quick and greedy with the same intensity he exudes with everything he does. My hands in his hair. His hands wrapped around my hips.

"You drive me wild, Ellie," he murmurs. The strain in his voice betrays his desperate need to get there. But knowing Liam, he'll make sure I get there first. Pulling back, his forehead meets mine, his jaw lax. Our eyes hold, but his gaze feels different. He's serious. It's intimate. Every part of me aches as he looks at me like I'm all he's ever wanted.

With my ass hovering on the edge of the cold, wood surface, his strong hands hold me in place as he moves deeper, rotates his hips and seconds later I'm crying out his name. Liam's shoulder covers my mouth as he harshly whispers into my ear. "Someone will hear us, and I don't plan on stopping, Ells. Bite my shoulder."

I press my teeth into the hard flesh of his shoulder to muffle the cries that I'm powerless to stop. My body shakes and tremors as I give myself over to him. The sensations are electrifying; they rip through me as the orgasm takes over my every nerve, every muscle, my very being. My head falls back, and I feel his warm mouth on my neck, only increasing the pleasure.

I rest my forehead on his chin while he continues to slam into me. Thrusting over and over until I see stars. He grabs the back of my hair and now it's Liam's turn. His hands move down my sides to my hips as he grips me even tighter, rocking into me deeper until he wraps his arms around my waist and holds me close, as close as we could ever be. He stills, finding his release.

"Oh… oh… God," he murmurs as he kisses my neck, my jaw and then my lips.

After several minutes, he slowly pulls out of me and helps me off of his desk. He puts himself back together then gently smooths my hair back in place. He unbuttons his dress shirt, taking it off, then turns towards a small closet near the back of the room. My eyes study the deep grooves and lines of his bare back, muscles that I can still feel on my fingertips, noticing faint red lines covering his shoulders and upper back.

"Are these marks from me? From the night of the club?"

"Yes. And no need to apologize. I loved it," he says, reaching for a new white dress shirt, slipping his arms into the sleeves. "I'm betting there will be a few new ones after today."

I watch Liam button his shirt and straighten himself back up. I can still feel my racing heart after what we just did on his desk. I don't remember ever feeling this alive. This is what happiness feels like, what it looks like. I know with everything in me that I'm falling harder every day for this man. And it should be terrifying because until Liam, I'd never allowed myself to fall for anyone.

He reaches for me and I'm quickly back in his arms. He presses my back into his chest- his very hard, broad, sexy chest - and softly kisses my shoulder. He whispers against my cheek, "That was a first for me, by the way."

I can't help but smile. "Sex on your desk?"

"Hmm," he murmurs, pressing a kiss to my temple. I sigh at the thought of being one of his firsts.

"I'm glad."

His chest gently shakes against my back as he chuckles.

He's the only thing I want. But this is starting to feel like it isn't enough. I want a life with Liam. An open and honest one where we let each other in, learn each other's hearts. I'm left with an ache in my chest and a panic in my stomach knowing I need to figure out what I'm going to do when he learns my secret. If Liam knew the whole truth about me, this thing between us would be over. He would walk away for good. And I would deserve the heartache that came with it for the stupid mistakes I've made. Tears burn, threatening to fall.

You're not a kid anymore.

You've grown up.

You made a mistake.

People make mistakes.

I close my eyes, swallowing the lump of pain lodged in my throat. I've been hiding from my past for a long time, but I've never had anyone in my life worth fighting for until now.

I know in my soul that Liam is worth the fight.

So that's what I intend to do.

Chapter Seventeen

Liam

There was something in her eyes when she left my office today that I couldn't make out. It's a look I've seen before, a flicker of uncertainty that I can't understand. I want to believe she wants more than just a casual fling, but the truth is I'm not sure. I can't get enough of her. I've decided that Ellie is the cure for everything. She's reckless, impulsive, spur of the moment - everything I thought I would hate.

Turns out the exact opposite is true. Ellie Reeves is everything -absolutely everything - I've never known I wanted.

Ellie forces me not to take things too seriously. She forces me to balance my work life with my personal one, to be in the present moment, to appreciate the little things. With Ellie, it's impossible not to enjoy life. The problem is I risk losing sight of my ambitions and forgetting why I've worked so damn hard all these years to make partner. All I want to do is lose myself in her.

Prime example: I have a meeting to get to, but I can't stop picturing her on my desk. Her long, soft hair in my fist. Her head thrown back as I give her what she wants. Her blue irises - those fucking goddess eyes that are full of emotion and heat, that sear right through mine in a way I've never known. She does something to me. She does everything to me. She sets my heart on fire. And I have zero plans of stopping it.

I shake my head, but I know it won't matter. She's always there, occupying my thoughts. Morning, midday and all fucking night long.

"Mr. Bennett. Your clients are running fifteen minutes late. Will that be a problem?" my assistant Silvia asks, popping her head through my door.

Perfect. That will give me just enough time to put into action a thought I had this morning. "That's fine, Silvia. Not a problem. I do need you to work on something for me immediately though."

"Happy to. What can I do for you?"

After giving Silvia specific instructions, she assures me she will take care of it and email me the details by the end of the day. I sit back in my chair. This is either going to be the best idea I've ever fucking had, or it will go down in history as the worst. Here's hoping for the former.

The afternoon passes quickly with back-to-back meetings and then I head to my parents' house to watch the Yankees game on TV with my brothers and my dad. Ellie is busy at the beach house with Olivia and my sister doing wedding things.

"Did you see that? Nice double play by Cole," Parker says, leaning forward in his seat with a beer in his hand.

"He's having one hell of a year," my dad replies from the leather armchair that has been "his" chair ever since I can remember.

"He's overrated," Miles interjects, and we all turn to stare at him. Cole Taylor, overrated? *Not a fucking chance.*

"Says the guy who knows nothing about baseball. Stick to acting," I tell him, because what the fuck. "Speaking of… what are you filming next?"

"An action, comedy, adventure film with Violet Michelson. We're shooting in Vancouver and LA. I've never worked with her before, and wasn't sure if I'd ever get the chance, so it's cool. I'm looking forward to it."

"Who's directing it? Anyone you know?" my dad asks, always keen to know the details of Miles' projects.

"Yep, Josh Lucas. The guy's a stud. He's unreal to work with and really involved with the cast. He's so damn artistic too. He's a genius."

"Sounds like a fantastic experience, son. When do you start?"

"In two months. I don't have my schedule yet, but filming starts in LA, then we head to Vancouver after that. They've put me up in a huge house overlooking the water." Miles swipes his phone to life, then types something into the screen. He turns the phone so Parker and I can see it. "Check out this house. It's crazy, right? You guys should really think about coming to visit. It looks like there is more than enough room, and Vancouver is gorgeous in the summer."

"Noted. That house is killer." Vancouver does sound like a good time and I've never been to Canada, but I'm temporarily distracted by my phone vibrating in my pocket. Digging it out, I check the screen, doing my best to hide a smile when I see it's from Ellie. Casually I slide my thumb across the screen to read it.

Ellie: Plans tomorrow night after work?

My reply is instant. And cheeky.

Liam: I was planning on watching The Bach-

elor at Applebees with Parker, but I can reschedule...

"I need a drink. I'll be right back," I say, pushing up from the couch and making a stop in my father's study to see what Ellie has in mind for us for tomorrow. I slide into one of his leather armchairs, checking the thread, watching the text bubbles float on my phone like a total idiot.

Ellie: I hate to tear you away, but I think you'll enjoy what I have planned much more. :) It's a class. That's all I'm willing to divulge at this time. Seven o'clock. Does that work?

Liam: Why does this feel like a setup? I draw the line at couples' yoga. Also, no cooking classes. And I refuse to watch you flirt with that cowboy again, so horseback riding is out.

Ellie: What cowboy? ;)

Liam: Good answer.

Ellie: Great. Do you mind picking me up at seven? It's either that or I double you on my bike. :)

Liam: Tempting... but I prefer the luxuries of four wheels and a proper seat. See you at seven.

Ellie: Can't wait.

Liam: Me too.

Wiping the smile from my face, I wander into the kitchen to fetch a glass of water, wondering what the hell I've just got myself into. This is Ellie we're talking about. She is one hundred percent unpredictable.

"Liam! Hi." My mom stops what she's doing and wipes her hands with a tea towel. "What can I get you? Are you hungry? I can make you something."

"No, Mom. I'm good. I just wanted a glass of water. I'll get it." I make my way to the cupboard and grab a glass.

"So, how's my son? Anything new?" my mother asks, a playful look in her eyes.

"Not much."

"Not much?" She crosses her arms over her chest and raises a brow at me. "Liam, there must be something new in your life you want to tell me." My mother has a way of getting people to talk. She should have been a shrink, if she wasn't so busy taking care of four kids. "Your sister told me about your night out at the club. She said you all had a great time."

I shake my head, filling the glass at the tap. "I'm betting that's not all she said."

"Then you would be betting correctly. She tells me you and Ellie were practically inseparable." There's no way for my mother to hide the smile overtaking her face right now.

"Jules has a big mouth," I joke, taking a sip of my water.

"Jules is excited for you, and frankly so am I. She said she barely recognized you, you were smiling all night." My mother beams as she rests her palm on the top of my hand on the kitchen counter. "And I can see that she's right. You look so happy, Liam."

"Not as happy as you do right now," I tease her.

"Oh, quit it. I can't help it. I'm just really excited for you, honey. You deserve a great girl like Ellie. You know how much your father and I like her."

I meet my mom's eyes. "Thanks, Mom. I really like her too."

"Have you told her how you feel?"

"Not yet."

"Well, I suggest you do. She's good for you, Liam. Your sister is right: you *are* more relaxed. And you're getting out more, having fun. It's good for you. You've been working your life away for as long as I can remember. You've always been my serious boy." She smiles at me, the lines at the corners of her eyes deepening. "You take after your father. I'll never forget you wearing your dress shirts and slacks when we would visit your dad at his office. Gosh, you were cute. You had to look the part. While your brothers played games underneath the boardroom table, you were begging your father to be put to work," she says, then chuckles. "Some things never change."

And she's right. I've put my job and schooling before everything else ever since I can remember. It was never enough to ace tests and get straight As. I needed to be the best in the class, then get into Yale, then graduate summa cum laude, then make partner before thirty. I've always had my sights set on the next prize, the next accomplishment. It's simply the way that I am wired. I've never let up on my goals, not even for a second.

"Any chance you'll be bringing her around anytime soon?" My mom asks, with a little hope in her eyes.

"I think you'll be seeing a lot of her, considering the wedding is right around the corner," I say, attempting to dodge the question. I'm not sure she's ever been as content as she has been since my brother popped the question to Olivia. All she wants is for her kids to be happy. No judgement, no expectations. Seeing her smile, I can't help but feel thankful. When it comes to parents, I definitely lucked out.

"I look forward to seeing her - and to seeing you two together at the wedding. And just remember that Ellie is always welcome here. We would love to get to know her better. Bring her by some time, would you?"

"I will, Mom. I promise."

She pulls me in for one of those hugs only a mom can give, and I wonder if she's right. Maybe it is time I tell Ellie exactly how I feel about her and not worry about the consequences.

And I know the perfect place to do it.

Chapter Eighteen

Liam

Looking back, I should have known. I should have realized "taking a class" meant a cringe-worthy event that would be horribly humiliating and end up with me wanting to escape out the bathroom window.

I lift a brow at Ellie as we both tie the strings of our smocks, telepathically telling her I-can't-believe-I-am-doing-this. When I scan the room, I'm not sure how there could possibly be eleven other guys who got roped into this scheme along with me. It's got to be down to duress or false pretenses. Nobody would do this willingly, would they?

The instructor at the front of the room looks to be in her forties. She's wearing a rainbow ombre fuzzy sweater and has her hair tied back in French braids. Introducing herself to the group as Emma, she motions us to our seats where she has an easel, a selection of paints and brushes already set up for each of us. The one saving grace in this Paint and Sip couples' class is the glass of Pinot waiting for me at my station.

"Is everyone ready to unleash their inner Monet?" she asks after we've all taken our seats.

I scan the other couples. Ellie pumps her fist beside me while the grown men and woman around me holler in unison that they're ready. I swear I've stepped into the twilight zone.

I inwardly gripe at the thought of spending the next 120 minutes painting a sunset or a palm tree, but it's also not lost on me that Ellie looks hot as hell in her off-the-shoulder sweater and miniskirt. I guess tonight isn't all bad. Her smooth, tanned legs are crossed at the knee and her dark hair is down her back in waves, beckoning me to run my hands through it.

Leaning in close, I whisper into her ear. "You look hot in that apron."

"I was admiring you in yours too," she says with a coy grin. "Have you done this before?"

"Paint a canvas?"

"Yes," she replies, tying her hair back into a ponytail.

"Not since elementary school."

"Well then this should be fun," she says, rubbing her palms together in enthusiasm. She then turns her attention to the front of the room where our overly eclectic instructor begins to guide us through the first stages of our canvas. Once we've started, she moves around the classroom helping to guide us with our strokes. She eventually stops behind me and is assessing my work when the middle-aged man behind us, who is dressed for the occasion in a knit beret, interrupts us. This man clearly takes his art seriously, and I'm relieved when our instructor heads his way. Extra attention is not what I'm looking for right now. It appears he is.

"Liam, I like what you're doing," Ellie says, leaning into my shoulder, pointing her paintbrush at my canvas.

I know what I prefer I was doing, and it has nothing to do with blending red and yellow to make orange. But Ellie is smiling and laughing so I'm choosing to make the best of it. Honestly, it's impossible not to enjoy myself when I'm with her. I'm not sure what it is about Ellie, but she makes me want things I've never wanted before.

"Thank you. I've been told I'm exceptional at mixing colors, so it's really no surprise you like my work," I deadpan.

"Is there anything you can't do?"

I shrug, arching my brow. "Write poetry, I suppose."

"That's a shame. I've always been a sucker for an impeccably written haiku, but I guess I'll keep you," she says, before dipping her paint brush into the pot of blue acrylic paint.

We continue to work on our paintings and to my surprise I laugh more than I have in ages. While my Starry Night resembles more of a crazed hurricane, Ellie turns out to be a Van Gogh prodigy.

"Drinking and painting is fun," Ellie says, taking a sip of her wine.

"Who decided painting and wine are a pair? That they would work well together? Shouldn't you have your wits about you when creating a masterpiece?" The question is rhetorical because the answer is obvious. Wine is an absolute necessity while participating in a Sip and Paint class. I never would survive it otherwise.

"You're not wrong. I doubt Michelangelo was half-cut when he created the Sistine Chapel." She says with a wink then takes a sip from her wine glass.

I laugh, trying not to spit out my mouthful of wine. This experience should have been painful, but with Ellie it's a blast. I've never met anyone who can make me laugh like her.

"Don't look now. She's back," Ellie says, wiggling her brows in the direction of our instructor, who is clearly headed our way. Ellie previously pointed out that Emma likes to gaze in my direction in an overly lustful kind of way, and she's not wrong about that. Emma is clearly eye molesting me.

Doing exactly what Ellie just told me I shouldn't do, I glance toward our teacher. Her eyes gleam. She steps closer so that she is only inches from my shoulder, narrowing her eyes on my canvas. "This would be even better with a little yellow in this corner," she practically purrs, her breath in my ear. I try very hard not to flinch when her shoulder rests against mine as she points out brush stroke techniques.

Is it weird the way she rests her hand across my forearm while describing shadowing? The way her bedazzled cat earring dangles against my neck?

Oh shit. Now her other hand is on my back, creeping down toward my waist. Yup, she's going for it. What the hell kind of class did Ellie sign me up for?

I look to Ellie for help, but she is clearly loving every minute of this. Her eyes tell me *good-luck-with-crazy-cat-lady* and her smirk says, *where's-the-popcorn*? Damn her. She's hanging me out to dry.

"I'll try that, thank you," I tell her, leaning forward in my seat, hoping to break contact with the hand that is still resting on my back. "Would you mind showing this technique to Ellie too?" I say, glancing at Ellie with a sly smirk.

Ellie blinks at me, mischief in her eyes. "I'm just fine over here but thank you, Liam. I think you could benefit from the extra instruction."

"But Ellie, I insist. I think you would really like this technique," I sneer, shooting daggers at her. Meanwhile, Emma's other hand hasn't left its position on my arm.

Ellie shakes her head, laughing as I attempt to dodge Emma's roaming hands. I take a gulp of my wine and clear my throat.

"I beg to differ," she replies, grinning. "This must be learned and learned by you."

And so it goes. I continue to do my best to counter our handsy instructor, and Ellie continues to do everything she can not to laugh. It's like she's in church afraid to get caught giggling during the sermon. Finally, after what feels like an eternity, Emma is impatiently beckoned by the beret-wearing man again and is finally forced to walk away.

"You enjoyed that a little too much," I say, tugging on the end of Ellie's ponytail. She squeals, throwing her head back in laughter.

"And you clearly didn't. I couldn't help it, sorry. You looked like your skin was in the process of strangling you, you were so uncomfortable."

"You were no help. Thanks for nothing. You could have let her know you didn't appreciate her feeling up your date," I say, my voice laced with sarcasm.

"Throw down on Emma? In front of all of these people?"

I laugh, my eyebrows rising in question. "What would be wrong with that?"

"Oh, nothing," she laughs. "It's just that typically I try my best not to beat up art teachers if I can help it. Especially ones in fuzzy rainbow sweatshirts."

We spend the next hour finishing our paintings while Ellie has far too much fun ridiculing my artwork. Despite the fact that it's at my expense, I crack up right along with her. It's a wonder Emma doesn't kick us out of class. When our masterpieces are finished, we both agree that we're not ready to call it a night.

"I'm picking the place, Ells," I say, slipping my arm around her waist. "Here's hoping I won't be groped by a random stranger at our next stop."

"Sounds like very little fun, Liam. How will we pass the time?"

Pulling her in close to my side, I kiss the top of her head. "I have a whole catalog of ideas, beautiful. I believe we will be just fine."

WE WALK the six blocks to an upscale cocktail bar. It's dimly lit but there's a buzz of excitement throughout the place. The walls are painted a jet black, accentuated with gold light fixtures and the floor is a black-and-white checkerboard of glossy tiles. Red velvet stools with gold legs are lined up along the white-and-gold veined marble bar. Moody but vibrant. The ambiance reflects how I feel as I sit across from Ellie at a marble table in the center of the bar: still high from our evening together but wound tight from wanting to touch her. Needing my hands somewhere, anywhere on her body.

I could stare at this woman all night. Ellie is captivating, and when I spend time with her I feel like I'm unraveling a mystery. She's confident when she's talking about what she wants but vulnerable in quieter moments. She's direct, but also secretive in a way that's completely enticing. She's a puzzle in the best kind of way, and just when I think I have her figured out she throws me for another loop, challenging me and bringing me to my knees in the same breath. My chest fills with a feeling I'm not used to when I'm with her. It's something I've never felt before. And I like it.

Ellie looks up at me from the menu she's looking at,

tapping her finger against her cheek as she deliberates. I watch her tongue absentmindedly run the length of her bottom lip and I am plunged back into memories of what it feels like to have my mouth on hers.

I sit back in my seat, crossing one leg over my knee, trying to remain cool. My body hums with anticipation. I'm lost in Ellie for a few more lust-filled seconds until she breaks the silence.

"You know, they're known here for their decadent desserts."

"They are, are they?"

"Yes."

"Then you should try every single one. I'll order them all."

She raises her eyebrows at me, apparently not convinced. "And I'm supposed to eat them all by myself? I haven't forgotten how you feel about junk food. Your body is a temple and all of that ridiculousness," Ellie says with a playful grin, her eyes travelling from my mouth to my lap and back to her menu. "I'm also in the mood for a night-cap," she adds, nodding at the drink menu, her gorgeous blue eyes meeting my gray ones.

I'm in the mood for a different type of nightcap, but I go along with her. "What's your fancy?"

"I think… an Old Fashioned. Join me?" Her eyes are darker than I'm used to as they sweep over my face to my chest then to my hands. I can see she's in a flirtatious mood and I'm happy to indulge.

"I could go for one myself."

"Look at us agreeing. We are two agreeable people. It's a sight to be seen."

I smile, laughing at her sarcasm, then turn the tables on our repartee. "It's starting to feel like we agree on a lot."

This makes her grin, and her eyes change again, this time alighting with what looks like hope. She leans in closer. My pulse quickens with anticipation. It always feels this way with Ellie. Then our waiter unknowingly interrupts our playful banter to ask if we've decided on drinks. I order the Old Fashioneds, silently cursing his timing. When he's left, I return my gaze to Ellie.

"So… how about that dessert?"

"I love a good chocolate cake. I can never say no to that. Share a slice with me?"

"None for me, but go ahead and order one for yourself."

"Worried about your delicious washboard abs?" she asks, letting her hair back down from the ponytail she cinched it in at our art class.

"You think they're delicious?" I counter, causing Ellie to roll her eyes and shake her head.

"Please. Anyone with two working eyes and a pulse would appreciate your midsection. I have eyes, Liam, and 20/20 vision," she says, then catches the attention of our waiter and orders the dessert.

Our drinks arrive minutes later, followed by a slice of chocolate cake that our waiter slides into the center of the table with two forks.

She scoops a forkful of the chocolate and raspberry cake and raises it towards me. "A toast."

I sigh, taking a forkful too. "To breaking my rules."

"To living on the edge." We clink our forks together and eat the chocolate cake. Admittedly, it's incredible, rich and decadent. But I'm not tempted to take another bite. The next taste I will have will be from Ellie's lips.

"So?" she asks expectantly. Her eyes lower to the half-eaten cake on the table between us.

I set down my fork, then take a swill of my Old Fashioned. "The cake was good."

She nudges the plate closer to me. "I promise you it's not going to kill you."

I laugh, and then she asks me her next question, catching me off guard. "You live to work. Have you always been this way?"

"Would you believe me if I said I have?"

"I wouldn't doubt a word you say to me. I know you're a straight shooter. I also believe you would never lie to me."

Lifting my glass, I swallow the liquor, enjoying the burn against the back of my throat. "I've always felt I had something to prove and I learned at a very young age that I'm a lot like my father. I think I started out just wanting to make him proud and from there it moved to never wanting to disappoint him. I remember visiting him in his office, watching him work, and wanting to be just like him. He has always believed in me and I guess, in a way, that has fueled me to work hard every day to prove him right."

"Did studying come easy for you?" she asks, reaching for her glass, taking a drink.

"In a way it did. I've always been determined. I believe determination is a necessity in getting what you want."

Ellie considers this, leaning forward in her seat. "I admire that about you, Liam. I appreciate your passion too."

"I'm passionate about you, Ellie. That reminds me. I have something for you."

I reach into the inside pocket of my jacket for the crossword puzzle book I selected for her, a shiny bow stuck to its cover.

"You bought me a gift?"

"I did. I think you might like it." I hand her the book,

watching her eyes brighten and a look of happiness flash over her face.

"*The (Almost) Impossible Crossword Book*," she says, briefly looking up at me, then back at the book.

"It's a rare first edition," I point out. "I hope you don't already have it. I noticed a stack of crossword books on your coffee table and it was obvious you really enjoy them."

She looks up at me again. "I do and I don't have this one. How did you find this?"

"It took a little digging, but I managed."

"It's incredible. I love it, Liam. Thank you," she says, leaning forward in her chair, reaching for my hand.

"You're welcome."

Ellie shakes her head, then pins me with a stare. "I really had you all wrong when I first met you."

"Is that so?" I have to admit that I'm curious. I want to know her initial impression of me, and how it differs from now.

She takes a drink, then sets the glass down and runs her finger around its rim. Her eyes never waver from mine. "It is. I saw your serious side and I took it for stand-offish. The confidence you ooze, I assumed that was arrogance. I didn't realize you were attentive and thoughtful, and possessed all these other amazing qualities that I didn't take the time to see."

"I get it. I'm pretty sure I did the same," I offer, but then realize she deserves so much more. "But I think they were all excuses, so I didn't have to admit to myself how I really felt about you."

"What do you mean?"

"I mean, I knew you were different from the minute I met you. I was insanely attracted to you, but I just knew you would be so much more than one time, and one time is all I've ever allowed myself. So, it was easier to tell myself you were too wild and spontaneous."

"I was wildly attracted to you, too. Right from the start. I used to wonder if you felt that zip through your chest like I did every time our eyes would meet."

Jesus. Her vulnerability is intoxicating. I feel a high, like she's the perfect hit of the best drug. Hearing that she's felt the same way I have this entire time makes me want to give her even more.

I lean in closer. It isn't easy to open up in this way, but it feels too damn good. "I felt it, Ellie. I felt it every damn time our eyes met, every time my skin grazed yours. I still do."

Her eyes widen and she smiles, carefree and stunning, and my body heats all over. Learning she was just as attracted to me as I was to her makes my heart beat triple time. I swear it could beat right out of my chest.

"Me too," she says softly, reaching for my hand across the table, running her fingers over mine. "You do crazy things to me, Liam."

Shit. Is there any other way to respond to this woman who has me teetering on edge *all* the fucking time from how sexy she is? I can't resist.

I lift up my glass and lick my lips while holding her gaze. I want to wind her right up, so she feels exactly like I do.

"Now, will you finish your cake? I'd like to take you home and undress you and do all kinds of crazy things to you."

Ice clinks in my glass as I knock the remaining liquor back.

Subtlety is not my finest attribute, but my direct approach seems to work. I watch Ellie shiver from my words. She studies my face, composing herself, but the blush across her chest gives her away.

I'm affecting her. She's worked up because of me. She's aroused and I caused it. *Perfect.*

"If you insist." Her lips curve into a smile that lights up her entire face. She takes a slow sip of her drink then sets the glass on the table.

"Ready when you are," she says, with pure sex in her eyes.

There's no way we can get out of here fast enough.

Chapter Nineteen

Ellie

His hand is on the small of my back as I walk up the steps to the door of the small plane that rests on the tarmac. My eyes are the size of saucers as I enter the cabin, which resembles an elegant living room with leather chairs and sofas.

Liam leans into me, his mouth inches from my ear as I take in my surroundings. "I hope you're not afraid of small planes, Ells," he says, his voice low and dreamy. "I promise you'll be safe."

Twisting my body to look at him over my shoulder, I smile nervously. "I've only been on a plane once before, but never one this small. And this one has *couches*, Liam. And dining tables. And a wet bar." *What the hell?* I mouth, and he chuckles.

Liam surprised me this morning after waking me up in his bed. In between kisses, his hands roaming my body, he informed me I would not be going to work today but would instead be boarding a private plane with him to a secret destination. He had everything covered; we just needed to swing by my apartment to pack my things and pick up my passport. *Where to?* He wouldn't tell me. In his words, *My lips are sealed, don't even try.*

The pilot steps out to greet us and a flight attendant offers us each a glass of champagne from a silver tray because how does one travel to their destination without a flute of champagne? Then she proceeds to show us around the cabin. There are couches near the front of the plane and a table and leather chairs near the washroom at the back. I haven't said a word during the rundown of emergency exits and safety briefing for the simple fact that I'm speechless. *I can't believe this is really happening, that this is really my life.*

Liam and I take seats next to each other while the staff disappear into the front of the cabin to prepare us for take-off. He asked that we were not be disturbed unless we call for assistance. The flight attendant then pointed to a button, instructing us to push if we needed absolutely anything. I'm not sure I would dare ask for a thing.

I drop my carry-on bag to the floor next to my feet while Liam pulls his laptop from his travel bag, setting it on the small table in front of him. He may have ditched his tailored suit for dark jeans and a gray pullover sweater, but he's been all business since we stepped into the town car this morning to bring us to the airport.

He looks over at me with a soft grin, and I take notice of his hair and the soft dark strands that my fingers are begging to run through. He apologizes in advance for needing to take care of some more work once we're in flight.

"Don't worry about me. I'll be over here enjoying the journey," I say, sipping from my champagne flute in dramatic fashion. He shakes his head at me, like flying in a private plane with staff to handle your luggage and serve you charcuterie isn't totally mind-blowing. I whisper playfully, "Do you always travel like this?"

"Not always," he says, "but it serves its purpose, every now and again."

We buckle our seatbelts and prepare for takeoff, Liam holding my hand as the plane takes off. Once we're in the air, Liam powers on his computer while I sip from my champagne and curl my legs up underneath me, pulling out the crossword puzzle book Liam gifted me. We sit together in silence, Liam occasionally running the tips of his fingers softly over my leg as he works.

We've been in flight for a half hour or so when he gets up to take a call, pacing the rear of the cabin with his moody-Liam face. Mr. Always-in-Control is agitated about something. It's sexy as hell. I want agitated Liam to bend me over this seat or have his way with me in the tiny aircraft's restroom. *Probably not the best time for that, Ellie.*

"What do you mean he didn't show up?" Liam's voice echoes off the cabin's walls, pulling my attention from my crossword. His posture is tense, his free hand pinching the bridge of his nose.

"I get that but come on, Noah," Liam says, stopping in front of a cabin window, his hand slipping into his pocket. "He's going to seal his own fate. What is he thinking?" I watch him listen to whomever it is on the other end of the call, annoyance written all over his face.

"I get it. Okay, keep me in the loop and let me know as soon as you track him down." Liam ends the call and walks towards me, fire in his eyes.

"Everything okay?" I ask, as he drops into the seat beside me, reaching again for his laptop.

"Everything's fine, Ells," he says, pressing a kiss to my

temple then turning his attention back to his work. "I'm just managing multiple cases right now that all require urgency, with looming deadlines and court dates, and some idiot is not making my life any easier. It's nothing I can't handle, though."

"I don't know how you do it all, Liam, and still make time for your family and Murphy," I tell him, adding, "and you obviously exercise like it's a full-time job."

Liam chuckles, but his eyes are laced with trepidation. He roughly drags his hand through his hair, clearly lost in thought. We sit in silence for a little while, Liam completely focused on his computer. Every so often, he'll reach for me, brushing his thumb over my knuckles or resting his hand on my knee. A reminder that he's here, that he knows I'm here, too. And it dawns on me he's not just stressed about work, but for the first time he's also trying to juggle his job and his relationship with me. This is new territory for Liam. He's never allowed himself the distraction of a relationship, and that breaks my heart. Liam deserves love.

Liam catches me watching him from the corner of his eye and flashes me a sheepish grin. "I've always been this way. I like to work. I like what I do."

"I get that. It doesn't feel like work when you enjoy what you do. But we all need a little downtime. A reset. And it's possible to have both," I say cautiously, afraid of pushing him too far. Liam has been wired one way for so long, and to some extent, I have been too. But Liam is who I want. I've been missing out on so much, never getting close to the men I've dated, always keeping them at an arms-length. I'm ready for more. I want more…with Liam. I want to surrender myself to this man who makes me feel things I'm not used to feeling. He makes me feel alive. He makes me feel whole. So I attempt to reassure him.

"You don't have to worry, Liam. I'm not going to push you. I like the way things are."

A crooked smile curves one side of his mouth, and he reaches for me, one hand brushing the side of my jaw. "I'm not worried, Ells," he says, his eyes on mine. "I'm happy with where things are at too. You know that, right?"

"I do. I just want it to be clear that there's no rush. We can take our time. No pressure."

"You are amazing, Ells. And fucking gorgeous. And I hope you're ready for what I'm going to do to you tonight when I get you alone."

"Counting on it," I say. My body heats at thought of Liam's hands on me, my mouth on him.

This feels like a turning point in our relationship, and my pulse quickens at that realization. We are accepting each other for who we are, flaws and all, and it feels exciting. And so damn worth it. There have been walls up guarding my heart for as long as I can remember, and the thought of letting anyone in is scary as hell. But if anyone is worth taking that chance on, it's Liam.

I close my eyes, leaning my head on the back of my chair, enjoying this moment, hoping I never forget it. My body softens and the frenzied beat of my heart eases.

We sit in silence for a while, Liam switching from his device to a folder of paperwork while I tackle my word puzzle. He seems to have relaxed, his jaw now void of tension and his shoulders less taut. Every now and then I sneak a glance his way and I'm reminded of how beautiful he is and of the overwhelming effect he has on me. The emotions he incites in me threaten to pull me under, to consume me.

"Pin," he says out of nowhere.

I shoot him a confused look. "Pin?"

"Bulletin-board material. A pin," he answers, barely suppressing a smile, motioning towards my crossword.

I laugh. "I hadn't gotten to that one yet, oh ye of little faith. That was an easy one."

"Are you saying I'm incapable of doing your crossword puzzles?"

"Maybe," I say with a coy smile. "Besides, don't you have work of your own you need to be doing?"

"I do. So please stop asking me for help and do your crossword puzzle on your own." He laughs as I swat at the side of his thigh. "Your glass is empty. Let me have the flight attendant bring you another drink."

Liam presses the button that I wouldn't dare to and seconds later a flight attendant appears. She leaves after taking the order, quickly returning with another flute of champagne for me and a coffee for Liam. She also informs us we will be starting our descent to our destination shortly. After we descend through the clouds, I watch as the sun streams in through the small window and wonder yet again where it is we are going.

I catch Liam gazing out the window and I can't help but admire his profile. His strong jawline, long dark lashes that cast a shadow over his cheeks, the curve of his nose, the thick dark hair that is starting to curl at his neck from needing a haircut. I reach for the back of his neck, running my fingers through his hair. He leans into my touch, moaning as I use my fingernails to increase the sensation. His eyes close.

The serious, focused side of Liam fades, replaced with the softer side that I know he doesn't share with many. His usual intensity is suddenly gone, his body relaxed as I rub the muscles at the back of his neck. I like being able to release some of his tension. I love knowing that I'm the one who has the privilege of touching him whenever I want.

A warmth spreads through me as I realize how much Liam has come to mean to me in such a short amount of time. He's captured my heart.

Liam is my person. My future. I've never been more sure of anything.

And…

I'm in love with him.

Chapter Twenty

Ellie

The doorman to the Seaside New York greets us as we step into the opulent lobby of one of the nicest hotels I've ever seen. It's a wonder there is any marble left in the world, because it looks like they've used every square inch of it in this hotel. A Verona black-and-gold stone fireplace stretches to the top of the vaulted ceiling on my left and a grand white-and-gold veined staircase is to my right. It leads from the lobby to a mezzanine overlooking a swanky bar called The Gold Room. There are pretty pastries on tiered displays sitting on top of a long marble waterfall island in the center of the room that my stomach is itching to sample, with three giant crystal chandeliers hovering over top. Looking around me in awe, I can't help but feel like Julia Roberts in *Pretty Woman. Minus the prostitute part, of course.*

"Liam, this is beyond incredible. It's so beautiful," I gush, overwhelmed by the opulence of the place. I take in the sheer beauty of Liam's family's hotel and can't help but feel proud to be here with him.

"You like it?"

"I love it," I tell him, finding it difficult to focus on any one thing.

"The look on your face is priceless," he laughs. "Come on. Let's check in. I have a feeling you are going to like the room they have reserved for us just as much as the lobby."

Liam clasps my hand in his and pulls me towards the front desk.

"Mr. Bennett. It's good to see you."

"Please, call me Liam, and thank you. We are excited to be here."

The man at the desk looks to be in his forties and according to his name tag, his name is Andrew. He seems well-acquainted with the Bennett family, greeting Liam with a wide smile.

"How's Parker doing? We all really miss having him around."

Looking around the lobby again, I can see why Parker liked living in this hotel while he managed it for eight years. That was before he reconnected with Olivia and they moved to Cape May. Who could blame him? Someone cleaning up after him, those mini-fridges no doubt stocked with all the best snacks. If I lived here, I would order French fries every day just so I could get those little personal ketchup bottles. I freaking love those miniature jars.

"You're all set. If you are in need of anything during your stay, please don't hesitate to ask. We are excited to have you and-"

Liam slides a glance my way before squeezing my hand in his. "Thank you. We look forward to it too. This is Ellie Reeves, my girlfriend," Liam says with a slow smile, like it's the most natural thing in the world. I blink and my heart threatens to burst right out of my chest. We stare at each other for longer than we should before turning our attention back to Andrew behind the desk. He's said something to us, but I haven't heard a single word. Not after Liam referred to me as his girlfriend. I'm surprised at my reaction. First because I liked it, and second because this thing between the two of us is starting to feel normal.

"Ellie, should we check out our room?" Liam asks, shaking me from my thoughts. He is already handing our suitcases off to a bellman.

"Yes, of course."

Liam leads us to an elevator that takes us up to the Grand Penthouse. "You ready?" he asks, opening the door and gesturing for me to lead the way. I nod, crossing the threshold into the most luxurious suite I have ever seen. My hand flies to my mouth as I take in the large living room decorated in gold and taupe. There is a bar in the far corner and a dining table large enough to seat twelve. Sliding accordion-style doors lead from the living room to a terrace where I notice a fireplace and a hot tub, and beyond that a view of the Hudson. My eyes travel upwards to a stone staircase to the left. Liam catches my eye. "That's where the bedrooms are," he says, a coy smile tugging at his lips.

"Bedrooms? As in plural? As in more than one?" I ask.

He chuckles, his smile reaching his eyes. "Yes, plural. But we will only be needing one of them."

Oh my god, I mouth to Liam, who just shakes his head and grins. I admit I've sometimes wondered how the rich vacation. Now I know.

There's a knock at the door and the bellman announces that he is here with our luggage. Liam strides through the foyer, digging his wallet from his back pocket, while I take off my shoes and slip outside to the terrace. I take in the stunning view, the turquoise blue of the sky dissolving into the deeper, sparkling blue of the Hudson River. I tip my face to the sun, soaking in its warmth.

For the second time today, Liam has blown me away. I can't believe the man I thought was surly and testy and only into himself has done all of this for me. *Me.* A completely selfless gesture, after I just told him it was a bucket list dream of mine to come to New York City. I'm falling for this new Liam; the one who holds my hand, who tells me I'm beautiful, who really listens to me when we talk. He's not the man I thought he was. He's proving to be so much more.

Liam has opened himself up to me in ways I never expected. He's been honest and vulnerable, and it kills me knowing that I haven't done the same for him. I want to let him in, but there are still things about my life he doesn't know, walls I haven't been ready to tear down. I know that I need to tell Liam about Mason. And I want to, but fear keeps stopping me from telling my story.

I can feel Liam's presence behind me on the patio. His hands drag my hair over my left shoulder, and his lips gently press a kiss to the back of my neck. I shiver.

"The view is pretty spectacular," he says softly, his arms wrapping around me as I turn in his embrace to face him. I run my hand through his thick dark hair. He closes his eyes, leaning into my touch, and murmurs, "Mmm, I love it when you do that."

I continue to drag my fingertips back and forth through his hair, enjoying the calm that has settled over us. He closes his eyes, leaning into my touch like a cat who is enjoying a massage.

"So, *girlfriend*, huh?" I ask with a grin, wanting to know where we stand.

He slowly opens his eyes and the way he smiles at me knocks me off balance. "I told you Ells, I want it to be just us. I'm serious. Unless you'd prefer a different label, girlfriend is what I'm going with."

My knees wobble ever so slightly and I'm completely lost in this moment with this man who destroys me. I'm not sure how I got so lucky to have Liam to want me. To choose me. He's standing here in front me, vulnerable, and I can't stand the thought of losing him. I need tonight with him.

"I'd like that," I tell him in a voice thick with emotion. He reaches for my cheek, brushing the back of his knuckles across my skin.

"Yeah?" he asks with a soft chuckle. His hands pull my body into his.

"Are you already having second thoughts?" I tease, crinkling my nose.

He laughs, smoothing his hands up my back to my shoulders. His mood is light, his shoulders relaxed, the usual tension in his jaw is missing. He looks like a different person. "Not for a second. I want this. Us. I want to be your boyfriend, Ells."

I lean into him, silently promising myself I'll do what I have to do to make things right when we get back to Reed Point. Liam planned this spectacular two days for me, and I don't want to ruin it for him. So instead, I tell him what's in my heart.

"Me too, Liam. I'm happy when I'm with you. Looks like we're officially official."

I go up on my toes, sliding my palms over his chest, and take his face in my hands. He bends forward, meeting me in the middle, and we kiss. A slow, deliberate, passionate kiss. A kiss that tells me everything I need to know.

I melt for this man.

Liam pulls back to face me, breaking the kiss. "I have

plans for us tonight, but if there's something you'd like to see this afternoon I can arrange for it to happen."

"Hmmm... A double-decker bus tour?" I ask, bouncing on my toes in excitement.

"If that's what you want to do then we'll do it," he says, although I'm sure he'd find a three-hour Zoom meeting with his camera on less painful than a sightseeing tour of a place he's probably been to countless times. But I'm starting to come to the realization that if it makes me happy, Liam makes it happen.

"Oh, and Central Park. And the Statue of Liberty. We can't forget about Rockefeller Center and the ice rink with the giant Christmas tree. Oh, and the Theater District."

Liam laughs and his eyes crinkle at the corners, "You realize it's May, and that Christmas tree isn't up all year long, right? And we are only here for two days? I'm not sure we'll have time to make it through your entire list."

And yet, the entire list is exactly what we attempt to do. We hit Rockefeller Center on the way to our pick-up spot for our double-decker tour. We spot Lady Liberty in the distance when our bus takes us through Lower Manhattan and we finish our tour right outside Central Park, where Liam takes me for the most incredible lunch at Tavern on the Green. Somehow, we manage to get a table in a cozy, back corner of the crowded restaurant that requires reservations weeks in advance. It's so Liam to have connections wherever he goes.

Five hours later, we shove off our shoes back at our suite and fall onto the large plush couch, exhausted from our marathon of sightseeing. Liam shifts our bodies so he's lying on his back and I'm lying beside him with my head on his chest. The fading sun peeks through the windows, casting a tangerine glow over the room.

"Everything about this hotel is unbelievable. They even

somehow know lilacs are my favorite flower," I say, admiring the fresh cut flowers in vases that are placed everywhere around the suite. The scent of my favorite blooms floating through the air.

"How could a Seaside hotel staff member possibly know that lilacs are your favorite flower?"

"Are you making fun of me?" I tease, tickling the dip of his throat under his chin. He squirms and grabs my hand away, linking his fingers through mine. "I think it's far too big of a coincidence to ignore."

Liam laughs softly, his chest shaking beneath my cheek. I look up to meet his eyes, which are brimming with mischief. "What?" he asks, feigning innocence.

"Was it you?" I ask, shifting so I can see him better. "It *was* you, wasn't it?"

"I know you love flowers, so I asked Olivia which ones are your favorites, then had them delivered. Not a big deal."

My heart melts into a puddle right there on Liam's chest, and I feel my cheeks heat. They might only be flowers, but they are more than that to me. It's one more thoughtful gesture by Liam, one more bit of proof that he really sees me, that he listens to me and wants to know me.

"Liam," I gush, amazed how in only a few weeks of spending time together, he has figured out the little things that make me, me. My love of flowers is so much more than owning my own shop. It started back when I was a little girl playing in my mom's garden, plucking flowers weaving them into tiny crowns for my pets.

Wanting him to know how much this night away means to me, I sit up and straddle his thighs, pinning his hands above his head.

"Thank you for bringing me here," I say, my voice low, raspy. "No one has ever done anything like this for me."

A slow, easy grin slides over his lips, his erection hard and heavy underneath me, causing an ache between my thighs.

"Kiss me, Ells," Liam begs.

I'm only too happy to. I love it when he begs. Dropping forward, I press my mouth to his, and when my lips part, he slips his tongue inside. A low moan escapes the back of his throat, and I smile into the kiss, loving that I turn him on.

Breaking the kiss, I slide my hands down over his pecs to his abs, feeling the hard grid of muscles underneath his shirt. I rise up off of him and walk towards the staircase that leads to the bedroom.

"Where are you going?" he pouts. His eyes follow me as I grip the edge of my t-shirt and I slowly pull it up over my head, glancing back at him. My eyes saying, *you like what you see?*

And then without a word, Liam is off the couch and we're moving towards the bedroom. We leave a trail of clothes scattering the staircase, the hallway, the foot of the bed.

His gray eyes are brimming with desire and lust as he crawls over my body on the bed where he's placed me. He's devastating on the eyes and I couldn't look away if I tried. Staring at Liam, I realize that everything I've always ever wanted is right here in front of me. This man owns me.

Everything feels like it should. Like it's right.

My heart is in his hands.

My eyes are on forever.

I never want this to end.

Chapter Twenty-One

Liam

I'm wearing one of my suits because I know they drive her wild.

Sitting in a lounge chair on the terrace of our suite, I drink from my tumbler of whiskey and work on my laptop, waiting for Ellie to finish getting ready. It's just after six and I have a car downstairs waiting to take us to dinner. I worked most of the flight this morning, but there's a case that is requiring a lot of my attention. Taking two days off is a luxury I would have never allowed myself in the past, so the fact that this getaway was my idea scares the living fuck out of me.

I'm in way over my head with Ellie. She's consuming me in every way. My thoughts. My dreams. She's everywhere. And it's been that way from the start. Minutes into meeting this woman, I knew she was different from all the rest. I not only needed to have her, I wanted to get to know her. Really know her. She has me thinking things I've never considered before, things like a future, a family. Someone to call after I've won a big case. Someone to come home to at the end of a long day.

Unlike the other woman in my past, Ellie means something to me.

She challenges me.

Excites me.

Energizes me.

It's terrifying as hell.

Seconds later, I hear the sounds of her heels clicking down the staircase. I shift, moving my laptop to the side to give her my full attention, and turn in my seat to see her. My breath hitches the instant I set eyes on her. Ellie strides onto the terrace, her big blue eyes meeting mine. She's got to know how fucking beautiful she looks.

"Come here," I command, widening my legs and holding my arms out to her. She steps between my parted knees and my hands reach around the backs of her thighs, gently squeezing her.

My eyes shamelessly travel up the length of her body, pausing at her cleavage. The dress is jade green, the neckline is sweetheart, and it ends mid-thigh, showing off all of her best assets. She has her long hair down straighter than usual with a jeweled clip behind one ear. She really is breathtakingly gorgeous. She's a study in contradictions. Her features are soft, but she's feisty, stubborn. She's gorgeous but grounded and unbelievably witty, uninhibited but so introspective. She looks so good it physically hurts. She always does. She looks good on the seat of my car, wearing my shirt in the morning, wearing nothing at all. And tonight, in a dress I picked up after I caught her admiring it in a window on our way to lunch. She looks breathtakingly stunning. There really isn't a better view in the world.

She steps away from my grasp and does a twirl, a grin on her lips and a twinkle in her ocean-blue irises.

"You look incredible, Ellie. That dress was made for you," I say, watching her smile widen at the compliment. I stand and take two steps towards her, closing the distance between us. Running the tips of my fingers down her bare shoulder, I watch her skin pebble under my touch. I have the sudden urge to kiss her and take her face in my hands. Seeing her in that dress makes me want to take her right back to bed. Or the bathroom counter. Right now, I'd settle for a wall.

"Thank you for the dress. You didn't need to do that, Liam, but I love it."

She goes up on her toes and kisses me, angling her mouth to deepen it. Her hands are on either side of my neck, my hands grip her waist. She pulls away with a coy smile and I tug on my collar because the temperature on this patio just skyrocketed to scorching. Unable to help myself, my hand travels down her thigh towards the hem of her skirt before she bats it away.

"When you kiss me like that, what do you expect?" I ask with a groan. There's something about her lips on mine, the sensation of the kiss, her tongue, that makes me feel things I've never felt before. I lose all self-control, lose all track of time. It's just us. And I want her.

"You don't play fair, Ells," I growl, running my knuckles along the edge of her jaw.

"You don't make it easy. But I didn't get all dressed up for nothing."

"If you don't stop teasing me," I say, kissing her again, "you can forget about dinner, and I'm going to take you back upstairs to bed."

She smiles against my lips and scratches her nails

through the scruff on my face. "I change my mind. You in a suit… who needs food?"

"Jesus, Ells. You. Kill. Me," I say, breaking the kiss and taking a step back. "As much as I'd like that, I've made reservations at the best restaurant in the city and I need to show you off in this dress. Shall we? The driver is waiting."

"We shall, Mr. Fancy Pants. We shall."

ELLIE

LATER THAT NIGHT, we are seated in a private room at Boulevard, a New York City hotspot. We've eaten a five-course meal chosen by the Michelin-rated chef and sipped wine that I'm sure costs more than my monthly rent.

The dress Liam surprised me with fits perfectly, which blows my mind considering I've never told him my size. He's been attentive and charming, the chemistry between us almost overwhelming at times.

We enjoy dessert and espressos and I feel satisfied and happy, lost in the glow of the candlelight as Liam motions to the waiter. Then suddenly he stands and walks around to the back of my chair, helping me from my seat. "We need to go now, Ells. I have somewhere I want to take you."

He catches me by surprise, but I grab my purse and allow him to guide me from the table, back into the waiting town car parked just outside the restaurant. Thirty minutes later, our driver stops in front of an old, weathered building with peeling paint. I meet Liam's eyes and the look in them makes it clear that he's up to something. Before I have a chance to press him on it, the door to the car opens and Liam scoots out. I watch him button his suit jacket then offer his hand, helping me from my seat. Stepping out into the cool night air, he immediately pulls me into his arms.

"Are you going to tell me what we're doing here?" I ask, staring up at him, still wrapped in his embrace. Somewhere in the distance, a musician is strumming his guitar and singing the lyrics to a Coldplay song. And it's perfect. So incredibly, heart-twistingly, straight-out-of-a-romance-novel perfect.

"Not yet."

"Liam. Are you sure you got the directions right? I didn't picture you for a man who frequents raves. You *are* full of surprises," I joke, reaching up towards his neck and adjusting his collar.

He raises an eyebrow and laughs. "Well, now you know all of my secrets. Closet raver, right here. I can't stop," he jokes and gives me a quick, chaste kiss on my lips before taking my hand and leading me down the sidewalk.

We walk for a block or so along the dark street when we encounter a crowd of people under bright lights. I don't think anything could have prepared me for what I see when I look up. My eyes go wide, and I gasp, covering my mouth with my palm. "No!" I shout. "Liam, are you serious?"

I whirl around to face him, tilting my head to the side. "Seriously? You did this for me?" I ask. Tears prick my eyes as he pulls me in close to his side and kisses the top of my hair. My palm is still covering my mouth.

"I did. I hope you like it," he murmurs into my hair, the vibrations of his voice sending goosebumps over my skin. I look up at the marquee sign again to make sure I didn't just imagine it. I didn't. It has *Cats* written across it in lights and just the sight of it makes me squeal. It's an off-

Broadway production since the original Broadway show closed over ten years ago.

"I had no idea the production had ended when I looked into buying us tickets, so this one will have to do. I hope that's okay?"

The tears in my eyes threaten to spill over. I'm overcome with emotion for this man who once again has rendered me breathless. I wrap my arms around his neck and kiss him fiercely. "Liam, it's more than okay. It's everything. *You* are everything. Thank you."

We are greeted at the door by a host dressed in an all-black suit who welcomes us and motions for us to follow him to our seats. Liam's hand is laced in mine as we walk down the steps of the theater to our row. We take our seats, which are center and five rows up from the stage. Liam presses a slow kiss to my lips, which surprises me, considering he does not do PDA. It's unexpected and when he pulls back I cock my head to the side with a puzzled expression. His eyes are bright, his grin laced in mischief, and his dimple is holding my heart hostage.

"I couldn't resist. You are killing me in that dress."

"I'm definitely not complaining. You can kiss me anytime, anywhere."

"Anywhere?" he asks, a smirk taking over his face, teasing and taunting me. *This man is irresistible in so many ways.*

"You know what I meant. Now, can you behave yourself until the show is over because I don't plan on missing a second of this play. No seduction on your part will be enough to take my eyes off of that stage. Is that understood?"

"Understood." He leans into my shoulder, his mouth at the sensitive spot just under my ear, and whispers, "That whole bossy thing you just did was hot as fuck. Can you do that again when I get you back to the hotel tonight?"

"I can," I say, kissing him chastely. "And I will."

We watch the two-and-a-half-hour show in silence. The entire time, his hands seem to always be in contact with me. His fingers laced with mine, on my knee, in my hair. Tracing circles on my shoulder. Every now and then he'll press a kiss to the top of my head.

The show is incredible. It brings me back to my childhood and Friday nights when my mom would transform the family room floor into a giant pillow bed with blankets and stuffed animals and popcorn and treats. We'd cozy up together and she'd ask me what movie I wanted to watch, knowing the answer would always be *Cats* because it was my all-time favorite. I can so clearly remember her snuggling up beside me, knowing all the showtunes, singing every line and every word right along with me. I imagine her voice and her laugh, and I miss her.

I wipe my weepy eyes with the tips of my fingers and Liam notices, squeezing my thigh in his hands. *You okay?* he mouths.

I nod, blinking my eyes to clear the tears that are blurring my vision. "The play just reminds me of my mom," I whisper. "I'm fine. I just miss her."

"I'm sorry, babe."

"I'm fine, Liam. Way more than fine. This is incredible."

He smiles back at me, that soft, shy smile that he seems to save just for me. It can bring me to my knees. That unfamiliar feeling creeps into my chest and this time I'm certain what it is.

This is love. What I am feeling right now is without a doubt love. The two of us together are tearing down the walls around our hearts that we've spent our whole lives building. We are learning to trust each other, to show each other who we really are. Those three little words have been on the tip of my tongue now for days, but I can't tell him, as much as I want to, for fear of his reaction. If it wasn't reciprocated the rejection would kill me. So, I swallow the words down and instead show him in the only other way I know how to.

Leaning into him, I take his face in my hand and kiss him, hoping that with this kiss, I'm saying everything I wish I could say to him. Everything I want him to know. Withdrawing from the kiss, I look into his eyes with a fierce, uncompromising honesty. My adoration for this man who has gone out of his way to make me feel special, to care for me. I feel exposed and euphoric and completely at ease, and there's nowhere I'd rather be than right here with Liam.

The look in his eyes tells me he feels the same. But it's mixed with something else, something that I'm unable to pin down. *Fear?* Liam never loses control and I'm sure the feeling of falling in love scares the shit out of him. Reaching across my lap for my hand, he entwines his fingers in mine and we go back to watching the show.

After a standing ovation and the curtain closing, the lights flicker back on in the theater. I turn to face him, an overwhelming look of gratitude in my eyes. "I still can't believe you did this all for me."

"And I can't believe you know every song by heart," he laughs.

I take his hand in mine, playing with his fingers. He lifts our joined hands to his mouth, brushing his lips across my knuckles. I'm completely unable to hide my emotions, I don't even try. He's looking back at me like I'm the one thing that means everything to him, a mirror image to the way I'm feeling.

"You know how happy you made me tonight, right?" I ask, my heart overflowing. No one has ever done anything like this for me and I'm still finding it hard to put into words how much tonight has meant. "I'm pretty sure that wasn't your idea of a good time, so thank you."

"Let's just keep this our secret. When the guys find out I sat through close to three hours of watching grown men in leotards on their hands and knees, they'll have smack talk on me for the rest of my life." He laughs, then kisses my forehead.

"I've got your back, Liam. I'll tell them you took me for all-you-can-eat hot wings at Hooters, that we shot-gunned beers all night then smoked cigars."

"Can you throw in that I'm a God in the sack too?" he deadpans.

"It wouldn't be a lie," I tell him honestly, running my fingers over the lobe of his ear and massaging it between my fingers. "Speaking of. I'm ready to go back to the hotel now, unless you have any more incredible surprises up your sleeve?"

And then, as if I couldn't want him anymore, he smiles the biggest, most heart-breaking smile and my heart tumbles in my chest. "Hotel. Now," he says, enunciating each word, his hand reaching for mine as we head up the theater steps to the street outside. It's dark and raining when we exit the building, so Liam tells me to wait under the awning while he finds our driver.

Watching Liam from where I stand, I am still amazed he went to all of this trouble for me. One night at the Seaside would have been more than enough, but the private plane, expensive dinner, surprise dress - not to mention sitting through a play for me… it speaks volumes to the kind of man Liam is.

He oozes sex, he's over-the-top alpha. Beautiful inside

and out. My heart swells when he turns to face me, looking up at me through hooded eyes as rain falls down upon him. I can't think straight when he looks at me that way. I wonder if I'll ever get my fill of this man, because right now it feels like I could never get enough. Returning to my spot under the awning, Liam pops open an umbrella that he grabbed from the car and holds it overtop of us. Tucking me into his side, he ushers me to the waiting car.

As we settle into the back seat, I think of all of the incredible things Liam has done for me and am suddenly slammed with all the reasons I don't deserve him. With the good comes the bad. And everything right now feels too good to be true. It can't last forever, *can it?* Especially not when secrets are involved. I would never want to see the hurt in eyes if he were to find out the truth. Besides, I've learned the hard way that people never stick around. They're here today and gone tomorrow and I know what it feels like when they don't come back. Tears sting the corners of my eyes for what feels like the millionth time today. I take a deep breath and tell myself to stay in the moment, to just be here with Liam. He deserves this night away from work, from the stress of his life. He deserves a reset, an unwind, and I want to show him just how grateful I am for this day.

I can do that.

And I intend to.

Chapter Twenty-Two

Liam

Not even the cool night air is enough to chill the heat simmering inside me as we step onto the sidewalk past the doors of the theater. Ellie in that dress, her legs on display beside me for almost three painstaking hours, her citrus scent tempting me all night. She doesn't need to know I have a hard on for her right now. But I do.

When we slip inside the waiting town car we're finally alone and I have her all to myself.

"I think it's safe to say you had a great time," I say, remembering the way she sang along to every song and then jumped from her seat in applause, tears in her eyes, when it ended. While I thought the show was a strangely torturous experience, watching oversized cats sing and dance while paw-licking and ear-slicking, Ellie clearly loved every single second of it. And that's good enough for me, because even though I didn't give a fuck about the spectacularly odd performance, I'm not sure I've ever seen her happier.

"Are you kidding me, Liam? It was honestly one of the

best nights of my life. I can't thank you enough for setting this all up. A dream came true. You realize that, right?" She looks back at me with sparkling clear eyes. "You made one of my dreams come true."

My smile widens, the passing streetlights casting shadowy hues across her face.

My chest fills with pride knowing I was able to give that to her, to make her feel that way. But I've never done feelings and expressing myself has always been strange, awkward. So instead of using words, I show her by tangling my hand in her hair at the base of her neck pulling her into me. I kiss her hard and deep, my tongue slipping inside her mouth to find hers. I'm rewarded with one of her sighs against my lips.

"You really have no idea what you do to me, do you?" I ask, a mostly rhetorical question.

She pulls her bottom lip under her teeth, a look of vulnerability in her gorgeous blue eyes. She knows, but she wants to hear it.

"You undo me, Ellie. I like the way I feel when I'm around you. I'm so fucking crazy about you," I admit, cupping her face in my hands and kissing her with a hunger that makes my head spin. My tongue slips in her mouth and she tastes sweet, like wine and passion. Our chests heave in unison, our need for one another so strong.

A shy smile covers her lips. "Me too, Liam. It's the same for me."

The look in her eyes tempts me even further, brimming with lust and desire. Her voice is gentle and steady when she leans into my ear and informs me she's never had sex in the back of a car.

That makes two of us.

I've had a lot of sex in my twenty-something years. Great sex. Filthy sex. In every different position. But never in places I might be watched. That's where I draw the line. I've always been an insanely private person in all aspects of my life and although I love sex as much as the next guy, I prefer it in privacy, behind a closed door. I broke my own rule when I had her on my desk in my office, and now I'm about to break another because I want her. That bad.

She cups me, squeezing the outline of me gently. A smirk on her lips taunts me to take her. Right here. Right now. I can't get enough of this woman and I doubt I ever will. It's all fun with her. Playful Ellie is my favorite.

I lean down to kiss her. My fingertips graze along her thighs then back towards her knee, feather-soft. Kiss after kiss, one after another; the intimacy in this moment pulls me under her spell. I check the sound-proof barrier is closed between the back of the town car and our driver and then I pull her onto my lap. Her thighs straddle mine as I crash my mouth into hers, slipping my tongue between her lips when they part. Our tongues collide while my hands seek her bare flesh. Reaching for the hem of her dress, I slide it up over the curve of her hips, gathering the material around her waist. Her hands tug at the ends of my hair while my hands grip the globes of her ass.

I desperately want her, like I need air to breathe.

"I want you, Ellie. So bad." The need to be inside her, filling her, is all I can think about. All other coherent thoughts are gone. It's just her and her body and the urgent need to have her skin against mine. She gazes back at me with a challenge in her eyes.

"Then take me. I'm yours, Liam. Take everything in me."

Fuck.

I cup her cheeks in my hand and control her mouth with mine, kissing her, tugging on her bottom lip with my teeth and then running my tongue over it to soothe the sting. She moans against my mouth and my dick hardens against my zipper.

Not able to wait a second longer, I pull her away from my lap and unfasten my pants, pushing them down, along with my briefs. Then I pull her thong to the side and line her up with my erection.

She lowers herself over me, until she is fully seated and begins to slowly rock back and forth. She rides me while my hands grip her thighs, digging into her skin, claiming her, marking her, wanting her to feel the depths of my desire for her. I want to lose myself in her, to taste her and feed this hunger that's been smoldering inside of me since she walked downstairs tonight in that dress. *That fucking dress.*

She feels so good. Her muscles clench around me, sparks go off under my skin with every motion of her hips rocking into me. She really starts to move, swiveling her hips, grinding her pelvis against my pelvis, taking what she needs. I'm more than happy to give it to her.

"Look at me, Ells. I want your eyes on mine. I want to watch you when I make you come," I command, squeezing her breast over the fabric of her dress.

"Don't stop," she pants, between thrusts. I listen to what she wants, driving up deeper. Harder. Her head falls back, and I take the opportunity to suck on the silky skin of her neck.

I've never needed her more than right now. Her eyes flutter closed from the sensations and I can feel she's getting close. "Open your eyes, Ells. Look at me."

"Liam," her voice is gravelly. The way my name sounds falling off her lips makes my arousal grow even thicker.

"I'm not going to last, baby. I need you to get there."

Pleasure spirals through me and I feel the pulses that warn me my orgasm is near.

She pants, her breaths shallow and even, and I'm shocked at how badly I need her. We breathe in unison, my eyes locked on hers. She looks back at me long and hard and I know. I know that I've found everything I never knew I wanted until Ellie. I want to tell her, but I can't find the words.

Watching me with those big dreamy eyes, she comes undone, flying over the edge into ecstasy and I follow her right over.

Afterwards, we are in bed at the Seaside, Ellie's cheek is resting on my chest. We managed to make it into the hot tub on the veranda once we arrived back to our suite before we had each other's clothes completely off. We moved from there to the stairs and then the king-size bed, finally getting our fill of one another. For now. With Ellie, I'm insatiable.

I'm on my back, one arm behind my head and the other wrapped tightly around Ellie's back drawing circles on her shoulder. Her long legs tangled with mine, the bed sheet pulled up to our waists.

"So, tell me the truth," she says, and I can feel her smile against my chest. "Scale of one to ten, how much did you hate the play tonight?" Ellie shifts so she is looking up at me through a fringe of dark lashes, a coy grin on her face.

"You don't really want to know. Some things are best left unsaid, Ells," I say chuckling, causing her lips to turn up at the corners in a soft smile. She doesn't need to know that in my head the entire time I was golfing. Then fucking her. Then more golf, followed by more of the same.

"I *do* want to know. Tell me, Liam," she pushes. "Like,

was it I'd-rather-be-operated-on-with-a-dull-scalpel or I-love-*Cats*-and-I'm-getting-a-face-tattoo-of-Grizabella?"

I wince, flashing back to all of the pawing and prancing around. "I definitely lean toward the former," I admit, laughing. "Let's just say I will not be watching the Netflix version. Ever."

"Okay, so a zero. You give it a zero. Am I right?"

"I didn't say that. Let's just say I couldn't wait to be free of it. My favorite part was the standing ovation at the end. But it doesn't matter, Ellie, you loved it and that was the whole point of tonight. To make you happy," I tell her. She smiles at me and I feel like I've won some sort of lottery. The woman in my arms, gazing back at me like she wants to remember every single second of being here, is mine. With all of her craziness and her sassy mouth and true-blue heart. She is mine.

Ellie takes my hand in hers and turns it over, tracing the grooves of my palm with her finger. "You definitely did that. It was the best night of my life."

I watch her lay her head back down on my chest, breathing a gentle sigh. I'd be lying if I said having her soft body pressed to mine in this quiet moment didn't feel fucking amazing. Ellie showing her affection for me, having her warm hands on my skin, makes me feel alive. Her free hand begins to move over the grooves and lines of my stomach, my skin shivering from her soft fingertips.

"Liam, what were you like as a little boy? I bet you were trouble, weren't you?"

She couldn't be further from the truth of who I was when I was a kid. "The complete opposite. Picture me ten years old and exactly as I am today. I've always been this way. It was Miles and Jules who were always getting into trouble."

"That, I can see. Those two are kindred spirits. There isn't a rule that wasn't meant to be broken with them."

I laugh, remembering the four of us growing up together. "I was the one continuously trying to bail them out of the trouble they got in. I was known as Jules' brother, her ferocious protector. It drove her crazy."

"You are still so protective of her. It's sweet." She reaches for my hand, tangling her fingers between mine. "You are fierce in and out of the courtroom. I happen to find that sexy."

Lifting our joined hands to my lips, I kiss the tips of each of her fingers. "Not even close to how incredibly sexy I find you."

I can feel her smile widen against my chest. "Liam, last question," she says. "Have you ever been in love?"

"No." I answer honestly. "You?"

"No, me neither."

"You've never been in love?" I ask, wanting to know why.

"Never." She shrugs and the air between us feels thick. I wonder how a girl like Ellie has never experienced love.

We share stories of old crushes, parties that ended too late, little pieces of our lives that have made us who we are today. We're opening up, really getting to know each other. It feels natural. It feels fucking perfect.

So fucking right.

The more I learn about Ellie, the more I want to know.

Then I wonder… how did I get here? How did I let this happen? How did I allow her to bury herself so deeply under my skin that she's all I can think about? All I fucking want. Every perfect piece of her. And I wouldn't want it any other way.

With sleepy eyes, Ellie searches my face from where she

lays stretched out beside me. "I never want this to end, Liam."

"It won't," I tell her, as she fights the sleep that is threatening to take hold of her.

"Promise?" Her eyes flutter close.

"Promise."

Chapter Twenty-Three

Ellie

My phone rings in my back pocket as I attempt to sprint to the end of the block in my 3-inch heels.

Forced to stop at a red light, I pull out my phone and see Olivia's face lighting up the screen. I also notice the time. *Shit.* I'm already six minutes late with another four blocks to go before I arrive at the bridal boutique where I'm meeting Olivia and the rest of her bridesmaids for our final dress fitting.

I answer the call, jogging across the intersection as soon as the walk signal appears. These damn heels. But they'll serve their purpose later this afternoon. I have plans for them. My temperature rises at just the thought.

"Everything okay, Ellie?" Olivia asks as I round the corner, suddenly distracted by a pretty little bakery with the most decadent desserts in the window. I look away, returning my focus to finding the dress shop. But I catalog the bakery in my brain for another day.

"Yes, Liv. I'm fine," I breathe into my phone. "Sorry, I'm a few minutes late. I'm almost there."

"Okay. Wanted to make sure you were fine is all. We'll see you soon. Oh, and Ellie?" she adds, in dramatic Olivia fashion. "We're all waiting on the details of your sex weekend."

A laugh escapes me as I end the call, continuing my dash down the street. Minutes later I'm looking up at the awning of the boutique. I tug open the door, met by the bridal shop owner, along with Olivia, Jules and Kate.

"It's five o'clock somewhere, I'm sure," Jules says, handing me a flute of champagne. She's wearing a fitted black pencil skirt, white silk blouse and red heels, office-ready after our fitting.

"I have no doubt it is. I can drink to that. Thank you," I say, taking a sip of the bubbly. "I'm sorry I'm late. You should have started without me. I opened Bloom for Leah and had to wait for her to arrive."

"We're ready now," the shop owner says. "You can all follow me. I'll take you back to the fitting area."

We follow her past rows and rows of white and cream wedding gowns to the fitting rooms. Wasting no time, Olivia ducks into a room to try her gown on first while the rest of us drop onto one of the couches, sipping our champagne.

While Olivia changes, Kate dives right in not wasting a second. "So," she begins in a hushed voice, one brow arched in my direction. "Are you going to make us beg, or come right out with the juicy New York City details?"

"I see there won't be any hemming and hawing today," I say. "Right to the point."

"When is there ever with us?" Kate's right. Beating around the bush with each other has never been our style.

Nothing is off limits. Getting to the good stuff is what we do best.

"We want every glorious, dirty detail, Ellie. Don't leave out a thing," Kate says, crossing one leg over the other and leaning in with a curious look.

"I'm one hundred percent sure I'm not up for certain dirty details," Jules groans, rubbing her temples. "A heads-up when the conversation takes a turn into your and my brother's sex life would be appreciated. I will hide myself in that row of gowns right over there, pretend I'm shopping for the most expensive one that I can find which my handsome husband to be - who lives in Italy and drives race cars, naturally - will adore."

Kate and I laugh at Jules' over-active imagination.

Flashing her a sympathetic look, I let her know that won't be a problem. I'd rather not discuss all the ways her brother pleased me. And there were many. Thankfully, I won't have to worry about that for now thanks to our conversation being interrupted when the curtain is pulled back, revealing a beaming Olivia.

My face must resemble the heart-eyed emoji when Olivia steps out from behind the curtain because the sight of my best friend in her wedding dress takes my breath away. We all ooh and ahh as she spins around for us, showing off the gown that highlights her decolletage and falls to the ground in a mermaid fit. Her long blonde hair is down, with one side pinned back behind her ear. She beams. Her eyes turn weepy.

Olivia steps up onto a pedestal in the middle of the room, the gown draping to the floor in a waterfall, spilling all around her. She's twisting her solitaire engagement ring on her left hand. She looks lost in thought for a second, like she's in the middle of a daydream. She blinks when I say, "He doesn't stand a chance, Liv." I mean every word.

"You think?" Olivia asks, a little wistful.

"I know," I tell her. "He will cry like a baby at the sight of you in this dress."

"Stunning," Jules adds.

Olivia smiles as she bends at the knees, allowing the shop owner to pin a jewelled clip to her hair. It sparkles like diamonds under the boutique lights.

"Breathtaking, Liv," Kate says to her sister with tears in her eyes. "I can't believe the day is finally almost here. I've never met two people who were so meant to be. You are a living, breathing love story."

"Thanks Katie-cat. The countdown really is on," Olivia says with a hitch in her voice. "Okay, your turn! I want to see us all side-by-side in our dresses."

Taking our cue, we each head to a fitting room, where our dresses are waiting for us. As we get changed, the shop owner excuses herself to answer a call and Kate takes her disappearance as a green light to resume her interrogation. She's persistent. I'll give her that.

"So, where were we?" she says from the next curtain over, loud enough for Jules and Olivia to hear. "How was it, Ellie? Where did he take you? What did you do? Details, now. I can't wait another second."

"It was one of the best nights of my life," I say, sliding into the satin gown, then slipping into my heels, remembering the night. I replay it in my mind: the jet to New York, the hotel room and the view from the terrace. My hand grasped in Liam's as we walked through Rockefeller Center. Talking together about the past and new promises while I was tightly wrapped in his arms. A rush of heat warms my chest. For the first time in my life I can see a future with someone, and it doesn't terrify me.

For years, I've been dead set against allowing myself to love someone. I've guarded my heart, built walls, shut myself off at anything more than one night. Okay, two nights tops. And it's worked for me just fine. I've never felt like I needed more. I've never felt like I deserved more. Until now.

I feel like a different woman. A woman who knows what she wants and is ready to take it. A woman willing to take a chance on love. Everything seems possible.

"He brought you to see *Cats*," Olivia says with happiness in her voice. "I'm not sure I've heard of anything sweeter than that."

"I know," I gush, remembering when Liam kissed me in front of everyone in the theatre.

Glancing at myself in the mirror, I zip the side of my dress, excited for Liam so see me in it. Ice-blue, with a sweetheart neckline and fitted bodice, the satin draping to the floor. I imagine my hair tied back into a knot, exposing my back and my collarbones for Liam to brush his fingertips and trail kisses over. My stomach flips at the thought.

With the hem of my bridesmaid dress in my hand, I step out from the curtain, meeting the rest of the girls in front of the wall of mirrors.

"If Liam couldn't keep his eyes off you before, he's going to be eye-banging you all night when he sees you in this dress," Kate teases, her eyes meeting mine in the mirror. "I love you two, by the way. Sparks fly when you're in a room together. The way he looks at you is enough to set the whole room up in flames."

I may be biased, but I have to agree with Kate. I blush, thinking of the spine-tingling, heated, flirtatious moments Liam and I have shared. "That obvious, huh?"

"*That* obvious," Olivia chimes in. "You two have major hot and heavy chemistry."

If they couldn't tell I was blushing before, they'll definitely see it now.

"Are you head over heels in love with him, or what?" Kate asks, with anticipation in her eyes.

The answer is yes but I'm not sure I'm ready to admit that out loud. Especially considering I haven't told Liam. So, I do my best to skirt the question.

"I like him a lot," I say, hoping it will be enough.

"You like him enough to want to tear off his clothes every time you're in the same room with him. That much is clear," Olivia says.

I laugh. It's true.

"Okay, enough about that," Kate interrupts, leaning toward me and lowering her voice to a stage whisper. "We want to hear the naughty stuff. Is he as huge as he looked in his ill-fitted suit pants?"

A laugh escapes me as I remember the photo that circulated in our wedding group chat. *If they only knew.*

Jules shakes her head beside us, holding up one hand like a stop sign. "Okay, nope. This is where I draw the line. So gross. I can't take it."

Taking the skirt of her dress in her hands, she turns on her heels, moving away from us towards the racks of bridal gowns on display in the showroom.

"So?" Kate asks as soon as Jules is out of earshot. She can barely contain herself.

"Let's just say there are zero complaints from me," I tease, biting my smile back.

Kate dramatically presses the back of her hand to her forehead, miming a fainting action. "You have all the luck. Both of you. What did the two of you do in your past lives to score such insanely attractive, successful men? I could scour every dating app, restaurant and bar and come up empty-handed. Actually, I think I literally *have* scoured every dating app, restaurant and bar. And… nothing."

Exchanging a look, Olivia and I can't help but laugh.

Kate is right. Never in my wildest dreams would I have thought I could be this happy.

"You'll find him, Kate. He's out there. You know what they say: you'll find him when you least expect it, and most likely you'll be in sweatpants with no makeup, dirty hair and a fleck of parsley in your teeth."

Kate tilts her head to the side, hands on her hips, and shakes her head. "I sure hope only the first part of that sentence comes true."

When the seamstress appears, Jules decides it's safe to return. A few tucks and pins later, each of our dresses fit perfectly, and we snap a few photos. After getting changed, our gowns are zippered into garment bags. Olivia will bring them to the Bennett estate today for safekeeping.

After saying my goodbyes to the girls, I decide to walk back to Bloom, enjoying the bright, beautiful day. The sun's rays cast a golden glow upon the streets of Reed Point and I smile, taking it all in.

There's an extra pep in my step and a smile on my face I haven't been able to erase in days as I round the corner to work. I'm walking on sunshine. I'm falling in love. Life is good.

A FEW HOURS LATER, I order an Uber to drop me off at the front entrance of Brooks, Gamble and Bennett. It's been two days since we returned from Manhattan, and I decided this morning I would surprise Liam at his office on his lunch break. Wearing fitted jeans and a pair of heels I know drive him wild, I cross the foyer to the elevators, hitting the button to bring me to Liam's floor.

Checking my appearance in the mirrored walls of the elevator, I re-apply my lip gloss and run my fingers through the waves I curled into my hair this morning. I check the time on my phone and am happy when it shows one o'clock, the time Liam typically takes his lunch break. The man goes about his day like clockwork: gym at six, green smoothie at eight, lunch at one. It makes it easy for me to always know where he is. My little control freak. I wouldn't have it any other way.

Once I've exited the elevator, I cross the hallway to the etched glass doors of his office. The door swings open and I'm greeted by Silvia, Liam's assistant, who smiles a hello and lets me know she's headed out for lunch.

I practically dance through the office door, excited to surprise Liam. Then my whole world tumbles down around me.

The man standing in Liam's office is taller than I remember him. His shoulders seem broader, and his wavy blond hair longer than it used to be. His Henley stretches tight over his bulging biceps.

I blink, trying to convince myself it can't be him. *There's no way.*

He makes eye contact, and then smirks that smug smile that has been etched in my mind for all these years, and my worst fear is confirmed. My mouth goes dry and I feel like I'm going to be sick. Like run-to-the-washroom-immediately sick. My body starts to tremble.

"Ellie. Hi," Liam says, acknowledging my presence, stopping his conversation mid-sentence when he sees me. It's just me, Liam and the man I'm currently married to standing in this way-too-small waiting room that feels like it's closing in around me. "Let me introduce you to Mason Ford, quarterback for the Green Bay Packers."

Mason.

My once-upon-a-time Mason.

The room seems to spin as I try to understand what is

happening. The man I married six years ago, my biggest mistake, is standing in front of me in my boyfriend's office.

How is this happening?

What is he doing here?

It feels like a cruel joke. I can see by the look in his eyes that Mason knows exactly who I am. He hasn't forgotten me. Despite that, his face holds almost no emotion other than the slightest glimmer of confusion.

I feel a chill go up my spine, and my hands turn ice cold. I know I should say something, but I am unable to form even a single sentence.

Liam doesn't flinch, he doesn't bat an eye. Like the ace lawyer he is, he holds his poker face, not reacting to my strange behaviour. The coffee cup I'm holding falls from my hand to the tile floor at my feet and I back away shakily, then turn and burst through the doors to the elevator.

"Ellie," I hear Liam shout after me as I stab the button over and over again before racing to the stairs, barrelling down them as fast as I can in my heels. It feels like it takes forever, but I finally push through the doors to the lobby and head out to the street. The cool air crashes into me when my feet hit the sidewalk and I gulp in what feels like the first breath I've taken since I saw Mason standing in Liam's office.

Realizing I need an Uber or a bus or a fucking bike for that matter, I try to force my body to stop shaking as I try to figure out what to do. I lose the opportunity when I hear Liam's booming voice call out to me. "Ellie!" I am rooted to the ground, my back towards him. How can I face him? Face the man that has quickly become my everything. My heart, my soul, my person. And I've lied to him. From day one I lied, never wanting him to know what a terrible mistake I made. Too embarrassed for him to know the truth. Knowing that when he found out, everything we have built would be ruined, and he would hate me.

"Ellie, what happened there? What the hell is going on?"

He knows. Shit, he knows.

"Not now, Liam. I need to go," I say in a small voice that sounds like it's breaking. My back is still turned to him, the heavy pain in my chest making it hard to breathe.

"Like hell you are. You are not going anywhere until you tell me what the hell that was back there. You look like you saw a fucking ghost."

I blow out a deep breath realizing that Liam doesn't know the truth. Not yet.

I shake my head.

"Look at me, Ellie. What the hell is going on?" I can hear his footsteps getting closer. His hand wraps around my bicep but I pull away, turning to face him. His eyes search mine, his expression muddled.

"Liam-"

"Ellie. What just happened in my office? You are not going anywhere until you answer me."

There's a long silence. My hands are trembling, and my heart is on the sidewalk at my feet knowing that when he finds out my truth, he will never want to be with me. *This is going to hurt so fucking bad.*

"Does this have something to do with Mason?" he asks. "Do you know him? Did he do something to you?"

I don't say a word. Fear is crippling me.

"God dammit, Ellie. Say something."

And suddenly I say it. The words stutter from my mouth but nevertheless, I tell him what I so badly hoped he would never have to find out. "We're married."

He stares back at me, clearly trying to wrap his head around what I just confessed to him. He drags his hand roughly through his hair, and his gray eyes seem to turn black, to something resembling gun metal.

"You're *married*? Tell me I didn't just hear you say that." His voice thunders, a look of shock flashes through his eyes. "Tell me, Ellie. Tell me!"

"I was young," I say, my voice trembling, my hands covering my eyes in embarrassment

Liam shakes his head, scrubbing his hand over his stubbled jaw. "I'm going to need a lot more than that from you right now. Mason? You are *married* to Mason?"

"Yes, Mason. But it's not what you think. We were young and stupid and way too fucking wild for our own good. It was a mistake." I shake my head, then force myself to focus, trying to read the expression on Liam's face. "It was a long time ago. It's not what it sounds like. Yes, technically I'm married but it's more, really, that I'm just not divorced."

"Dammit, Ellie. That is bullshit and you know it," he snaps, shaking his head. "It's you. Of all people, it had to be you."

It's me? Panic is overtaken by confusion, but I barely have time to process it before Liam is on the attack. His voice ricochets off of the pavement beneath us.

"This is so you, Ellie. So very fucking you. Married, not divorced - what is the damn difference? *You are married* and you didn't think I had the right to know?" The muscles in his jaw tense, his hands curled into tight fists at his sides. "All this time, I've been sleeping with a married woman and you didn't bother to think to tell me? What kind of warped, fucked up world do you live in?"

Tears pool in my eyes. I never meant to hurt him. Rage flashes over his face and he looks like a tornado about to destroy everything in its path. The vein in his neck pulses and I brace myself for what's to come next, knowing Liam well enough to know that he feels betrayed, and that breaks me. *You caused this, Ellie. You put that hurt in Liam's eyes. This is your fault. You deserve this.*

"I need to know what happened. You owe me that much, don't you think?"

I'm trying not to cry. I know the enormity of what I've done. If I could go back and change it all I would. The last thing I wanted was to cause this man standing in front me, this man I love with everything in me, this much pain. I swallow the tears and tell him the truth. The truth that I should have told him that day at the coffee shop when I first began to feel more for him.

Wringing my hands, I take a deep breath and do what I know I need to do. I need to tell him what I've never told anyone except for my mother. My deepest, darkest secret. The skeleton in my closet.

"It was six years ago. I'd only known him for three weeks when we wandered into a Las Vegas chapel and got married. We had been drinking." I blow out a long breath and shake my head. "I got married and I can't even remember doing it, that's how much I had to drink that night." I hang my head in shame, my eyes glued to my hands. "When I realized the next morning what I had done I regretted it, but he was already gone. I tried to track him down but with no luck. He wouldn't return my texts or my calls and then one day his phone number changed. I was young. I was stupid. Honestly, I was just so embarrassed. I didn't know what to do."

"Did you love him?" he asks, his voice cold and hard.

I pause, knowing he'll see right through me if I lie. And I've lied enough. But admitting I married a man I had merely fallen in lust with is humiliating. "No. I didn't even know him. I met him at a party. He was charismatic, the life of the party. Everyone wanted to be in his presence. I got caught up in it all. It was just lust."

"Well, that answers that," he says flippantly, rolling his eyes, and turning away from me. My body instinctively wants to go to him, to wrap my arms around him and take away his pain. But I don't. I stay where I am, my feet firmly planted, while my body aches for his touch.

"I couldn't tell anyone for just that reason. I know how awful it sounds."

"You're right, Ellie. It sure as hell does. Jesus. Why would I be surprised that you got married in Las Vegas of all places, and that six fucking years later you're *still* married - but only on a technicality." He blows out a breath, turning to face me again before lifting his head to the sky, avoiding my eyes. I'm sure wanting to look anywhere but at me.

"Liam, when you and I started getting serious, I tried to get in touch with him, to fix this." My voice breaks. "I swear, Liam. His agent wouldn't put my calls through to him. I didn't know what else to do."

"*Now*, Ellie? After how long? It only took you six goddamn years to remember to do something about it."

My eyes follow him as he paces the sidewalk, his hands raking through his hair, rage and agitation radiating off of him in waves

"Liam," I plead. "What do you want to know? That I feel stupid? So stupid that I've never even been able to tell my best friends what I did? I'm so ashamed by the idiotic choice I made that night. I swear to you I was trying to fix this."

I take a step closer and he quickly raises his hand up to stop me. "Don't, Ellie."

I stare at him, tears blurring my vision, willing him to

say something. Willing him to understand. My lips quiver as I try to swallow the gravel in my throat to speak.

"Talk to me, Liam. Please say something." My aching heart feels like it's coming apart at the seams. I'm not sure how I'm still standing, how my legs haven't given out. Devastation takes hold and a sob escapes me, a tear sliding down my cheek. Another follows it and soon I'm standing in front of him bawling. I frantically swipe at the tears with my hands, choking back the lump in my throat. I struggle to breathe, the intensity of the pain in my chest is so strong, it feels like the air in my lungs is being pummelled from my chest.

Liam finally looks right at me, and I see the storm, the fury in his eyes. His jaw grinds in a punishing rhythm.

"We are done here. I'm done." His words feel like they were meant to destroy me.

"Liam, no!" I beg, so desperately that I barely recognize my own voice. "Please. I never meant to-"

"Save it, Ellie, for someone who cares, because that guy isn't me."

His words are like a sucker punch to the gut. The pavement beneath my feet feels like it's dropped out from beneath me.

I'm going to lose Liam.

I can't lose him.

My teary eyes search his one last time before he turns and leaves me standing there. I can't bear to watch him walk away from me. I double over, shivering as I wrap my arms around my chest. The world around me continues to spin while mine has come to a screeching halt. I want to scream, punch something, anything to relieve this searing ache in my chest.

People stare. I can only imagine what I look like.

Broken…watching the one man who has meant anything to me walk away.

I straighten my spine in time to see Liam disappear into his office building.

He's gone.

The words *I'm sorry* left unsaid.

And I'm left here to pick up the pieces of my shattered heart.

Chapter Twenty-Four

Liam

"Are you going to tell us what's going on or are we just going to sit here all night? I know I'm not going anywhere until you admit what's got you in this mood, and I'm pretty sure Parker isn't either."

Miles sizes me up with a stare over the lip of his beer bottle, resting his feet on the coffee table. Murphy looks up at me from where he lies on the floor at my feet. Even he knows what a pathetic loser I've been over the last twenty-four hours. *I know, Murph. Believe me, I know.*

My day was going great until I woke up. I somehow dragged myself through the day at the office, and just as I'd collapsed on the couch this evening I was surprised by a knock on my door from Parker and Miles. I made the mistake of opening the door without checking to see who it was, and now, after ordering take-out and watching a few innings of the Yankees game, the interrogation has begun. *Fan-fucking-tastic.*

"I just had a shit day at work," I lie, knowing these two

will probably see right through me but not having the energy to come up with a more creative excuse.

"If you think we buy that, you must be drinking your bath water. You thrive on bad days at the office. It's what gets you off, so let's try this again. Why the mood?" Parker asks, leaning forward on the couch, his elbows resting on his knees.

"You expect me to believe your fiancée hasn't told you?" I say, assuming Ellie has talked to Olivia by now. It's been almost two days since the proverbial rug was swept out from underneath me and work has been the only thing I've managed to accomplish since. Work is the only thing keeping me going. I've managed to suck hard at everything else in my life.

"Tell me what? Olivia hasn't mentioned a thing except for the usual shit I hear every day. You know: Parker, you're hot as hell. Parker, your dick's so big."

I roll my eyes. *Why are these two still here and why won't they stop talking?* Talking is shit that women do. I sure as hell don't feel like hashing out the entire story and then getting my ass handed to me for not seeing *it* coming. I blow out a breath, slouching back into the couch.

In the end I decide the only way to get them to leave is to confess everything and get this over with. Now or never. Do or die.

"Ellie and I broke up."

"What? I didn't see that one coming," Miles says, his cocky grin replaced with a look of confusion.

"I didn't either," Parker says. "What the hell happened?"

"Ellie's married. That's what happened," I say, causing both of my brothers to look at me like I just told them I'm taking up knitting while learning to sing on a tennis court.

"You're joking, right?" Parker asks, confirming that

Olivia really didn't tell him. It makes me wonder if Ellie has told her. If Ellie has told anyone.

"Why the hell would I joke about something like that? I'm dead serious. She married Mason-fucking-Ford six years ago in a Vegas ceremony, drunk out of her mind. Didn't remember a thing."

"*The* Mason Ford? QB of the Green Bay Packers?" Miles asks, with an open mouth stare. His eyebrows raise and then drop back down again in astonishment.

"The one and only."

"Shit." Parker shakes his head.

"Yup."

"Well, you definitely have to give her credit for the Mason Ford part of the story. The guy is a legend. What was she doing with you after landing a guy like that?" Miles laughs, looking from me over to Parker, clearly enjoying the rise he's getting out of me. *Now's not the fucking time, asshole.*

"Fuck you," I tell him, emptying my beer and cracking open a new one to drink away the sting of the pain. I shouldn't expect anything less from Miles, he's been giving me the gears since we were kids. "I'm not in the mood for your jokes."

"You have to admit it was funny, though," Miles says, peeling back the label on his beer bottle in little, tiny pieces. I must be completely fucking out of it because I can't even find the strength to care about the scraps of paper that are falling to the floor.

"Not even a little. The guy can throw a solid pass but he's obviously a total dick off the field. He has to be to leave the chick he married the night before in a Vegas hotel room, and then ghost her for six straight years after that." The guy deserves my fist in his face for not manning up and taking her calls. For ditching her in Vegas in the first place. I'm obsessed with hating him. I fantasize about running him over with my car.

"Ouch. He really did that?" Parker asks.

"According to Ellie," I answer grudgingly. "He had an appointment with me today in my office if you can believe it. Ellie walked in right in the middle of it."

"What was he doing in your office?" Parker asks.

"Ironically, he was in my office to discuss filing divorce papers. How effed up is that? Apparently he was flying in for one day only to get the divorce started. His assistant chose my firm because we are the best in Reed Point, and they knew she lived somewhere around here. We didn't have time to get to the rest of it though because Ellie practically dropped dead on my floor at the sight of him."

"You've got to be kidding me. Or did he come looking for you on purpose wanting to meet the guy who's sleeping with his wife? I think that would make you the mistress. Or… I guess the mister in this case?" Miles chokes back a laugh, then continues on at my expense. "Was he pissed that another man has been banging his wife all this time?"

Not amused, I flip him off and take a pull of my beer. They can laugh all they want. None of it matters to me anymore. Ellie's no longer mine. She's not my problem. She can ride Mason Ford off into the sunset for all I care.

"Well at least we've gotten down to the real reason you are a miserable bastard. Now what are we going to do about it?" Parker asks.

"What do you mean what are we going to do about it? Zip, zero, zilch. It's over. She can live a long happy life with her husband. I'll send them a belated wedding gift," I say, the grip on my bottle so tight, my knuckles are turning white. "Those two deserve each other."

"You don't really mean that. Take a deep breath, bro.

You wouldn't be this upset if part of you didn't really feel something for her. This can all be fixed."

"Why in the world would I ever want to fix this? She's a liar. I'm done, man. It's over." *Because you know she didn't mean to. You know she is a good person who is only guilty of making a stupid mistake.*

"She's not a liar, she just didn't give you the full picture. There's a difference," Parker says, raising his beer bottle to his lips.

"Tomato, fucking tomahto. It's semantics." I argue the point, something I enjoy doing, then drain the rest of my beer. My brother looks unconvinced. I want so badly to get the hell out of here, to get in my car and drive, to forget all about Ellie and this pain in my chest. She lied to me and over what? Didn't she know I would have understood? I could have helped her. I would have been on her side. Now, all I feel is betrayal, knowing that what we had was built on a lie.

"We are going to need something stronger than a couple of cold ones to get you through this." Miles gets up and fumbles through my kitchen, returning with a bottle of Jack Daniels and three shot glasses. For the first time tonight, I actually agree with my little brother. He lines them up, pours three shots and we each down them. The Jack burns my throat but leaves me on edge. I need it to burn. I grab the bottle, pouring two more. I start with one and then another, trying to erase the memories of Ellie.

"She's under your skin, man," Parker says.

"Why the hell would you say that?" I know Parker is not at fault, but I'm still so angry that I just want to lash out, at anyone.

"You will argue to the death about anything." He shakes his head at me.

"It's my fucking job to, dick-shit."

"Back to the point at hand. I said it because until Ellie, I've only ever seen you give a fuck about work and family. But you care about her. We've all seen it. You've never really cared about a woman. You have been the Olympic gold medal winner of fuck'em and chuck'em for as long as I can remember, and that all changed the night of my party at the beach house. You've been crazy about that girl for months. Admit it, Liam. There's something about her that's different from all the rest," Parker says, tapping the edge of his empty shot glass against the coffee table.

My eyes focus on the bottle of Jack on the table. I wonder if I'll ever find the answers I need, if I'll ever be able to get over the one woman I could actually see a future with. I try to shake off the questions circling through my head. I've never wanted a future or a commitment or any of the other crap that comes along with a relationship. I like my balls right where they are, not in the hands of a woman who has the power to bring me right to my knees.

"Pour me another." I feel a million emotions all at once. I look around the room and everything makes me think of Ellie. I remember bringing her here, I remember bending her over the dining table. The look in her goddess eyes, that desire and want just as strong now as the day I first saw her. I rub my hands over my eyes. This isn't helping. *Keep drinking, Liam. You'll feel a hell of a lot better.*

"Don't walk away over this. You can work this out. *She* can fix this. Shit - you are the guy to help her fix this. She tried, Liam. You said it yourself, the asshole made it impossible for her to get a divorce," Miles says.

My head feels like it's taken a ride on the tilt a whirl, spun too fast. I'm full of rage, doubts, questions. I like my life a certain way. I like to be in control. I like schedules and order, and everything in perfect, predictable, neat little piles. But right now, my life is anything but. It's a mess. I guess that's what I get for letting someone in.

I push up off the couch and walk to the glass doors overlooking the yard, needing space, needing air to breathe. Murphy follows me, dropping to my feet sensing there's something wrong. Man's best friend and all that shit.

Memories from our first day together eating lunch on the patio hit me out of nowhere. I can still see her long legs stretched out on the lawn chair, throwing the ball for Murphy. I can still smell the scent of her shampoo, I can taste her on my lips. I curse under my breath, pissed at myself for letting her in. *Like I ever had a choice.*

Ellie had my number from the start. I never stood a chance.

"Ellie accepts your broody shit, she deals with your tantrums. She loves you, bro. You need to be a man about this and admit you love her too," Parker says.

How do I tell them that I fell for Ellie? That I fell in love with her and saw the white picket fence and all the rest of the crap that I never wanted? That I didn't want to run in the opposite direction when she agreed it was just us? But I trust my brothers. I should be able to tell them.

"You need to get out of your head. You love her. Forgive her. This can all be worked out. Sure, she fucked up, but ultimately is what she did really that unforgiveable?" Miles adds as I blink away the old images of a future with Ellie. "Drink tonight until you can no longer feel, then sleep it off and wake up tomorrow and remember what fucking matters. Ellie."

"Pour," I demand. "I need another."

I flop onto the couch next to Parker, my jaw still clenched. I keep going back to what could have been with Ellie. She's the only thing I can see. The only thing that I want. The only thing I can't have. I clink my glass with my brothers.

"To forgetting," I say.

"To forgetting," they reply, and we all toss back the shots. The warm amber liquid feels like a blanket around my soul.

The only thing that will make me feel any better is polishing off this bottle, numbing the pain and forgetting about this hole in my heart that is making me a miserable bastard. So, I knock back another, and another after that, looking for answers at the bottom of a glass. But even the damn bottle tastes like her, feels like her teeth scraping over my shoulder when she's coming undone. She's in my head and fuck if I know how to get her out of it. Turns out my whiskey-jumbled brain isn't helping.

"Listen," Parker says. "Do what you want. I'll be here to support you with whatever you decide. But man, I've never seen you happier than when you're with her. That's all I'm saying."

I raise my hands in surrender and give my brothers a hard look, signalling the end of this interrogation.

I thought a drink would get her off my mind, but I'm not sure that I will ever be able to erase this never-ending highlight reel of thoughts about Ellie. No hangover will ever be enough to make me forget her. I miss her. Hell, my dick misses her. I'm reminded of her everywhere. The crossword puzzle she left here sits on the side table, her hair scrunchie is on my bathroom counter. My bedsheets still smell like her, the ones I haven't been able to wash because I'm afraid of losing that scent. There's only one way to fix this - sell this house or set it on fire. I need to be somewhere that doesn't constantly remind me of her.

I miss the sound of her voice. How did her voice become the one I want to hear at the end of a long day? I miss her sarcastic comebacks when I've said something to rile her up. I miss her quiet smile, the one that undoes me and strips me bare.

I just miss Ellie.

Fucking Ellie.

Chapter Twenty-Five

Ellie

Why does the little one have to be so mean to the big one? It's one of many questions I've asked myself this morning while watching an endless loop of puppies-in-sweaters videos, in between crying fits and shoveling down spoonfuls of cookie dough. Anything to take my mind off of Liam and how badly I hurt him, knowing he deserves so much more.

Tying my hair into a knot with a scrunchie, I sink deeper into the couch, yawning. Tossing and turning the last two nights, I've hoped that when the sun rose in the morning, the lump in my chest would a hurt a little bit less. *Wishful thinking.*

Liam has been my first thought when I wake up and my last thought before my eyes finally succumb to what tiny bit of sleep I've managed to get. It's his cocky grin I think about when I sit alone in my apartment, his arms I miss when I crawl into my empty bed and that overwhelming sense of loneliness sets in. Getting over Liam will be the hardest thing I've ever have to do.

The next video starts, and I can't help but smile through the tears at two Pomeranians wrestling one another in turtlenecks. Moments later, the doorbell rings and my heart instantly skips a beat. The doorbell rings a second time, and the thought that it could be Liam flickers through my mind. Maybe he's ready to talk. My pulse races a million miles a minute as I turn the handle and open the door. But it's not Liam. Instead, I find Mason standing on my doorstep.

"What the hell do you want?" I ask.

"Still the firecracker I remember." He grins. "Some things never change."

"Cut the crap, Mason. Why the hell are you here?"

"Is that your way of inviting me in? Yes, thank you, I'd love to." He takes a step towards me and I move aside coolly, allowing him inside my apartment.

I've seen Mason on TV a few times over the years, despite trying my best to avoid it. But seeing him here, in the flesh, I notice the subtle ways he's changed. He looks leaner, stronger. A little older, but still undeniably handsome. And judging by the way he drops onto my couch and makes himself at home, still confident as hell.

I was drawn to him right away when we first met. He was good looking and a ton of fun to be around and our chemistry was off-the-charts. But it was more than that. Mason Ford was magnetic - he pulled me in, made me want to get lost in him. And that's exactly what I did. So lost that I married the guy after just a few weeks.

"Get to the point, Mason," I snap, shaking loose of the old memories. "Why are you here after six fucking years?"

"Ellie, I'm not here to fight with you. I'm here to give you what you want. A divorce. I thought you'd be happy about it."

A laugh escapes me. He's got to be kidding. Did he

really think I'd welcome him with a hug and a plate of pastries? I'd like to slam a fist into his face, and he would deserve it if I did.

"I would have been happy about the divorce if you'd offered it six years ago, Mason. Scratch that. I would have been even happier if you hadn't married me and then disappeared the next day!"

Rage simmers beneath my skin, and as I look at Mason I feel it threatening to boil over.

"Obviously the wedding was a huge mistake, but then to just take off and never talk to me again? Are you fucking kidding me? I didn't deserve that!" I feel my anger start to burn away, replaced by the hurt that I've lived with for so many years. I turn my head, not wanting him to see the tears that I feel welling up. "All this time I've wondered how you could be so cruel. You treated me like garbage. You humiliated me. You fucking broke me, Mason."

When I look at him again, he's standing and the cocky grin is gone from his face, replaced by something softer, something I can't quite place.

"Ellie, I..." he starts to speak, then stops again, running a hand through his hair.

"Ellie, listen. I know I was a dick back then, that I could've handled it all so much better. But I swear to God, I had no idea I hurt you this much," he insists. "I thought...I guess I thought we were just having a good time together. I really liked you, Ellie, you were so easy to be around and you were just as wild as I was. And gorgeous, obviously. But we only knew each other for a few weeks. And my career was just starting. Football was it for me. That Vegas trip was my last crazy weekend, after that I headed straight for training camp. Things got a bit too out of control with the wedding," he admits with a wince. "I still can't believe we actually did that."

He finally looks up at me, taking a deep breath, and there is sincerity in his eyes when he speaks again.

"I couldn't do a real relationship back then, Ellie, and I honestly thought you felt the same way. But I guess I got that wrong. Or maybe I just wasn't paying attention - I had a pretty huge ego back then, I probably didn't notice a lot of things," he says sheepishly. "Either way, I'm sorry."

His words sting, but I can see that Mason is telling me the truth. But an apology isn't enough to make me forget how embarrassed and angry I've been.

"It wasn't just that you left, Mason. You didn't say goodbye. You wouldn't even return my calls," I remind him. "You acted like I suddenly didn't exist."

He sighs, flashing me a guilty look. "I know. It's not like I set out to ignore you, Ellie. I woke up the next morning, after that insane night, and you were still passed out. So I left you a note and figured we'd connect at some point, decide what to do about having the marriage annulled or whatever. I was on a flight out to meet my dad that day and then straight to camp from there. And then I ate, drank and fucking slept football and the wedding just got pushed to the back of my mind."

"Mason, I never saw a note. I don't have any idea what you're talking about."

"I left you one, Ellie, on the side table next to the bed."

I think back to that morning, but most of it is a total fog. Could I have missed a note? Could it have been knocked to the floor and swept under the bed? *I guess it's possible.*

"There were times over the years when I thought about contacting you, but it all just felt like so long ago. I had sponsorship deals by then and I guess part of me worried what a bunch of 'drunken Vegas wedding' headlines might do to my reputation. God, I really sound like such an asshole," he says, shaking his head. "I know it doesn't mean much at this point, but I'm a better guy now than I was back then, Ellie."

I look at Mason, the man I was once so attracted to. The man I've hated for so long. I see the remorse in his eyes, and I believe that he's telling me the truth. He treated me carelessly, there's no erasing that. But in a way it's kind of healing to finally be able to tell him how much he hurt me. After all these years, maybe I can close this chapter.

"You know, I half expected you to appear one day, but you never did," Mason adds. "Until now, that is. I got your message from my agent a couple of weeks ago and decided it was a sign to finally deal with it. So here I am."

He apologizes again, and I accept it. I am just so tired of feeling embarrassed and angry. What's done is done and I am so ready to move on. Besides, it's no longer Mason who makes my pulse race, who makes me wish for things I never thought I deserved. It's Liam. When I think of my future, Liam is the only man I want in it.

"So, how about that divorce?" Mason asks.

"A divorce sounds good."

IT'S BEEN three days since I've seen or talked to Liam. They say time can heal a broken heart, but I'm not so sure. I'm cranky and irritable, I haven't slept, I can't eat. I collapse on the sand next to Olivia and pull my legs into my body. I've been inconsolable since that gut-wrenching scene on the street with Liam.

"Ells," Olivia says, wiggling her body closer to me and resting her hand on my thigh. As soon as I confessed everything over the phone she came straight to my apartment and forced me out of the house. She brought me to the one place she has always been able to find peace, hoping it will do the same for me. The ocean. And although I know she is disappointed in me, she is still here supporting me when I need her the most. Even through the overwhelming shame brimming within me, it feels good to have her here.

I don't deserve her.

"I'm sorry I never told you," I say, tears stinging my eyes, mortified that she now knows the humiliating mistakes I've made. Olivia's hand wraps around my back and I lean into her. "I just never knew what to say. I was so embarrassed. I mean who does that? Britney, that's who!" I add, feeling her laugh against me. "And then he just left me without saying a word. I felt like a fool. It was all so humiliating."

"I just wish you had told me, Ells. I would have understood. I'll admit it, at first I was really pissed at you. I'm your best friend, the one person you should have known you could turn to. That's what friends are for, to be there for each other in both the good times and the bad. I hate that you felt you needed to keep this from me. I would have been there for you." She sighs and I squeeze my eyes shut, so grateful that she is still here beside me. "But I know you and I know you think you can handle anything life throws your way. You are as stubborn as they come, always trying to prove you can manage your own life without the help of others. But you don't have to. I'll always be there for you."

I swipe a tear from my cheek. In hindsight, that's exactly what I should have done but I was too chicken shit to admit to anyone what an idiot I was. I look up towards the pale blue sky, breathing in the salty ocean air. I understand now why Olivia finds peace in the sounds of the waves and the feel of the warm sand beneath her toes.

Leaning my head against her shoulder, I exhale a slow

breath, hoping to calm the nerves buzzing like electricity beneath my skin.

"Yes, I'm acting as your shrink today. Don't worry, your bill is in the mail," Olivia says, and I'm thankful for an excuse to laugh, needing a break from all the seriousness. "Let's talk this out. You've gone far too long as the only soldier in this battle."

"He won't speak to me, Olivia. He won't return any of my messages," I say, my mind drifting to the calls left unanswered and the voice messages left pleading Liam to hear me out. I've told him how much I miss him, begged him to call me. I've stared at my phone screen, willing him to reply. In response, I've gotten nothing but silence.

"Give him time. You're going to have to be patient. It's a pretty big bombshell that was dropped into his lap. You're going to have to give him space to come to terms with it all. It's not going to happen overnight, especially with Liam. He's as stubborn as you are."

"And what if he doesn't?" I manage to ask, trying to prevent my voice from breaking. My stomach churns at the thought of never hearing his voice again, never feeling his touch.

"Then we'll deal with that if it happens. Together."

I press my fingers into my temples, wondering how I'm ever going to face anyone again. How am I going to look Parker in the eye? Jules and Miles? And what about Mr. and Mrs. Bennett? I shrink back into myself at the thought of it.

"Is Parker pretty mad at me?"

"Don't worry about Parks. I'll handle him. Everything is going to be okay but Ells, you're going to have to explain yourself eventually to everyone now that's it out in the open."

"I know," I murmur, looking up at the clouds then back

at my best friend. There is forgiveness in her eyes. I'll do whatever it takes to see that same emotion in Liam's eyes. In his family's eyes.

"I fell for him," I confess, a hitch in my throat, admitting what I've been holding in for weeks but have known all along.

"I know. We all saw it. I'm sorry, Ells. I know how much this hurts."

My eyes are drawn back to the shore, the breaking of new waves helping me to get back to me. It reminds me that while we may not be able to stop them from coming, it's up to us to decide how to ride them out.

"It will take some time, but he'll realize how much he misses you."

And what if he doesn't? What then?

Liam doesn't let people in. People need him, not the other way around. Until me - and I broke his trust. I'm not sure I'll ever be able to find a way to earn that trust back.

I squeeze my eyes shut. I'm drowning. I want to scream, to cry. Nothing has ever hurt like this. I would do anything to ease the ache in my chest that has taken up the space where my heart used to be. It's there every second of every day and I'm not sure how to make it stop.

I want to go back to New York City and the terrace. His arms wrapped firmly around me when he asked me to be his.

It's as if Olivia can read my mind. Maybe we've been friends for that long. Running her hand down the length of my spine, she says, "It's going to be okay, Ells Bells. There's a morning waiting for you when this will hurt a lot less."

I drop my head into my hands and pray to God that she's right because I'm not sure how much more of this I can take.

"I'm never getting over him, Liv," I confess. Olivia

pulls me into her arms, and we sit there for a moment longer, before we are both suddenly drenched by a spray of water on our backs. It snaps me out of my misery, and the two of us are immediately on our feet, shrieking. Beside us stands a huge, shaggy, black-and-white dog, apparently on his way to find his owner after a run through the waves. He stops to rub against my legs, his tongue flopping out of his mouth and his tail wagging a mile a minute. A man jogs along the sand, calling the dog by its name and profusely apologizing for the sneak attack on the two of us.

I can't help but laugh because how can I not? This is how my day has gone. This is the perfect end to a disastrous two days. Before I know it the laughs turn into tears and the tears turn into sobs. Anger, fear, sadness, humiliation - I'm just so tired of all of these emotions coursing through me, threatening to strangle me.

The dog wanders down the beach and its owner follows closely behind, fortunately managing to avoid the crazy woman who is having a total breakdown on a public beach. This is my life now. Olivia and I sink back to the sand and sit in silence for a little while, time stretching on. It wasn't supposed to end like this. Liam was supposed to be my person.

Feeling restless, we eventually decide to walk. The beach is pretty vacant, except for a few families, kids splashing through the surf, a man throwing a ball for his dog who darts across the sand. The fresh air and the sound of the waves hitting the shore are the balm I need to take the edge off. Olivia walks beside me, allowing me the quiet I need to work through the mess in my head. This overwhelming sadness reminds me of the first year after my parents left, how my heart shattered watching them go. I didn't know when I would see them again but sensed it wouldn't be soon.

I wish my mom was here to ask for advice. She'd make me one of her teas and then sit with me and know exactly what to say. I wish my dad was here to tell a corny joke and make me laugh, so I could forget for a few short minutes about the relentless throb in my chest. *If only.*

My phone vibrates in my pocket and a spark of hope ignites in me. I will Liam to be on the other end of the text, wanting to talk and hear me out. I want him to say he misses me, that he accepts my apology, that we can move on from all of this. Together.

I pull the device from my back pocket, anxiously checking the screen. My shoulders sag and my head drops. It's Kate. She's next in my long list of apologies to get through.

Olivia notices my disappointment

"Give him time, Ells. It's only been two days."

"I don't know what I was thinking." I shake my head. "I was a fool to think I could make it work. What did I expect? Liam and I are too different. I've made too many mistakes. What made me think we could find love and hold onto it?"

"There are no rules for relationships," Olivia says matter-of-factly. "You are powerless to what your heart wants. The best thing about love is that you can fall into it with the most unexpected person in the most unexpected place, even when you aren't looking for it."

"That was really profound, Liv." I smile, nudging her shoulder with my elbow. "Like, really flipping profound. That impressed the hell out of me. Do you have, like, a podcast or something I could subscribe to?" I joke through my tears, needing to take the edge off.

"I'm right up there with Dear Abby," she says, nudging me right back. "But on a serious note, you know you're going to have to see him. The wedding is in two days. Are-“

“Olivia, it’s not even a question. There is no way I will allow the shit going on between Liam and I to interfere with your day. I promise you that.”

“That’s not what I was going to ask, but I appreciate it. Although, you two on a good day are like bottle rockets on the Fourth of July. What I was going to say is, will you be alright when you see him? Do you think you can handle it?”

I haven’t thought that far ahead yet. I’ve been too busy crying my eyes out and binge-watching insane YouTube videos to even realize I’m going to have to face him. Not mention his entire family. *Holy balls.*

Just the thought of seeing Liam makes shivers run up my spine, makes the hollow in my chest seem larger and sends a panicked fear through me. Because I miss him. God, I fucking miss him, and everything in me wants him back. I want it all back… mornings in bed with him, lunch dates in his office, sex on his desk, the steamy banter that lights a fire in me. *But what if he doesn’t?* Losing the one thing that has meant anything to me in forever isn’t a reality I can think about.

I can still feel him all over me, I can still taste his kiss on my lips.

I’m fighting with all I have to stop from crying because deep down I know the answer to Olivia’s question is *no.*

I definitely will not be alright.

Chapter Twenty-Six

Ellie

Olivia's stunning silhouette stands in front of a window of gauzy curtains in an upstairs bedroom of the Bennett estate. The sunlight of a perfect, late spring day casts a warm glow all around her. Her long blonde hair is twisted in a loose bun of curls at the nape of her neck. Her wedding day is finally here, and she looks absolutely beautiful.

Bending down in my ice-blue dress, I adjust the train of Olivia's mermaid gown to the click of a camera while the wedding photographer documents the day. Olivia's gaze drops over her shoulder while her hand dips to her waist, the largest engagement ring I've ever seen reflecting the sunlight and casting a kaleidoscope of light over the bedroom walls.

"You are going to blind everyone with that ring, Liv," I joke. "Parker must really want every guy in America to know you're taken."

"It's ridiculous and I've told him that, but Parker does what Parker wants. You know how my fiancé is."

"He'll be your husband in a matter of minutes. Are you ready, Liv?" My voice drops to a hushed tone as I give her hand a squeeze.

"I've never been more ready." She beams, dabbing the outside edge of her big brown eyes with a tissue. "How are you holding up? Have you seen him yet today?"

Her head is angled to the side as she awaits my response and it's clear as day she is referring to Liam. I tell her that I'm fine, but in reality I'm anything but. I managed to sneak into the Bennett home this morning and up to Olivia's "bridal suite" without seeing Liam and I haven't left the room since for fear of running into him. My heart cannot survive the sting of Liam's rejection and I need to not only get through this day but to enjoy it. My best friend is getting married. That's what matters today.

"I haven't seen him."

"He's here, you know."

"I assumed he was, considering it's his brother's wedding day and that would make him the ultimate asshole if he skipped it," I tease, and we both laugh an awkward, forced laugh because she's Olivia, the closest thing I have to a sister, and she knows my heart is twisting in two.

Needing to change the subject, I pull her in close to me for a hug. "You are honestly the most beautiful bride I've ever seen, and you've found your forever. You two deserve all the happiness in the world. I'm really happy for you."

I just finish my sentence when Mrs. Bennett walks into the room looking elegant in a floor-length navy-blue evening gown. Her hair is neatly styled in her signature bob with a diamond collar necklace wrapped around her neck. My hands tremble in anticipation. I know we need to talk. I know I need to apologize. Her heels clatter across the floor, closing the distance between us.

"Olivia, that dress was made for you. Parker is not going to know what hit him," Mrs. Bennett gushes with an approving smile, leaning in to press a soft kiss to Olivia's cheek. "You have made me the happiest woman in the world marrying my son today."

Olivia's eyes mist over with tears and there's a mad dash to get her a tissue, so she won't ruin her makeup. Olivia's mom swoops in with a box just as Mrs. Bennett's warm eyes meet mine.

"Ellie, sweetheart, come here," she says, holding her arms out to me with a smile that reminds me so much of Liam's. "It's good to see you."

I've met Mrs. Bennett a bunch of times before, but this all feels so incredibly different. I smile warmly at her, wanting to make a good impression. Needing her approval. I hope she can understand why I did what I did, and that she can see in my eyes the love I have for her oldest son.

"It's really nice to see you, too. Mrs. Bennett, I was hoping I could talk to you for a minute," I say carefully after she pulls back from our embrace. My eyes search hers, looking for a hint of how she is feeling towards me.

"Of course, honey, but please call me Grace. Come over here." She ushers me over to the opposite side of the room and sits on the edge of the bed, motioning for me to sit down beside her. I take a seat next to her. She is a woman I greatly admire. She's the epitome of wealth and affluence and yet she understands that money cannot buy you happiness, and lives life as joyfully and abundantly as possible. She's a wife, and a mother who has raised four of the best people I know.

"I'm not sure if Liam told you-"

"He did," she says, stopping me from finishing my sentence and having to say the words that until very recently I've never been able to admit out loud.

I continue, taking my time choosing each word carefully. I swallow nervously. "I'm so sorry I wasn't honest with Liam. I never meant to hurt him. It was never my intention."

"Shush, sweetheart. It's okay. There's no need to apologize to me. It's between you and Liam and I will support him in whatever decision he makes."

Her words catch me off guard. It's not the reaction I was expecting. Wasn't that the part where she was supposed to rip into me for hurting her son? I'd deserve it, but I'll happily go along with this instead. I bite my bottom lip, sure that she can see the fear and the guilt in my eyes. I'm not sure what to say but I know I need to say something. "I'm happy he has you to talk to. I'm just so sorry I wasn't upfront with him from the start. I should have known better. I know I really hurt him."

She places her hand over mine. "He'll be fine. He's feeling things for the first time and I think it scares the heck out of him. Be patient with my son. I know he feels the same way you feel about him," she says with kindness in her eyes. "And if it's meant to be, it will be. If you really love someone, you won't let them go."

Love.

I know what I felt for Liam - what I still feel for him - is love, but I'm not convinced that he was ever able to get there.

"I don't know that he ever loved me," I say softly, opening my heart to the only other woman in Liam's life.

"Oh sweetheart, the writing was on the wall. He might not have fully understood what he was feeling, but my boy loves you," she says, a warm smile spreading across her lips. I can't help but notice the way that pride fills her eyes when she speaks about her son. "Come here."

Removing her hand from mine, she wraps her arms

around me in a hug and speaks softly in my ear. "It will all be okay. Thank you for talking to me. Now come on, we have a wedding to get to."

The sound of the photographer interrupts the moment, but not before Jules, in a pale blue dress that matches mine, kneels down in front of us and places her perfectly manicured fingers on my lap. I force a smile, making light of an awkward situation. "What she said, Ells. Well, I'm not exactly sure what it is she said to you, but I know my mother well enough to know that I would agree. We all have a past. We all make mistakes. We aren't judging you for yours."

Squeezing my knee, she stands, reaching out her hand to me. "I was sent to grab you two for a picture. We don't want to keep the bride waiting now do we?"

My heart expands in my chest and I blow out the breath I didn't realize I was holding. A strong wave of relief flows through me and for the first time in days, I feel a small sense of happiness. It's nowhere near perfect, but it's better than the gut-wrenching, cry-like-a-baby, near-paralyzing sadness I've been feeling since losing Liam. And as I walk towards my best friend on the most significant day of her life, I allow myself to feel this pure, simple joy, even if for only a few minutes.

The next twenty minutes is spent taking photos, drinking champagne and watching Olivia open the gigantic diamond earrings Parker sent her for their wedding day. My first instinct is to take a refill of bubbly to ease the nerves that have had me on edge all day at the thought of seeing Liam - and then another and another after that - but the need to be present to witness Olivia and Parker convinces me not to. I want to remember today and besides, walking sideways down the aisle is never a good look. Haven't we all seen *Bridesmaids?*

"You look beautiful, Ells Bells." The unexpected voice sends shivers down my spine.

I blink, frozen in place. My back is to the door, but I don't need to see who just walked in, I would know that voice anywhere. I turn slightly to my right at Olivia with a did-you-know-about-this look and she shakes her head in a no. I quickly turn around in shock, a single word falling from my lips in a whisper. "Mom."

I run to her and wrap my arms tightly around her small frame. "You're here…I've missed you, Momma, so much."

"I've missed you too, my Ellsie Bells," she says, letting me go to take a step back and take me in. "It is so good to see you, baby. You look even more beautiful than the last time I saw you."

I can't help the tears that are streaming down my face. It's like the damn has broken and years and years of missing my mom have spilled through.

"I can't believe you're here. Is Dad here too?"

"He is, and he can't wait to see you. He'll be the guy crying in his seat at the sight of you walking down the aisle looking so beautiful tonight. I'm guessing he won't be the only one."

I laugh. It's just like my mom to think the whole world is as crazy about me as she and my dad are. "No, I'm pretty sure it will just be dad," I tell her. "But that's good enough for me."

"I'm betting not. I'm sure that handsome man of yours who picked us up from the airport last night is going to weep like a baby at the sight of you in that dress."

My jaw drops. *What did she just say?* Liam picked my parents up from the airport last night? I must be hearing things.

Lifting my eyes to meet my mom's, I ask, "I'm sorry, what? Who picked you up?"

"Liam did. He called your dad and I and told us how happy it would make you if we came up for the wedding. He booked us two first class tickets and my gosh, did you know they give you warm nuts and steaming hot hand towels when you sit down? That's a whole other story because we missed our first flight. Our goat yoga fundraiser ran late, and we couldn't miss the part where they dress up the goats in party clothes and parade them around like a pageant. It's the sweetest thing, baby. If you haven't tried goat yoga, I highly recommend it."

"Mom, that all sounds fantastic, but get back to the part about Liam."

"He's a good guy, baby, and easy on the eyes too. He's a little serious but that's something you can work on with him. He would really benefit from some crystal healing and a little meditation. He also has excellent taste in hotels. I told him, your dad and I would have been happy at the Reed Point Inn, but he insisted on putting us up at the Seaside. He got us a suite!" Her answer is unexpected but makes perfect sense. Liam must have arranged all of this before he found out the truth about me. He wanted to surprise me with the two people on Earth I love the most because he knew it would make me happy. My heart swells in my chest and shatters all at once for the man I love - the same man I lost.

"I better head downstairs, baby, and take my seat. The wedding is going to start soon," my mom says, before wiping a lone tear away from my face and kissing my cheek. "I just couldn't wait another second before seeing you."

"I hope you have tissues, Momma, because you are going to need them. You've always loved love."

"Oh baby, you're right about that. But don't you worry about me," she says with a smile, then she is gone just as quickly as she came, leaving me rooted in place, too stunned to move. And then it's time for us all to go, and panic sets in, replacing the overwhelming surge of happiness that just engulfed me. I will be seeing Liam in just a few minutes.

Carrying the train of Olivia's dress, I follow her and the rest of the bridal party downstairs to the living room where we are out of sight of guests who have taken their seats in the backyard garden. Olivia is greeted by her dad in a warm embrace, allowing me the opportunity to sneak a peek at the ceremony outside. It's a perfect warm day, rows and rows of white and gold chairs are lined up just past the pool, and there's an altar made up of hundreds of peonies in a giant arch.

I spot Liam next to Parker, waiting in their places under the arch of flowers. He's leaning into his brother's shoulder, whispering something into his ear that causes Parker to throw his head back and laugh. Seeing him gets my heart racing and my libido roaring.

He looks incredibly handsome, like he belongs on a cover of a magazine. His charcoal suit hints at the muscles underneath, his dark hair is perfectly styled and his five o'clock shadow is trimmed neatly just the way I like it. The sight of him makes my skin heat all over and emotions hit me like a freight train. Love. Regret.

I force myself to tear my gaze away and walk back to where the rest of the bridal party is lining up.

I hand Olivia her bouquet.

I find my spot in line.

I try to remember to breathe.

Chapter Twenty-Seven

Liam

"You realize after today your balls are going to shrivel up and fall off, right?" I tease, leaning into Parker's ear, his head falling back in laughter. The two of us are standing in front of our family and friends at the altar alongside Miles and Dylan, waiting for the ceremony to begin.

"Is that so? From all the incredible sex I'll be getting on my honeymoon?" he says, then adding - because it's Parker and he can never leave well enough alone - "My future wife can never get enough of me. It's like my dick has cast a spell on her."

"Not the time or place, Parks. I swear Grandma just heard that," I say, nodding my head towards where she sits next to our dad in the front row.

"It's always the time or place when my dick is begging for more."

I roll my eyes at him but straighten my spine when the officiant takes her place, signalling that it's time to get the show on the road. I look to my right at my younger brother who has now pulled himself together. He looks like the happiest man on the planet, finding that real love that some people spend their entire life looking for. I know he is more than ready to make Olivia his wife. He has always known it was Olivia and I'm envious. It goes without saying that I'm happy as hell for my brother today. There's no doubt he's found his soulmate. Olivia and Parker were always meant to be together, but I have to admit that for some fucked up reason I am equally excited to see Ellie in her dress today.

I know I shouldn't want to see her. I realize I should still be madder than hell at her. But it's Ellie, my vice, and when I think of her I forget everything else.

The music starts, the glass doors open to the house and I watch everyone in attendance stand to their feet. Heads turn to see the first bridesmaid, my sister Jules, as she steps out over the threshold. Kate follows closely behind her and then I take a sharp breath, knowing who will be next.

It feels like slow motion. I can feel Parker's eyes shift to me, knowing the effect the next bridesmaid will have on me. I squeeze my eyes shut for a moment then open them up to see *her.*

Ellie walks down the aisle in a pale blue gown that ends at the floor and dips at her cleavage, hugging her curves in all the right places. With every step she takes, I'm reminded of what's under that dress and what her body does to me.

Shit, she's beautiful.

Her eyes twinkle, so wide and blue, and they do me in, like they always do. My body wants her, and I have to fight my immediate instinct to step towards her, reach out and pull her into me. But I can't for more reasons than the obvious.

Halfway down the aisle, her gaze flicks over to me and

our eyes lock. Her blue meeting my gray. Her expression shifts almost imperceptibly, but I see it change, from joy to sadness. I can't look away. I can't move. More than anything, I want to see her smile. I want to see that smile that I feel in the very depths of me. The one I melt for.

Ellie's eyes travel to the opposite side of the altar and I feel an immediate sense of loss. She walks towards her place in line beside Kate and I still can't take my eyes off of her. Her hair is pulled up into a twist, her shoulders exposed. I itch to touch her. I crave the scent of her skin.

When Pachelbel's Cannon begins, I force myself to look away and I see Olivia take her first steps down the aisle on the arm of her dad. When she reaches the end of the aisle, Olivia's eyes meet Parker's. They whisper words to each other only the two of them can hear and take their places in front of the officiant. And for some fucked up reason, I find myself imagining Ellie in that white dress, and what it would feel like if it was me standing there with her, her hands in mine, pledging our love.

I take a deep breath, trying to compose myself, to calm the racing of my heart. But for some reason I can't shake the feeling that we left money on the table; that this really isn't the way our story was supposed to end.

We could start over.

We could try again.

My eyes find Ellie's again, causing my breath to catch in my throat, and our eyes hold while the backyard and everything and everyone in it seem to fall silent. We stare at each for longer than two people who just broke up should. Something flashes through her eyes which I can't quite decipher, but then slowly her lips curve up in a sheepish smile. *Her smile.* There it is. I can't help but smile too.

A moment is shared between us and I can't let it go by without doing something. "Gorgeous," I mouth from across the altar, flashing her the grin that I know that makes her crazy. As I watch a blush slowly cover her skin I almost forget the hell and back we've just been through.

"Thank you," she mouths back, with that quiet smile that sends a shiver of heat rolling down my spine and suddenly it hits me all at once that I want her. I want her back. No, I need her back. I don't care about the rest of it. I fucking want her. I want her crazy, her sassy mouth, I want it all. Ellie Reeves was made for me.

I remember why we are all here and turn my focus to Olivia and Parker, but the soul-shattering realization that I need to have Ellie back keeps my eyes wandering back to hers, making me wonder what she sees when she looks at me. Does she see the forgiveness in my eyes that I so desperately want to give her, or the three words that sit at the tip of my tongue but I haven't been able to say?

Not willing to wait for the ceremony to end to continue, I mouth, "That dress." There is a heat between us, and it feels like our old selves finding our way back to one another. She's smiling like she's not sure whether to believe it or not, that I might be having a change of heart.

"Sometimes too much." She mouths the words back to me, her eyes running the length of my suit.

I heave a sigh, remembering those exact words she said to me the night I took her to Catch 21, when she told me I looked handsome, and it was *sometimes too much.* I chuckle. This woman is everything I need, everything I crave and everything I never knew I needed. I'll give her what she wants. Whatever she wants. I just need her back in my arms.

Our eyes leave one another's momentarily, returning to Parker and Olivia when the officiant announces, *You may now kiss your bride.* Guests stand, clapping and whistling, while the bridal party files one-by-one down the aisle towards the pool, lead by the newly married couple.

With each step I take my mind narrows to thoughts of Ellie, needing to get to her and make things right. I'm a carnival ride of emotions and my heart pounds in my chest when I see her hugging Olivia. I bide my time, congratulating my brother then embracing Olivia. I can't wait any longer. I inch closer to Ellie until I'm standing behind her, so close I could reach out and touch her, smell the sugary citrus scent of her skin. I run my fingertips feather soft from her elbow to her shoulder causing her to turn and face me. Her eyes, so blue under her dark lashes, meet mine over her shoulder.

I'm so far gone.

And I'm completely okay with that.

"Ells," I say in a low voice as she turns to face me, knocking the air from my lungs. I'm always trying to catch my breath around her. Adrenaline begins to pump through my body.

"How have you been?" I ask, needing to know if she's okay. Her eyes meet mine, glimmering with what I think looks like hope. I've ignored every attempt of hers to talk - the texts, the calls and even a knock at my door have all gone unanswered.

"I'm okay," she whispers. Her voice is soft, uncertain, and her gaze drops to her hands that are fiddling with the ribbon on her bouquet.

"Can we talk?" I ask. I hope she'll say yes. I raise my eyebrows, waiting for her answer.

She nods, so I lead her away from the guests now gathering around the pool towards the white tent that has been erected for the reception, where we can have some privacy. A flutter of hesitation crosses her face when we step inside and I face her, as she nibbles on the corner of her lip. Now it's just the two of us. She sets her bouquet on a table and when she looks up at me there are tears in her eyes.

Her lips part, and a faint, soft sigh falls from her mouth. "This is all my fault. I'm sorry, Liam. I never meant to hurt you. You have to believe me."

I can see her struggling and it kills me. Her hands are tangled together, her fingers worrying through one another. Trying to put her mind at ease, I take her hands in mine and step a little closer, so our bodies are inches apart.

"It's okay, Ells. I promise you, it's okay. None of it matters anymore," I say, squeezing her hands a little tighter in mine. Her eyes scan mine and there is a cautious hope in them. She blinks, like she's trying to decipher my words. "We'll get through it together...if you want to."

Please say yes.

"Of course I want to. I've been so fucking miserable without you," she says. Relief pours through me, but I remain quiet, letting her get out whatever she needs to say. "I hate myself for not telling you and I hate myself even more that I hurt you. I promise I'll never shut you out again."

"Come here," I say, pulling her into my arms, resting my chin on the crown of her head and enjoying the feeling of her body back against mine. I close my eyes and remember how good it feels to be *us*. There's so much more I want to do with her like sit with her on my patio and watch her do her crossword puzzles while we throw the ball for Murphy. Watch her eyes light up when I surprise her with one of her bucket-list destination vacations. Enjoy a bath with her in my tub that I've seen her admiring when she stays the night. A million other ideas float through my mind now that she's back in my arms. I drop a kiss to the top of her head.

Ellie eventually breaks our silence.

"Liam?" she asks.

"Mm-hmm?" I murmur into her hair, which smells like her shampoo that I love.

"You brought my parents home to me." She says it quietly, just above a whisper, while running her hands down my suit jacket from my lower back to my hips. "I still can't believe they're really here. I don't know how I will ever be able to thank you." She pulls back, eyes as blue as the deepest part of the ocean staring back at me. A tear rolls down her cheek and I pad it away with my thumb.

"I can think of a few ways," I say, chuckling. She steps back into me and her hands slide up the lapels of my jacket. We stare at each other in a moment of clarity, knowing we both want this. We both want *us.* And it feels so damn good.

"I bet you can, and Liam, count me in for them all." That flirty gleam in her eyes is back. I fucking love it. I've missed the way she looks at me, draws me in.

Then those same eyes fill with lust as they lower to my mouth, and I can't wait another second. I frame her face in my hands and press my lips to hers, kissing her with everything in me. The kiss feels intimate and full of passion and it still amazes me how much her touch affects me. Angling my head to the side, I slip my tongue between her lips and when my tongue meets hers, it tastes like hunger and want, but more importantly like love.

This is *love.*

Her face softens when I pull back to meet her eyes and she starts to say something, but I raise my finger in the air between us to stop her. "Wait. Not yet, Ellie. It's my turn. Just listen. There is so much I need to say to you."

I can't hold it in anymore. I want to tell her everything in my heart. Everything that needs to be said. Everything that should have been said before. I start to speak and then stop to make sure I have every word right. I pick up her hand and hold it in mine. "When you told me you were married, I was livid. I've never let anyone into my life, into my home and my family, until you. And then finding out that you're married made it all feel like one giant lie."

"I know," she whispers, visibly shaken, slipping back in time momentarily.

"I didn't want to forgive you. I swore to myself I wouldn't. But seeing you today changed everything." I rest my palm on her cheek and for several seconds, the two of us stand in silence. We take each other in, our eyes never leaving one another's, and I realize that the love I have for her is boundless.

"How so…?"

"You stole my heart a long time ago. I'm crazy about you." I take her face in my hands as she blinks back tears. "And I'm very much in love with you."

Her eyes go wide and her breath hitches and everything in me needs to feel her lips on mine. I seal my mouth to hers in a long, slow, torturous kiss before pulling back, unable to stop looking at her.

"What are you saying, Liam?"

"I'm saying I was never going to be able to stay away from you. The other stuff doesn't matter. It can all be fixed. But what we have is perfect. No one can make me feel like you do. Nobody, Ellie. It's you."

I watch her bite down on her bottom lip as tears begin to spill over and flow down her cheeks. "It's you, Ells," I say against her mouth, my heart soaring. "I am so crazy in love with you."

The motherfucking one.

I wait for my words to settle in her mind. I lean forward, pressing soft kisses to her forehead, her nose, the corner of her mouth. I rest my forehead against hers. "I love you, Ellie. I've loved you for weeks but didn't know how to tell you."

"I love you too, Liam. Madly. And I've wanted to tell you, too. You mean everything to me."

I kiss her, like it's the first time. A scorching, fiery, heated kiss that feels like more than any other kiss we've shared. It tastes like the salt from the tears streaming down her cheeks, like promises and above all - love.

Breaking the kiss, I meet her gaze.

"I just have two conditions."

"Anything."

"One, you need to divorce that Mason asshole."

"Already in the works."

"Good. Two," I say, raising my eyebrows in a devilish smirk. "I need you now, Ells. Come with me."

Her eyes pop. Then she smiles. Taking her hand, I lead her towards the pool and inside the house, catching Parker's eye along the way. He flashes an I've-got-you-covered smirk and I nod my head in his direction. Leading her up the stairs to my old childhood bedroom, I look at her over my shoulder, my intent made clear in my eyes.

Pulling her into the bedroom, I shut the door behind us and turn the lock. Within seconds, her body is up against mine and I'm walking her backwards towards the bed. I inhale her, my favorite scent in the world. "I love the way you smell," I tell her, dragging my nose along her neck.

"I love *this*, Liam. Being with you, when you kiss me like that," she gasps, all hot and wrecked in anticipation of what I'm going to do to her.

Our mouths crash together in a kiss that feels reckless. It's a rush. Her arms snake around my neck and my hands travel down her back to her thighs.

When we break apart, the anticipation of what's to

come is pumping through my veins. My skin heats, the hair on my arms rise, a needy moan falls from my lips.

"Take your clothes off, Liam," she pants. The feeling is mutual. There's no time for foreplay. I can't wait another second, I just need her naked before me. Together we undress. I shed my suit and shirt and her dress is removed and thrown against the bed and finally we're both completely naked and ready for one another.

"My hair, Liam. We need to walk out of this bedroom looking presentable. We still have photos to take."

Taking her hand in mine, I walk us to the adjoining bathroom, trapping her body between mine and the bathroom counter. My front is pressed up against her back, her hands grip the edge of the sink and my hands grasp her waist. My aching hard-on is pushed up against her back and my mouth is only inches from her neck. I breathe her in, the scent of Ellie I've missed, and her head tilts to one side giving me access to her long neck. I drag my tongue from just under her ear to the base of her neck, earning me a strangled moan, making my balls tighten.

"I'm apologizing now, Ellie, because this is going to be fast and hard. It's been way too long since I've had you." Pumping my dick in my hand for good measure, I position myself at her entrance, needing this connection I've missed so damn much. More than my last breath.

"Ellie…" her name falls from my lips as I hold her gaze in the mirror in front of us as I sink inside of her. She welcomes me, tightening around me, needing every inch of us connected. "Oh, God."

"I know, Liam. I know. I love the way you feel."

I fist my hand behind her neck, kissing and licking and sucking the soft skin of her neck. I take everything I need from her to claim her, to taste her and remind her that she's mine. Every emotion that has built up over the past week - from not having her, not seeing her, needing her - washes over me and my body vibrates and pleasure builds. A groan works its way up my throat when I reach my release at the same time as Ellie. White-hot fire and bliss shoot through me as I give in to every single sensation ripping through my body.

I grip her thighs tight, holding her as close as I can, not ready to break the connection that joins us. I'm enjoying every last second of the woman I have missed madly. Leaning over her, I kiss the center of her spine, not able to get enough of her now that she's back in my arms. I exhale, meeting her eyes in the mirror. The look she gives me tells me she feels the same way I do. That was so much more than sex. That was making love.

"I love you so fucking much," I tell her, looping my arm around her waist, pressing a kiss to her shoulder.

"I love you too. With my whole heart. Always."

We get cleaned up. I help her into her dress and shoes, and she straightens my tie. "Do you think anyone downstairs noticed we're missing?" Ellie asks in a post-sex voice, startling a laugh out of me.

"I don't think I'd care if there was a search party sent out to find us," I say, and her grin grows wider. "But I guess we really should get back to the party. But Ellie, we will continue this later tonight at my house."

Ellie's mouth lifts in a smile that I want to see for a lifetime. "I'm holding you to it."

A LITTLE LATER, the sound of a fork clinking a glass echoes across the tent as a Michael Bublé song floats through the air. We've just finished dessert and the dancing is about to begin, but not before a rowdy table of my brother's friends join in on the glass clinking, hoping to see Olivia and Parker kiss.

"I need another. I'm hitting the bar," I tell Miles who is sitting beside me at the head table.

Pushing up from my seat, I remove my suit jacket and drape it over my chair.

"I'm right behind you, right after I eat your dessert you tossed aside. Jesus Liam, sugar is not the enemy. It's your friend. You need to live a little."

Rolling my eyes, I turn and make my way to the bar where I order a Macallan on the rocks and wait as the bartender with pink-tipped hair pours my drink. My mom, Jules and Kate join me with a whistle directed my way from Kate's lips that feels all kinds of wrong; my girlfriend's best friend ogling me like I'm street meat. Lifting the glass to my lips, I take a drink, then lick the liquor from my bottom lip.

"Liam you look so handsome," my mom says, straightening my tie and the collar of my white dress shirt.

"Yeah, Liam." Jules smiles, practically bouncing on her toes in excitement. "I've never seen you look this happy. I'm really glad you and Ellie worked things out." Her expression is one of happiness and it means something to me to have her approval. Not that it would matter in the least if I didn't. Nothing would be able to keep me away from that woman.

"Her parents seem awfully sweet and that was extremely thoughtful of you to surprise Ellie with them. I'm proud of you, Liam. That heart of yours is remarkable," my mom says, patting my chest where my heart is. "Ellie's mom offered to gift me a few of her homemade roller oils. She said she makes one that will make me sleep like a baby. I told her to meet me for lunch at the Seaside so she could get them to me."

"That's nice of you, Mom. I know Ellie will appreciate the gesture."

Speaking of the girl who has stolen my heart, Ellie catches my eye from where she's standing on the edge of the dance floor talking to her parents. Her face lights up at whatever they're saying and those fucking goddess eyes of hers sparkle. I watch, mesmerized, as her head tips back and her smile goes wide. Watching her, my balls tighten, and my temperature rises. I can't look away from her for more than a second before my eyes are back on her, following the curve of her waist, the dip of her cleavage, the hollow of her neck. I'm watching her over the edge of my tumbler, my gaze running over the course of her body in that dress.

How did we get from there to here? I can't stop smiling. It's impossible. I trace my finger along my lower lip, remembering three hours ago upstairs in my old bedroom.

I'm forced from my thoughts just in time when Miles clasps me on the shoulder. "Jesus, you are fucking whipped for her," he mutters. "She's got you by your balls, Bennett."

He couldn't be more right. My dick is exactly where I like it to be, wrapped tightly in Ellie's grip. "Yup, I guess she does."

"What?! You're not going to fight me on this? You're just going to allow me to insult your manhood and not say a thing? What happened to my no-strings-attached brother? Where are you hiding him?"

I laugh and shrug my shoulders. "One day you'll understand. When you find the one, you can't fight it. There's no point. It's a losing battle."

"Man, first Parks, now you. You both need to hand over your man cards. My bros are dropping like flies."

"Think about it this way…there's more fish in the sea for you now," I joke, nudging my elbow into his bicep while my eyes follow Ellie to the dance floor where she joins Olivia and two of their girlfriends. A fast song plays over the speakers and Ellie and the girls dance suggestively, rolling their hips and raising their arms in the air. Jesus hell, this woman is going to be the death of me. What a crazy wonderful way to go.

Dancing to the beat, Ellie turns and catches me staring. She smiles my way. It's an I-love-you smile, and I flash one right back to her. Except mine is a you-are-sexy-as-hell version.

Minutes later, I feel Ellie's arms wrap around my center and warmth zips through me. I shift her body from behind me, slipping my arms around her waist and pulling her back into my chest. My voice is in her ear. "You know what that does to me, Ellie. You dancing like that. You're not playing fair."

"I have no idea what you're talking about," she purrs, her body vibrating against mine as she laughs.

"Is something funny?" I ask.

"Nope."

"Your body is so fucking hot. I am so turned on right now and what am I supposed to do about it?" I groan, dipping my mouth into the curve of her neck. My warm breath is next to her ear and I feel her skin tremble from my touch.

"I'm sure that filthy mind of yours can think of something," she says, tilting her head to the side to gaze up at me.

"Do my filthy thoughts turn you on?" I ask her.

She smiles, and I feel it deep inside my soul. "Isn't it obvious? Everything about you turns me on."

My smile widens against her jaw and my dick is at half-mast pressed up against the curve of her back wanting a little attention. I know she's aware she's playing with fire, but my girl has never been afraid of getting burnt. The back and forth between the two of us feels too damn good to stop, but I know I need to put an end to this before I do something I'll regret in the morning.

"You better go before I drag you from this tent and jump you on a pool chair." The warning is clear. She knows all the rules that I have continuously broken for her. I will take her on that chair if she doesn't walk away. My restraint when it comes to Ellie is nonexistent.

She laughs, turning in my arms to face me with a smile in her eyes that says *I dare you*. "You never stop, do you?"

"Nope, not when it comes to you," I say as she takes a step back, dragging my hand out between us. "And I don't plan on it either, so you better get used to it."

Chapter Twenty-Eight

Ellie

"Fetch, Murph!" Liam hollers, throwing the plastic chicken across the yard from where he soaks in the pool. Liam's thick dark hair is wet and messy while beads of water drip down his bronzed skin.

It's been three weeks since the wedding - the day Liam realized he didn't want to lose me. We're both tired from a dinner party last night at the beach house welcoming Parker and Olivia home from their honeymoon. Everyone who mattered was there: Liam's parents, Miles and Jules, Kate and even Olivia's parents who have been getting along remarkably well since Olivia's dad returned back into their lives. It was a traditional clam bake on the beach like the ones Liam's family used to have when he was a child, followed by after-dinner drinks and chocolate pie around a fire.

The Bennetts are really starting to feel like family, taking me in like I'm one of their own. Parker, Miles and Jules have become the siblings I've always wanted. Six days into my parents' stay they told me they felt in their bones they were needed elsewhere. I told them I understood. Liam promised them he'd take care of me. Then he promised me he would make sure it was months and not years until the next time I would see them. That was that.

After sleeping in until ten and the best morning sex of my life, we are now lounging by his pool. Well, *I'm* lounging. Liam prefers doing laps while I lie stretched out on a lounge chair. I turn my attention back to the crossword I'm working on and shift in my chair, enjoying the warm afternoon sun on my skin.

Stumped at my next clue, I ask Liam from across the yard, "Dated American cocktail?"

"Isn't it obvious?" He answers with a smug smile, his dimple in his left cheek catching my eye. *Arrogant fucker.*

"Listen, smarty pants, if it was, do you think I'd be asking you? Indulge me."

Liam pushes up from the edge of the pool with his hands, lifting one leg over the side. He runs one hand through his wet hair once he's standing and his other hand trails down his chest to the board shorts he's wearing deliciously low on his hips. The sight of his bare chest and hard abs and the dusting of hair leading into his swimsuit, spikes my heart rate.

I stare at my devastatingly gorgeous man.

My pulse races.

My skin pebbles.

My eyes wander shamelessly over every inch of him. I don't think the burn in my chest will ever go away when I look at him. My God, this man knows exactly how to light a fire in me. It seems I spend far too much time waiting for it to smolder.

He stalks towards me, taking a seat on the end of my chair, reaching for a towel and rubbing it through his hair. Droplets of water drip slowly down his chest and I fight the urge to reach out and touch them. His eyes then roam shamelessly down my body and my black triangle string bikini. My core heats, knowing that I'm turning him on. Knowing that I'm the woman he can't resist.

"So…" I say, tapping my pen against my bottom lip in thought. "Dated American Cocktail. Twelve letters. Begins with an O."

Liam is straight-faced. "Old Fashioned, of course."

"Bingo." I snap my fingers and point at him. "You are my human thesaurus."

He laughs, then lowers himself to the edge of my chair and reaches for my ankle, pulling it into his lap. He massages the arch of my sole in small circles with his thumb. I close my eyes. Liam knows exactly how to touch me. "And *you* are a crossword junkie. You eat and sleep word puzzles. You could live off of letters and boxes."

"Guilty. How do you think I got so smart? I exercise this muscle daily," I say, pointing to my temple. "While you exercise all those other muscles." I smirk, waving my finger over his torso. He's already done, I bet, a ten-hour workout, followed by a thirty-mile run and seventy-six laps across his pool.

His grin is wry. "You are the smartest. I don't know anyone who holds a candle to you. You could crossword your way out of a burning building and that's sexy as hell in my book. You're a triple threat, Ells."

"Triple threat?" I question him, because I've never really considered myself very good at anything. I tried ballet when I was a kid and learned that I had two left feet. My mom begged me to quit soccer after I spent an entire season cartwheeling over the field when I should have been running. And a singing class when I was fourteen only proved that my voice should be solely heard by the deaf.

"Smart, funny and gorgeous as hell. Triple threat."

"That, Liam, will earn you a kiss. Come here, baby." He leans in closer to me, his muscular arms pressing into the cushion of the chair on either side of me. The scent of his aftershave and the light eucalyptus of his shampoo flood my senses, intoxicating me. Sitting up, I take his cheek in my hand, brushing my thumb over the scruff that covers his jaw. I pull him in for a slow kiss, then pull back before we take the kiss any further because let's face it, we have neighbors, and we've never been particularly good at restraint when it comes to one another.

"Biased boyfriend, but I'll take it. By the way, this is the third time this week I've seen you in the pool. For a man who hates to relax, you're doing a good job of looking footloose and fancy free."

Liam rolls his eyes like I've insulted his manhood. I know what he's thinking. Relaxing is reserved for those born with a missing work ethic chromosome. That's definitely not Liam.

"You're looking pretty relaxed yourself, princess. I think you like it here with me and Murphy. Admit it, you can't resist us. Nor can you resist the good time we bring. You're secretly bored out of your mind when you go back to your apartment."

The cheeky bugger.

"Pull-ease, Liam. I've never needed anyone else to show me a good time. My middle name is *full-time-fun-haver*."

Liam's expression shifts suddenly from laid back and playful to pensive. His face turns serious and he shifts a little in his chair. "A good time would be you coming home to us instead of just coming over. Move in with me, Ells."

His question takes me aback. I was not expecting it but can't deny the burst of excitement that quickly spreads inside my chest. *Isn't it too soon? Wouldn't we be rushing things?*

There must be an appropriate amount of days before it's considered okay to make a big move like this.

I shoot him a quizzical look. "Liam, don't you think we're moving a little fast?"

"Hard no. What's the point in waiting? You sleep here most nights anyways. Why pay rent on a place you use only a few hours a week?"

He has a point. Then again, Liam always thinks he has the upper hand. Persuasion is one of his strongest traits. He's used to getting what he wants, when he wants it, but I won't give in to him without a skirmish. *What fun would that be?*

"We're not leaving here today, Ellie, until you see things my way." His gray eyes have never looked at me so piercingly. My body tingles all over. Bossy Liam is my favorite. I continue, serving him back a quip, earning me a point in this battle of wills because let's face it – I can never resist working him up. It's what we do. It's *us*.

"Always so bossy. You know you can be a big bully, right? I like my apartment and besides, it's much closer to work. It would take me three days to bike to Bloom from here. And in heels, Liam? I believe you've seen me in my heels, right?"

He pretends to be annoyed, but I know he loves our banter. He scoffs. "Three days? My God, you and your drama. You really deserve to star in your own soap opera because you are a soap opera to deal with. It would take you ten minutes longer. Don't dare ninety-eight percent me," he says, referring to the nickname I earned in college, because *allegedly*, with air quotes, ninety-eight percent of what I say is to spice up my stories. *Yeah, right!*

"But I like my neighbors, and the coffee shop down the street," I insist, riling him. Poking the bear, if you will. I swear I can see his temperature rising.

"But you like it here with me much more." He runs his hand across my sun-drenched skin to my back and fiddles with the strings of my bikini. Reason number one why I like bossy Liam the best: he knows how to get my heart racing. His face is inches from mine. His mouth brushes over my jaw. My hand reaches for his bicep when he suddenly pulls back with a cocky smirk.

"Not happening until you give me an answer, Ells, and I'm going to need it to be a yes."

"Liam…" my voice gives me away. It comes out feathery and wistful and I know he realizes he's won this particular battle.

"Say it, Ellie."

Of course, my answer is yes. It's possibly the easiest question I've ever had to answer. So, I tell him enthusiastically, "Yes! Yes, Liam. I'll move in with you."

"Get over here," he growls. If I wasn't already in love with this man, I would be now. It's the singing-in-the-rain type of love, the shout-it-from-the-rooftop kind. The cherry on top of the sweetest, most delectable strawberry, chocolate, banana split in the history of the world kind of love. He skims his fingers over the flesh of my thigh, and it feels like I'm soaring. This feels like a dream. I'm positive it doesn't get better than this.

"Your negotiation skills are impressive. I can see why you're unstoppable in the courtroom," I say into his ear, my arms wrapped tightly around his neck. I feel his lips dust a kiss on the edge of my shoulder.

"I'm unstoppable in more ways than one," he says as I break the hold I have on him to look him in the eyes. My fingers weave through his thick hair as he flashes me his most devastating smile.

"Hmm, is that so?"

"That is so."

He stands, dropping the pool towel onto the end of the chair. His abs glisten in the sun, lines and delicious grooves that make my mouth water.

Liam takes note of my drifting eyes, currently seared to his mid-section. He raises a brow then flashes me a *like-what-you-see* look.

"You are incorrigible," I scoff, fighting off a laugh.

He doesn't let up. "You like to ogle me. Admit it. You like my body."

It never fails. Liam has me on edge. I ache for this man. It feels like I'm free-falling and he's the only one on this planet capable of catching me. I'm jumping in with two feet. I'm all in.

I stand from my lounger and run my hands up to his neck, kissing him with all that I am because time flies and life is short, and *this* feels right. I'm not willing to waste another second without Liam by my side because if you're lucky enough to find that once in a lifetime, earth-shattering love… you better be smart enough to seize it.

Thankfully I am.

LIAM

3 months later

THE PAST FEW months with Ellie have been a blur of dinners on the patio, lazy Sunday mornings in bed and as well as some ridiculous things that she insists couples do together - axe throwing, couples' massages, cooking classes. I'm not even surprised anymore at the crazy shit this woman has me saying yes to. It's almost unbearable at times, but the sex she rewards me with at the end of each activity makes it all worth it. And then some.

She's my kind of crazy in all the best ways. And I fucking love her.

Our relationship has moved quickly, thanks to Ellie's divorce becoming finalized last month and her officially moving in with me. My house, now our house, has little touches of Ellie everywhere. Her canary yellow throw blanket is draped across the arm of the couch, her porcelain mugs with ridiculous sayings fill up the dishwasher, the fridge is covered with Polaroid photos of her parents' adventures and those God-awful *Cats* magnets. And I wouldn't change a thing.

Surprisingly, none of it drives me insane. Ellie is the furthest thing you can get from a neat freak- she's all clutter and chaos, the polar opposite of me. But I wouldn't have it any other way. She's everything I've ever wanted and a million things more, and if it means I need to navigate through boat loads of knick-knacks and tchotchkes to be able to get into bed next to her every night, so be it. Paint the walls purple and string fairy lights across the ceiling as far as I'm concerned. *Zero fucks given.*

We've also found ourselves settling into an easy rhythm together. One of the best things about Ellie is that it's always easy with her. That's not to say her easy doesn't come without a hefty serving of crazy. But it's entertaining and endearing and has a way of making a hard day at the firm seem easier.

My family loves her as much as I do. She fits in. Effortlessly. We spent a weekend in Cape May visiting Parker and Olivia and have a trip to Canada planned to visit Miles when he films in Vancouver. We also try for weekly dinners at my parents' place, where my mother and Ellie happily plot against me, thinking up new activities to torture me with. I'm pretty sure that's where the axe-throwing debacle got started.

I return home after work today to find her in the kitchen in a Yankees ball cap and cut-off shorts, a glass of ice water in her hand and Murphy by her side. When I told her I had to stop by the office on a Sunday, she wasn't happy. *You're breaking a sacred rule,* she said when I kissed the tip of her nose and left her in our bed. Weeks into living together, she made me promise I would take weekends off whenever possible to unwind and try new things, and I've kept up my end of the bargain. Until today.

She greets me with a kiss. "I missed you."

"And I missed you," I say, pulling her body into mine. "I picked up a few things on my way home. Help me unload the car and I'll take you for lunch."

"A picnic on the beach? We could stop by Sammies along the way and pick up lobster rolls and your favorite pressed grapefruit juice," she suggests, batting her lashes.

"Since when have you known me to eat a lobster roll?"

"Since never, but there's a first time for everything, isn't there? Besides, lobster rolls are sent from heaven."

I tsk her at the ridiculousness of her statement but then relent because I'm powerless to Ellie. Always have been and always will be. "Have I ever said no to you?"

"Never. Come on, let's do this," she says, slipping on her sandals, and heading for the front door. I'm right behind her when she opens the heavy front door leading to the driveway.

I know when she sees it because she stops dead in her tracks, causing me to collide with her back. "Liam…" she says, looking from me to the white Range Rover with an enormous red bow parked in our driveway, and then back to me again. "What's happening?"

"It's yours, Ells. It's for you."

"What?" she demands in a high-pitched squeal. "Liam, are you insane? I can't accept this."

"You can and you're going to. Let me do this for you."

"Liam…" She hurls herself at me, wrapping her arms around my neck. "This is too much. Way too much. Like on a scale of one to ten, it's one hundred too much."

"You and your one-to-ten scales. Go sit in it, Ells. See what you think."

She hurries to the SUV, where I open the driver side door for her and watch her climb in. Her hands wrap tightly around the steering wheel as her eyes roam the interior. Her smile is impossibly bright, and it makes me grin too, because every emotion Ellie feels is contagious.

"You like?" I ask, already knowing the answer to my question.

"I'm obsessed. Thank you, Liam. My heart might burst. I might die on the spot."

"Please don't. I'm just getting used to you," I deadpan.

"Very funny. But I can't even be cheeky with you because holy mother-of-pickles, you bought me my first car! And a Range Rover at that."

"No girlfriend of mine shall be car-less. I had to remedy that right away."

"Well, you did. And then some" she says, flipping her ball cap backwards. She takes my face in her hands and kisses me breathless. "I love it, Liam. And I love you."

"I love you, too. Drive us to Sammies? I'll ride shotgun."

"Get in, my insanely handsome shotgun rider. Let's go."

2 months later

"I blame you, you know."

"Blame me?" Ellie replies to my mother nervously. It's Sunday and we've just arrived at their place, joining them in the backyard. Clearly unsure of where the conversation is going, Ellie shifts her gaze to me with a concerned look on her face.

"Yes, you, sweetheart. I'm completely and totally crossword-obsessed thanks to you." My mother smiles from where she's sitting on a deck chair, picking up the crossword book from the table in front of her and waving it in Ellie's direction. "Come here, you two. Give me a hug."

"It's true. She is obsessed," my dad agrees, as he walks the perimeter of the pool with a net, skimming the surface of the water. "She crosswords all over the house. The deck, in bed, the backyard. I've even caught her working on a puzzle while making her Bolognese." My father shakes his head and laughs, then sets aside the pool net, striding towards us. He greets us after my mother does, hugging me and kissing Ellie on her cheek.

It's Sunday, and Ellie and I are here to have lunch with my parents. Reluctantly setting her crossword book to the side, my mom excuses herself to the kitchen to get us cold drinks and a few pre-lunch appies. Ellie offers to help her in the kitchen, but my mother insists everything is done, and to sit and enjoy the sunshine.

"Ellie, honey?" My mom hollers from the kitchen window. "Will you look at my crossword and try your hand at the next couple of clues? I've been stumped on those all morning, and you are a genius when it comes to solving word puzzles. I could really use your help."

I watch Ellie shift in her chair, reaching for the book. She's beautiful. Today she's wearing a sundress that ends just above her knees and a pair of ankle boots. Her long hair is tied back in a ponytail.

Shifting my focus to my father, I ask, "Dad, any idea on the Yankees game? Do you know what the score is?"

"I haven't looked, son. Why don't we check?"

I press a kiss to Ellie's temple and follow my dad inside, where I can hear my mother and Ellie chat through the kitchen window.

"A flower the shade of lavender. I think the first one is lilacs," Ellie calls out, reminding me of our New York trip and the lilacs I ordered knowing they were her favorite.

"Yes, you're right. See honey, I knew you would know the answers. What's the next one?" My mom asks, catching my gaze from where she stands in the kitchen. There's a twinkle in her eye, and her smile is a mile wide.

"Broadway musical inspired by T.S. Eliot. Well, I better know the answer to this one. It's *Cats*! Only the best musical ever invented," Ellie calls towards the kitchen, and I can't help but smile. "This crossword was made for me. It's all of my favorite things," Ellie says, while I do my best to swallow a chuckle.

My mom keeps her going. "Of course. How did I not get that one? The answer should have been obvious considering you were just at the production with Liam a few months back. Okay, two more and I think I can take it from there."

"Famous last words asked in every *Bachelor* finale episode." Ellie says, and there's a pause as I wait for her to answer. "Will you marry me. The answer is will you marry me." The end of the sentence trails off to a quieter tone in her voice as if she's deep in thought.

"That's it. One more, sweetheart. I'll be right there."

I smile. Then I try to calm my raging nerves by taking a deep breath. My smile remains plastered over my face. I couldn't wipe it away if I tried.

I inch closer to the patio door and I feel the strong clasp of my father's hand on my shoulder. I can see her sitting on the couch, the book in her lap, filling in the small boxes with her answers. My heart races in my chest.

Ellie continues to the next clue. "The gorgeous half of Liam's *just us*."

And that's my cue. I shoot a wink at my mom and step through the patio doors towards Ellie. Anticipation zips through my body seeing the woman I want to spend forever with, wondering if she's figured out the answer to the most monumental clue she's ever been given.

"Ellie." I say her name like it's the only name that will ever really matter in my life. Her head whips around to face me. In four long strides, I'm standing in front of her. I drop to one knee on the stone patio beneath us, pulling a blue velvet box from my pocket and flipping it open. "The answer is Ellie." Her hand covers her mouth, and her eyes go wide, her shocked expression telling me that I pulled this off. "Ellie-"

"Liam, are you serious?" she gasps, shifting forward in her seat, moving towards me, taking my face in her hands.

I nod, and her tears begin to escape her. Tear after tear, smile after smile. It all comes, she's powerless to stop it. My face is inches from hers when I tell her. "You're my reason to come home. My reason to smile. You're my every reason. Every I love you. Every little thing. Marry me, Ells."

"Yes! Liam, yes! So many times, yes," she says, leaning in to kiss me. We kiss through smiles and laughter, while my heart beats like a drum in my chest. I slip the emerald cut diamond ring onto her finger then watch her jaw almost drop to the pavement. "My God, I've never seen anything more beautiful."

She waggles her ring finger, unable to stop herself from staring at the shiny rock on her hand. It fits perfectly, just like the way she fits in my life. Seamlessly.

"I can't wait to marry you, Liam."

"Neither can I," I tell her, kissing her like it's the very

first time. "I want it all with you. A future, a family. You are it for me. Forever and always."

"Liam…" she murmurs, clutching her heart, her blue eyes shimmering with happiness. "I want it all too. With you. I can't wait for our life together."

I kiss her chastely because I know my parents are waiting for her answer, waiting to celebrate one of the biggest days of our lives with us.

"She said yes!" I holler, and my parents come running. Fifteen minutes later, the rest of my family are here: Parker, Olivia, Miles and Jules, lunching on the patio and toasting to our engagement.

"I can't believe you were all in on this. It makes the proposal even more fantastic," Ellie says to my family once we finish the lunch my mother prepared for us on the hunch that Ellie would say yes and we would have something to celebrate.

"That's only because Liam couldn't be trusted to pull this off by himself," Miles shouts from the opposite end of the rectangular table we're all gathered around, under a trellis of lavender morning glories and bougainvillea.

I roll my eyes, flipping him off, then press a kiss to Ellie's cheek. Knowing Ellie has longed for siblings and a family she can see frequently, I thought she might like a proposal surrounded by the people who now consider her part of theirs.

"He deserves a gold star," Olivia says. "The crossword puzzle proposal was brilliant."

"He definitely does. It was perfect." Ellie squeezes my thigh under the table. "I'll never forget it."

We finish dessert and say our goodbyes. In the car before pulling away, I lean over and kiss her neck. I am happy to finally have her all to myself.

"Hi," I say into the column of her neck, my voice smoky, savoring her scent.

"Hi to you too, my fiancé," she says, with a fevered smile. "Liam, remember back when we drove each other crazy? When I thought you were too cocky and serious, and you thought I was too wild and impulsive?"

"Of course I do. I never forget a thing when it comes to you. And for the record I'm absolutely in love with your wild, impulsive side. It's one of the sexiest things about you."

"I would like to also go on record, Liam Bennett. That broody, serious, cocky thing you do is insanely hot as fuck," she says, mock fanning her face with her hand. "And look at us now. Hopelessly in love and getting married, about to spend the rest of our lives together. It feels like I have everything I've ever dreamed of and somehow more," she says, holding up her hand, admiring her engagement ring as it glints and gleams.

I couldn't agree more. I thought my life before Ellie was good. I thought I was happy. I thought I had everything I needed.

I know now that I was wrong.

It was missing Ellie.

"I think deep down, maybe I knew early on that you were the only one for me. I've wanted you since the first day I met you. I knew I had to have you," I confess, setting my hand on her cheek. "That's how I know it had to be you, Ellie."

I must be doing something right, I figure, to have landed a catch like this gorgeous, witty brunette sitting in my passenger seat. They say you know when you know, and I couldn't be more certain that Ellie is the one I want to spend forever with.

"Really, Liam? You always knew?"

"I did."

"Me too," she says, leaning across the console that separates the two of us, her chin up, her lips parted, inviting me to kiss her. And that's exactly what I intend to do because it's all I ever want to do when I'm around her. But most of all, I want to love her. For eternity. Curling my hand around the back of her neck, I kiss her, then rest my forehead against hers and repeat those five perfect words.

"It had to be you, Ellie. It had to be you."

Epilogue

A FEW WEEKS LATER

Ellie

I turn my head to find Liam leaning against the bedroom doorway, bare-chested with a pair of joggers hung low on his hips. That V shape muscle and the hard lines of his abs taunt me. I'm not sure I'll ever get used to the sight of him.

"Are you ready?" His morning voice does that sexy, throaty thing that slays me.

"Are you planning on putting a shirt on?"

"You don't usually complain when I'm half-naked," he says, absently running his hand across his stomach. *Such a smart ass.*

"Oh, believe me, I'm not complaining, but a shirt might be appropriate when Facetiming my parents."

Sitting cross-legged on the bed, I reach for my laptop while Liam pulls a T-shirt from his drawer. He sits on the bed next to me, pulling it over his head. A ray of sunshine streams in through the patio doors, casting a beam across the monitor. Shifting the laptop on the bed, I find a spot where we can both see the screen clearly.

We take the chance and by some sort of miracle, my parents answer. I smile at my mother through the screen, looking every bit the hippy in her floral sundress, my father next to her with his layers upon layers of crystal necklaces. They're smiling, both at me and at my fiancé, as we get ready to deliver big news.

"It's so good to see you! I miss you both. So much," I say with a smile, my chest aching to hug them. I have to give credit where credit is due - they've called, emailed and Facetimed almost every other week, wanting to be kept in the loop with our lives. And although it's not the same as having them live in the same city as me, it does help to know that it won't be months until the next time I hear their voices.

"Hi, honey. Hi, Liam. I can see you're keeping our girl very happy. She's glowing. Do you have something to tell us?" My mom leans into the camera so all we can see is her chin. Liam and I look at each other and laugh.

"Mom, sit back. We can't see your face," I tell her as my dad reaches around her to her shoulders, gently pulling her away from the screen.

"That's better," I say, carrying on with the conversation. "I'm the happiest, mom. Never been better. And yes, we have news. How did you know?"

"I talked to Stella."

"Stella?" Liam and I both ask in unison, looking at each other with who-the-hell-is-Stella stares on our faces.

"Yes, Stella. My psychic."

"Ahh. Of course," I say, pinching my fingers into Liam's thigh. He quietly laughs and I do too, wondering what Stella the spiritual, supernatural supernova had to say.

"Well hurry up, sweetheart!" My mother's eyes light up

like she's walked into a surprise party and we all just shouted her name. "I've been waiting for this call."

Not able to hold it in a second longer, I blurt out: "We're pregnant! I'm pregnant!" Then I watch as my parents both burst into huge smiles, unable to contain their joy.

"Oh sweetheart, we are wildly happy for the two of you, even though we already knew, of course. We are so happy you finally shared the news with us." My dad beams as Liam pulls me into his side, setting his hand on my belly. I melt against him. If Liam ever wondered where I got my crazy from, he definitely knows now.

"But…you two are the first people we've told," Liam points out, clearly confused.

My mother replies with a cat-that-ate-the-canary grin. "Stella knew two weeks ago, darlings. Your father and I almost fell out of our seats in happiness when she broke the news. We've been waiting for the two of you to spill the beans ever since."

I shake my head. We both crack up. We fill them in. The shock of finding out, surprising Liam with the news one morning in our bed, the thrill of hearing our baby's heartbeat for the first time last week. I grumble over Liam's fiercely protective side, and his long list of things he already considers too high-risk for me to be doing now that I'm carrying our child. Standing in front of the microwave while my popcorn is popping is deemed too risky if you ask Liam. I'm also pretty sure he thinks I cooked the baby during my half-hour bath last night. My parents seem to side with his overprotective ways. *It figures. Liam can do no wrong in their eyes.*

As soon as I end the call, Liam lays me out on our bed, straddling my hips. He slips his hand beneath my shirt, resting his palm on my belly, an easy-going smile on his face.

"I think that went well. Would you agree?" he asks, running his finger down the center of my chest and back to my belly, which is still flat for now. Soon it won't be, and I can't wait for that day.

"I would. There's only one way that could have gone better…if me having their grandchild might make them want to move back home."

"You never know. Maybe it could. And if it doesn't, I will make arrangements to have them flown here as often as you would like," he says. "You know there's nothing I wouldn't do for you."

That, I do know. For all life's uncertainties, I never doubt the strength of Liam's love for me. He shows me in different ways every day. Like when he sends my favorite soup and sandwich to Bloom because he knows I have a bad habit of working through lunch. Or when he massages my feet at night while we're watching TV because he knows how much I love it. Or the sinfully sexy text messages he sends, detailing all the naughty things he plans on doing to me when he gets home from work. My reply is always *I can't wait, hurry home.*

Home.

It all feels too good to be true. Liam will always be my home and I wouldn't want it any other way. Of course, things weren't always this easy, but I vowed every day to earn back Liam's trust. I've learned the best way to do that is by letting down my walls and opening my heart to him, trusting that he won't break it. In turn, Liam has been opening up to me too - showing me his softer side, letting me in. It means everything to me.

We are meant to be. There's no other way to explain it. Liam and I were always meant to find one another. He is my future. My one and only - and soon, my husband and the father of this miracle I'm carrying.

I think about our baby growing inside of me, the very best surprise of my life. Of *our lives.* And I'm positive our little boy or girl was written in the stars. Fate.

I imagine Liam and I in our backyard ten years from now, with our baby, and maybe one or two more. I broaden the image, so that I can picture Parkers and Olivia's children with ours, playing in the pool. Miles and Jules are there too, and their families as well. Liam's parents and mine watch *their* children with their own kids, with pride in their eyes. My chest expands with love as I picture our life together so clearly. It's a life I am ready for.

Wrapping my arms around Liam's neck, I slide my hands through his hair, relishing his familiar scent and the feel of his skin against mine. He presses a light kiss to my lips, staring into my eyes.

"Want to know something?" Liam asks, with a far-off look in his piercing eyes. Of course I want to know what he's thinking, but first I have to tease him just a little.

"I already know. Stella called me," I joke, playing with the short strands of his hair near the back of his neck.

Liam's eyebrows raise in mock curiosity. "Is that so? What did Stella have to say?"

"That I'm quite the catch and my fiancé is one lucky man," I tell him, wiggling my brows in amusement.

"She did, did she? Anything else?"

Tapping my finger to my lips, I go for an award-worthy performance. "She said we will have twelve kids and star in our own reality TV show someday."

"Really? Was our friend Stella drinking again?" Liam says with a wise-ass smile. I hold back a laugh, continuing on with my theatrics.

"Stella? Definitely not," I say, upping the ante,

spreading my arms wide open over my head. "I believe she's known all over North America for her exceptional ability to see into the future. People go to her from far and wide."

Liam shakes his head in amusement, then his fingers inch down my abdomen. I squeal as he tickles my sides, squirming under his solid, muscular body. He keeps going, gently and agonizingly tickling me until I beg him to stop.

"Now, do you want to hear what I was going to say to you, or are you not quite finished with the theatrics?" he asks, sweeping my hair from my face, his hips still pinning mine to the bed. The mood in the room shifts from playful to pensive as he twines both of his hands between mine.

"I'm done. I swear," I tell him. "What is it, Liam? What did you want to tell me?"

He inhales a deep breath, looking into my eyes. "You are without a doubt the best part of my life. You and this baby," he says with pure joy in his eyes, gesturing to my belly. My skin pebbles all over in goosebumps. He drops his lips to mine in a slow, heated kiss and I tremble at his intense love for the two of us. "I'm going to spend my life making you happy. Making our family happy."

This man.

The day I told Liam I was pregnant he was in bed, lying on his stomach, his arms buried under his pillow and the bed sheet pulled down to his waist. I remember my breath catching in my throat at the handsome features of his profile and the sculpted lines of his back. I held the pregnancy test in my fingers. I suspected I could be pregnant when I was six days late. The test confirmed my suspicions that morning with two pink lines. I stood there watching him, excited and scared to tell him, but I knew I couldn't wait.

I know you're watching me, he'd said, and that's all it

took for the tears to flow over my cheeks. He nearly jumped out of bed, afraid something was wrong, but then quickly noticed the test in my hand. I nodded through the tears and he smiled the hugest grin. "Say something," I told him. He asked me how this could be true. I told him I thought he was a little too old for the "birds and the bees" talk then he tugged me into his arms and whispered in my ear how happy he was. It was perfect.

"I know. This baby and I are the luckiest to have you, Liam. You are going to make the best dad and husband."

"You think so?"

There is no doubt. The fierce love and devotion Liam shows his family and me every single day is proof enough. "I know so. You've spent your entire life looking up to your father and he's one of the greatest men I know. And you are just like him in so many ways. This baby won the daddy lotto. We are going to have a great life together, babe."

He bends lower, resting his forehead to mine. "Have I told you that I love you yet today?"

"You have, but I'll never get tired of hearing you say it. But Liam…"

He sits up and nods with an arch of his eyebrow and a look in eyes that's too damn sexy for words. I almost forget what I was about to say but a flutter in my stomach reminds me.

"I am starving. I could eat a horse. What do you say to making your world-famous chicken Caesar salad and we eat it together on the patio like old times?"

He kisses me and it tastes like forever. What starts out as a chaste kiss turns into more because it's always more with Liam. I kiss him back harder, taking his jaw in my hand, then break the kiss remembering my need to eat.

"I can definitely agree to that," he says, moving off of me and helping me from our bed.

And that's exactly what we do.

THE NEXT FEW days are a whirlwind of pregnancy announcements and phone calls. We tell Liam's family over dinner at Catch 21 and from their reaction, you would think we hung the moon. Tears immediately filled his mom's gray eyes - eyes the colour of her son's. She jumped from her chair, her hand on her heart, squeezing us both in her arms. "This baby is a gift. Our family is beyond blessed," she said, dabbing at her eyes. His dad's eyes went glossy, and he too joined in on the hugs. I will always be grateful for the Bennetts and the love they continuously show me. Liam also devoted an entire afternoon to finding us a suitable obstetrician and booking an appointment to begin monitoring the baby. In other news, I've been napping daily after work, utter exhaustion being a side effect of pregnancy that has hit me the hardest.

A few days after telling Liam's parents, we headed to Vancouver to visit Miles. Parker and Olivia joined us, jumping at the chance to stay with Miles in a gorgeous west coast home right on the edge of the Pacific Ocean.

I stand at the water's edge and take in the view, soaking in Vancouver's perfect balance of nature and city. It's picture perfect - the mountains in the distance, the salty scent of the ocean, the sun a fiery ball in the sky. "I can see why people love it here," I say to Liam, as we stroll along the seawall, which winds along the coast, around Stanley Park and the aquarium. We wait for Parker and Olivia, who are a few feet behind us, having stopped to take a selfie. Our plan is to wander, eat lunch at a hot spot Miles recommended, and then meet him back at the house once he's done filming for the day.

"You realize it rains here? I'm not sure you could handle it." Liam's expression is dubious when he turns to face me.

"You don't think I could handle a little liquid sunshine?"

"I'm not sure. You tell me," he says, looping his arm around my waist, pulling me closer. He rests his palm against my belly. "How's my little dude today, by the way?"

"Liam, I'm not sure how many times I need to remind you. We have no clue what the gender of our baby is."

"I know it's a boy. Your mother's psychic also agrees this baby has an X and a Y chromosome. Therefore, it's a boy."

I shake my head as a breeze picks up from the ocean, blowing my hair across my face. Liam reaches for the wild strands, pinning them behind my ear. He does have a point. The psychic did predict I would get married this year. Then she predicted my pregnancy, making her two-for-two. "And if it's a girl? What then?"

"Then, I'll be wrapped around her finger. But there's no need to worry about that, Ells. It's a boy."

A laugh bursts out of me as I watch his gaze turn to the ocean, and the tide crashing against the stone wall below us. Truth be told, I'd be happy with a boy or a girl, as long as it's healthy. It might be cliché, but it's true. But the idea of a miniature Liam with his dreamy eyes and dark hair running around makes my heart thump in my chest.

Seconds later, Parker and Olivia catch up with us. Olivia asks again about my pregnancy and we get lost in baby chat while the boys stroll ahead of us. My heart fills to the brim then spills over, watching Liam and his younger brother who have this incredible bond. They've been there for each other for their entire lives. Miles and Jules too.

"It's ridiculously cute how you can't stop smiling around Liam," Olivia says.

"Seems I do that a lot," I admit. I let my eyes linger on him for a few seconds longer, enjoying my view. Faded jeans show off the curve of his ass perfectly, a dark gray Henley hugs his firm chest and shoulders, and a pair of Ray-Bans that I swear he wears to slay me. His hair is perfectly messed up from the wind moving in from the ocean. I take him in - chiseled jaw, cocky grin - and he's everything I love in the world. He's the reason for my happiness, the piece of the puzzle that makes my life whole. He's my forever, my one true love and the fierce protector of my heart.

"I'm not sure what you are doing to that man, but I've never seen Liam so relaxed."

I laugh. "I doubt that's a word that's ever been used to describe Liam."

Olivia laughs too, because it's true. Although Liam has learned to find balance in his life, he's definitely still the wound-tight, intensely focused control freak he's always been. That, I'm sure, will never change. It's who Liam is and always has been, and I liked him that way from the moment I met him.

"Are you still happy in Cape May?" I ask Olivia, checking in with her. Their move was always only temporary with their plans being to return home to Reed Point once Parker had the newest Seaside Hotel up and running smoothly.

"I am because I have Parker, but I miss Reed Point and all of you," she says a little wistfully.

"Any idea of when you two will move back?" I ask as we walk past a family of four on bikes. There's a woman too, pushing a stroller, and I can't help but think how that will be me one day soon. My heart does a back handspring in my chest at the thought.

"Parker thinks November. I refuse to get my hopes up."

I do the math in my head. That's only two months away. "Seriously? That's just around the corner."

Olivia laughs. "Sort of, I guess. two months feels like an eternity, especially now that you are pregnant. I don't want to miss a thing. I'm beyond excited that it's you, Ells, who is going to make me an aunt." Olivia pulls me into her side, and I rest my head upon her shoulder. I sigh in agreement, knowing that I don't want her to miss a second of this pregnancy either.

We spend the rest of the day doing Canadian things, making our way back to Miles' rental just after six. The home is incredible, overlooking the ocean with six bedrooms, a theater room and an outdoor pool and spa. Hearing voices echoing from the basement, the four of us pad downstairs where we find Miles in the games room playing pool. But he's not alone. Across the table is a pretty brunette with golden skin and green eyes the color of emeralds. She's a knockout to any man's standards. Hell, I might even have a crush on her.

"Hey," Miles greets us, rounding the pool table. His guest does the same. "Everyone this is Rylee. She's a set PA on the movie I'm shooting. Rylee, these are my brothers Liam and Parker, Parker's wife Olivia and Liam's fiancé Ellie."

"It's so nice to finally meet y'all." She says, holding out her hand, greeting us with a model-worthy smile and an ever so slight twang to her speech. "Miles has told me so much about all of you."

He has, has he? Interesting.

"I hope Miles hasn't been too much of a diva. We

know how he can get when he's hungry or needs a nap." Parker says, then shakes her hand. "It's great to meet you too."

"It's nothing I can't handle," Rylee says with a laugh. "I just send him to his trailer when he throws a tantrum."

I like this girl already.

After introductions, we decide on ordering Thai food from a local hot spot Miles recommends. Parker serves up a round of gin and tonics - a mocktail for me, of course - and we start a game of pool while we wait for the delivery.

Rylee tells us a little bit about growing up in a small town and the last two years working under different producers and directors on various television and movie sets. Miles listens intently the entire time, never looking away from her, hanging on her every word. In turn, Rylee holds Miles' stare, touches his forearm or shoulder whenever she can, and softly laughs whenever he says something charming. *It's too darn cute.*

I know first-hand the feel of a gaze like the one Miles is searing through Rylee. It's the same way Liam's eyes have always stared at me when he's unable to look away, like I'm the only woman he's ever wanted and will ever want. *They're flirting. And I'm loving it.*

I catch the eye of Olivia with a do-you-see-what-I-see look, and she smirks. Yup, it's not just me. She's seeing what I'm seeing. Miles and Rylee have chemistry.

A little while later, we've finished dinner and I'm watching Parker and Liam take on Miles and Rylee in a game of pool. I'm feeling the first trimester fatigue so I'm sitting this one out, resting on a bar stool.

Liam is up. His brows knit together as he studies the table then bends over the edge of the felt lining up his shot. He skillfully sinks a striped ball into the pocket then strides over to me with a twinkle in his eye. I pull him into me, needing my hands on him, where he settles between my thighs. "Nice shot, babe. You can add pool shark to the list of hot things you do that turn me on."

"Maybe one day I'll let you in on my pool shark secrets."

"Only if I'm lucky," I say, kissing him chastely with my hands wrapped around his waist. "By the way, seems like Miles is very much into the set assistant," I say under my breath, looking at Liam's brother. He smiles, all flirty, moving next to Rylee where she's leaning against the pool table about to take her shot.

"Really? You think so?"

"Liam, are you joking me? What's the matter with you? You have two eyes. It's as plain as day." I swat at his bicep playfully. "They look like they're well on their way to matching tattoos or adopting a puppy together."

He arches a brow at me. "You realize this is Miles you're talking about? Neither one of those things are happening. The guy is a legend at playing the field and he's smart enough to know not to cross lines with a PA on set."

"Fine. Think what you want, but there is definitely something brewing. Mark my words. They are feeling each other, and you of all people should know you can't fight love when it gets a hold of you," I argue, shooting him a *trust me* stare.

"Your move, Liam," Miles calls out. "You think you can tear yourself away from Ellie long enough to sink the white ball?"

Liam leaves my arms, rubs chalk over the end of his cue, and taunts his brother. "Since when did you become a pool shark, show performer?"

"Show performer? Seriously?" Miles wrinkles his forehead. "Try A-list Hollywood action star. That's more like it."

Rylee laughs while Liam shrugs and rolls his eyes. Liam bends over the edge of the table, lining up his shot, sinking a striped ball. He sinks three more after that.

"You see that Ells, I told you I'm ridiculously good at everything," Liam jokes. Some things never change.

"Hmm. I didn't notice," I say. He just shakes his head with a mock-annoyed grin on his face. My pulse speeds at the banter that never fails to turn me on. Liam must notice the hungry look in my eyes because he suddenly announces he needs to get his pregnant fiancé to bed. I don't argue because it's exactly where I want to be.

With my man.

The man I love with everything in me.

He's devastatingly gorgeous.

He's totally and completely irresistible.

He's the most mouth-watering combination of wit, sex-appeal, confidence and flirtation, and he's mine for a lifetime.

When we're finally in bed, Liam narrows in on his favorite freckle, pressing an open-mouthed kiss to my collarbone. He moves over me until we're chest to chest, his heart beating against mine. He kisses me - a slow, lazy kiss - and whispers my three favorite words: "I love you."

"Mmm… I love you too," I murmur, reaching for his lips with mine, kissing him deeply, making it known just how much I do, in fact, love him. He pulls away with a look in his eyes that says forever, then slides his naked body down to the bed beside me. His palm finds the subtle curve of my belly.

"I can't wait for this belly to get bigger, Ells."

"It won't be long now. You sure you'll still love me when I'm as big as a house and an emotional mess?"

"I'll only love you more." His response is sweet and swoony, and one that no one on this earth would expect to hear from his mouth. Affection typically kills Liam. Except with me.

"Your love for me and our baby makes me melt, you know?"

"That stays between us three," he says. "I can't have the reputation I built as a ruthless attorney tarnished."

"Then that's where it will stay," I tell him, pointing from me to him then to my belly.

He raises his head to meet my gaze, his cocky grin on full display. "That's not your typical sassy response I've come to expect."

"Should I try this again?" I pretend to re-think my answer, tapping the tip of my finger against my chin. I mess with him. It's far too much fun so I keep going. "I'll make sure the word on the street is that you watch Monday night football with one hand down your pants and a beer in the other. On Tuesdays, Wednesdays and Thursdays too. Better?"

"Yes, much. You want to know why?"

I nod, in between kisses. I've worked him up. Mission accomplished.

"Because that mouth of yours is such a turn-on. That witty mouth that winds me up."

I smooth my hand over the stubble of his jaw, burning for him. "Ditto, Liam. Ditto."

Another Epilogue

Liam

We're lying under umbrellas, baking in the sun. The biggest decisions we will make today is whether we should lie out on a striped beach chair or take a dip in the ocean. Whether I'll have a beer or some fruity drink Ellie pushes on me. A mid-day siesta or a bowl of shave ice. It's a rough life but someone has to live it.

I surprised Ellie with a trip to Maui. It was on her list of places she hoped to visit. I plan on getting through that entire list, checking off each and every one of her most wished for vacation spots, by the time she turns thirty.

The timing seemed right, what with how busy and chaotic our lives have been lately. Making partner at the firm came with its own set of stresses and commitments, and my practise has been growing by the day, keeping me busier than ever. Ellie has been busy too, between the pregnancy and working hard at Bloom. She's also been setting up a nursery and getting ready for our baby to arrive. *I'm still convinced it's a boy, by the way, and I'd be willing to bet the house on that.*

She's nearing the beginning of her third trimester and our lives are about to change. I'm told sleepless nights for the next five years are coming at us full force, so ten days away in a tropical paradise at the Fairmont Kea Lani seemed fitting. And I was right.

We've luau-ed, played in the surf, swam beneath waterfalls and attempted the road to Hana. Turns out a three-hour drive in a rental car on a narrow, winding road is not ideal for a pregnant woman. We turned around fifteen minutes into it and shared fish tacos with a view of the Pacific Ocean at a beachside dive bar instead.

Ellie is stretched out on a chair beside me under a floppy hat with, of course, one of her crossword puzzles. She's in one of her bikinis that threaten to kill me with her baby belly proudly on display. She has her phone in her hand and a smile on her face. Gorgeous in every way.

"What's making you smile, Ells?" I ask, turning my gaze towards her.

"It's just your brother. You would know if you checked the group chat," she says, not looking up, furiously typing away at the screen.

"So help me God with that wedding group chat, Ells." I tell her. "Parker and Olivia have been married for almost a year. Why the hell am I still being tortured with that thing?"

She smiles in amusement. "We're in Hawaii, Liam. The happiest place on earth. Stop being so grumpy. It will mess with the zen here."

"That's Disneyland, Ellie," I say sarcastically, but not really meaning it. "Besides, I thought we were taking a break from our phones this trip? If I remember correctly it was another one of your sacred rules."

She tsks me and continues to type, giggling away at whatever she's messaging. I admit, I'm curious as to why she's gone from smirking to bust-a-gut laughing so I begrudgingly reach for my iPhone and open the app.

I scroll through the messages.

Miles: You two should really think about one of those portraits. Matching Hawaiian shirts, leis and grass skirts. A neon sunset in the background.

Ellie: Good thinking. I could blow it up to almost life size and hang it above the mantel.

Miles: Liam would prefer it on the wall in his office behind his desk. Trust me...I know my brother well.

Fucker.

I keep scrolling.

Miles: Speaking of...How *is* my brother? Is he bringing his laptop and a stack of files to the beach everyday?

Ellie: His hands are full of other things

Miles: That a boy! Enjoy your vacation love birds.

Reading enough, I toss my phone to the side. Ellie side-eyes me and shakes her head.

"You're just throwing a fit wanting my full attention on you, Liam."

Maybe I do. I stretch out my arms over my head, flexing my ab muscles like a dog who's begging to be petted. It works. She notices me with a smirk.

I reach for the phone in her hands, wanting more of her attention.

"Don't even think about it," she says, whipping her phone to the side, clutching the device in the air. "Let's quickly send the group a selfie then I'll put my phone away and will happily gawk at your abs." *Works for me.*

She snaps the photo, sends it off to the group chat and slides her phone into her beach bag. Her gaze shifts to the ocean then back towards me. Right where I like it.

She lowers her sunglasses to the tip of her nose and drinks me in. I laugh. She's humoring me and enjoying the view all at once.

Reaching across our chairs, I press my hand on her belly, running my palm across her smooth skin, slowly back and forth. She closes her eyes for a second and sighs. This baby is going to be here before we know it. Ellie rests her small hand over mine, her diamond engagement ring catching my eye.

"You know, I could make a call and have someone here to marry us under one of those palm trees over there. Just like that, you could take my name and officially be mine."

"Liam Bennett. If your mother heard you right now, she would disown you. You must be temporarily insane to even suggest that. Do you have some sort of death wish?"

She's right, but it doesn't change the fact that I'm in a rush to marry Ellie. I agreed to a wedding after our baby is born but it won't stop me from trying to change Ellie's mind every chance I get.

"Should we take a dip, babe?" I ask her.

"We should. Pool or ocean?"

"I'll follow you," I say, knowing damn well I'd follow her to the ends of earth and back any day of the week. Luckily for me, today it's to a kidney-shaped pool under the sun on a tropical island.

"Are you coming?" she asks, looking over her shoulder, her hair streaked from the sun and her body looking good enough to eat. *Damn.* So sexy.

I smile as I watch her.

"I am. Just enjoying the view."

. . .

THE END.

(for real this time :))

Acknowledgments

First and foremost, to our incredible readers. We hope you enjoyed Liam and Ellie's story. We are forever grateful you took a chance on two indie authors who love this genre endlessly. This is the second novel that we've written and what a crazy ride it has been. We've learned so much about ourselves and the world of publishing and marketing. We are humbled by the support we've received, including so many of you we've never met. Our most sincere thanks to everyone who has read our books and encouraged us and taken the time to contact us.

Thank you to our Beta readers, ARC readers, bloggers and bookstagrammers for sharing our love of romance and getting our books out to readers. We are appreciative of every share, post, review and mention. It means the world.

Thank you to our editor, Carolyn De Melo, for her wit and brilliant mind - you always come through with the most genius insights. We are indebted to you for your eagle eye and key fixes. We know we are the luckiest to have you. You mean EVERYTHING to us.

Thank you to Carmen for being insanely hilarious and always available to brainstorm. We kept waiting for you to change your phone number on us but somehow you never did. Thank you for being a huge part of bringing this book to life.

Thank you to Brandee and Erin for reading HTBY ten times over and still being excited to discuss plots and characters. You are two of our biggest cheerleaders and we are blessed to be on this journey alongside you. Thanks also to Leah and Natalie for your friendship and continued support.

Thank you to our author friends for cheering us on and sharing our posts. We love celebrating each other's successes and feel grateful to belong to such an incredible community.

Thank you to Kim Bailey of Bailey Cover Boutique and Alyssa and Tricia of LitUncorked. We loved working with all of you on Book 2.

Finally, thank you to our friends and families, who make this dream possible. You love us fiercely and constantly support us when we need it most. It seriously means so much to us, having you in our corners pulling for us. We could never have finished writing this book without you.

Lily and Miller XO

Also by Lily Miller

Always Been You, a second chance contemporary romance and Book 1 in the Bennett Family Series. Read Parker and Olivia's story today.

Manufactured by Amazon.ca
Bolton, ON

24849609R00177